# NEVER WAKE

## AN ANTHOLOGY OF DREAM HORROR

EDITED BY
KENNETH W. CAIN & TIM MEYER

CRYSTAL LAKE
PUBLISHING

# NEVER WAKE

## AN ANTHOLOGY OF DREAM HORROR

Edited by Kenneth W. Cain & Tim Meyer

# NEVER WAKE

Published by Crystal Lake Publishing—Tales from The Darkest Depths

Join the Crystal Lake community today!

# WELCOME
## TO ANOTHER

## CRYSTAL LAKE PUBLISHING
### CREATION

Join today at www.crystallakepub.com & www.patreon.com/CLP

# CONTENTS

INTRODUCTION                                              xi
Sadie Hartmann

SHE WHO BRINGS THE RAIN                                    1
Kristin Peterson

SLEEP WELL AND DREAM OF DARK THINGS                       13
Laurel Hightower

NOT EVERY LIVING THING WILL ROT AWAY                      25
Eric LaRocca

THE SEVEN-YEAR WAR                                        43
Lee Murray

LABYRINTHINE                                              61
Michael Bailey

THANK YOU FOR PARTICIPATING                               73
TJ Cimfel

THE LOOKING GLASS PILLOW                                  87
Angela Liu

PERMANENT INK                                            105
Michelle Tang

CAREFUL ON THE ICE                                       115
Jara Nassar

FEAST OF THE DREAMER                                     129
Pedro Iniguez

ARMINGRAABER                                             139
Joe Koch

MEMORY DIPPED IN SEPIA                                   155
Anaea Lay

P IS FOR PHANTASIES                                      163
Steve Rasnic Tem

NIGHTTIME RITUAL                                         175
Cynthia Pelayo

ONEIROPHOBIA                                    187
Todd Keisling

PRAYERS TO CHTHONIC GODS                        197
Lyndsay E. Gilbert

OUR DARKEST THOUGHTS ARE INKED IN
CARBON                                          209
Catherine McCarthy

LEONORA DRIVE                                   225
Gwendolyn Kiste

SPECTER                                         241
Philip Fracassi

NEVER WAKE                                      275
Kenneth W. Cain & Tim Meyer


THANK YOU                                       279
ABOUT THE AUTHORS                               285
ABOUT THE EDITORS                               291

*For Laird Barron,*

*Wishing you a speedy recovery, friend.*

# INTRODUCTION

## SADIE HARTMANN

My mom had this big dictionary of dream interpretations my sisters and I liked to use. I've tried to find it online; I think I would recognize it if I saw the cover. It was so cool! If you had a dream about a dog, you could look up the word dog and then the book would break that down into different kinds of dog dreams. For instance, if the dog was scary and chasing you, that would have a whole different meaning than if the dog in your dream was friendly. And if you were bitten by a dog, that had its own meaning as well. I remember looking that up once and the book suggested that if a dog bit me in my dream, I needed to stay alert because someone close to me could be trying to take control of me or harm me. Clearly a warning about my parents ruining my life by disciplining me for no reason!

I went through a weird season of my life where I was having these horrible nightmares about my teeth falling out. They were so realistic. It wasn't like I would just open my mouth and all my teeth just tumbled out; that wouldn't be as bad. In my dream, my teeth were loosening; wiggling, one by one. One tooth would fall out and I would just be beside myself and then, soon after, another tooth would start loosening. The anxiety and fear I felt were so intense, I would wake up and immediately start checking my teeth to see if they were loose. Dream interpretations claim this kind of dream could indicate that you're going through some significant life changes or difficult loss. At the time of those dreams, this felt accurate.

I mean, who knows if there is any validity to these interpretations? Regardless, our brains are manufacturing vivid stories while we sleep and it's entirely possible there could be hidden messages in these stories that would prove to be useful to our waking life if we could somehow unlock the code. The code to the *"...bad videos in my head."*

In this book, Kenneth W. Cain and Tim Meyer have curated an anthology of dream horror, nightmares, hallucinations, and phantasmagoria.

Experimental sleep studies.

Dream journals.

Lucid dreaming.

A memory box.

A future where people visit *"pillow cafés"* and *"pop pills to dream for days."*

Strange persistent dreams coincide with a couple's growing penchant for violence.

Some of these stories are ethereal and dreamy—nightmarish fairytales.

Others are cold, calculating, and cruel.

A particularly memorable story begins with, "Six months following his death I began having my father's dreams."

One story gave me a nightmare about a doll that rattles when you shake it. You'll have to read all these gems to find out which one it was and what was inside the doll.

I loved the ending to a story that reads, "No, John. Unlike death, tattoos are meant to last forever."

There's even a character named Sadie in this anthology! So, of course, I'm partial to it. I'll let you discover which one it is.

Friends, I'm concerned that human beings crawl up inside a bed every night and wiggle down under the covers so that we can close our eyes and become totally vulnerable for several hours. Our brains tell our bodies to shut down while it goes into some kind of low-battery mode. We just lie there, barely operating, a captive audience to whatever distressing movie the theater of our mind is showing that night.

We're not especially equipped to protect ourselves, naturally, under any kind of distressing circumstances. We don't have sharp teeth or claws, or poisonous secretions. We're basically defenseless at all hours of the day and remarkably so while we're sleeping. Perhaps this is why some of us NEVER WAKE.

Sadie Hartmann
March 2023

# SHE WHO BRINGS THE RAIN
## KRISTIN PETERSON

Winter

Ara's voice is crackling ice that whispers, "Gilda." She and I will soon be reunited after this long, cold winter. I will know the blue of her hand, and she will know the flush of my cheeks.

Spring

THE AIR LIVES, seething with flowers and pollen, butterflies and bees. Grasshoppers flick by on a warm breath that melts my marrow made solid by winter's chill. I run to the swimming hole to meet Ara in a secluded cove of the lake, hidden in the deep shade of black and blue oaks, ponderosa pines, big-leaf maples, and willows.

Before I fish her out, we peer at each other, imitating

clouds and their reflections. One looks like a rabbit. Another could be a goat or a blackened flame. A heavy pillow smothers the face of the sun, and the dark pits of Ara's eyes lead inward to a place where light can neither survive nor be destroyed, only crushed under the grief of a billion dying stars. Shadows reveal her skeleton, her clacking jaw, her empty ocular orbits. She's a wraith who extends her bony hand to touch me, wisps of skin and flesh hanging from her fingers, maggots weaving over one another and dripping from her decaying forearm, her raven hair flowing around her face.

The cloud passes, and my reflection overlays hers. We mirror each other. My left eye is smaller than my right, and her right eye is smaller than her left. Her beauty mark is on one side, mine on the other. I reach for her as she reaches for me. For a moment, when I pull her from the water, I'm overcome with the fear she's not who I think she is. But she emerges and is smiling. We laugh, holding hands, curling our muddy toes together. My long hair glows golden where sunlight cascades through the trees. We trace freckles on each other's faces, then check our reflections in the water. They're identical maps leading to the sea beyond the wilderness. She reads my palm while I read hers. Their bifurcated creases tell us the same story.

Ara calls, "That which is above is from that which is below." She's off, running through the trees, into a meadow of blurred yellow and purple flowers on a green background.

I follow, thinking only of touching her long, black hair, the way it flows and shimmers silver like the frothing, forked river that feeds the lake. I respond, "And that which is below is from that which is above."

Summer

Aʀᴀ and I have gorged ourselves on the delights of spring and summer, lazing in and around our swimming hole, near where the river becomes tame, splintering in protest before it cedes its wild nature to the reservoir. We vow to always be the river, never the lake.

Our mouths bleed magenta from the blackberries we pick to eat as we walk along the rails. Today the circus train has stopped in our little town to feed and water the animals. The crew opens the doors of the train cars that hold cages. Tigers and lions snarl for their meat. Elephants respond with blares for hay. Camels belch for oats. But we're not here only for the animals. We're hoping to see celebrities. Little people, tattooed people, and most of all, aquatic people.

We linger long, but only those who must work emerge from the train. Ara pushes me toward the tracks as the crew slides the boxcar doors closed, begs me to speak for her, reminds me no one else should see her. Maybe the performers meet on the other side, but a childhood of living next to trains has taught me never to cross over or under one, especially when it's blowing its whistle to warn us of its imminent departure.

Next year, we'll watch from the station side. I am patient, but she is not. The town's annual harvest parade and fair is soon. As usual, the townsfolk will come for her.

Fall

Wᴇ ʙᴀꜱᴋ in fallen oak leaves, their lush scent honeyed and floral, swathing the ground with layers of damp color. There's a snap to the air that carries the smell of autumn: burning leaves, mist, and morning frost.

"I love you, Ara." The words spill from my lips without forethought.

"Will you take me into your heart?"

"You are my heart."

She stands and walks into the water, bubbles rising as it devours her.

THE NEXT MORNING, I return and wait to greet Ara before the townspeople arrive. She finally emerges, dripping black water, a sludge that clings to her hair like a long, black veil. Hollows lined with matte coal are where her eyes should be. Her jaw hinges weaken, and her entire face threatens to complete its rot. But it's her body that horrifies. Fish and turtles have torn and eaten chunks of her. An eel consumes its way through her abdomen until it exits and plunges into the water. Sickening, translucent worms hang from her wounds, a legion of blind tentacles rippling in sea anemone waves, reaching for the scent of fresh sustenance.

"Please hide me." Her body is dying like it does this time every year.

"But where? All the places I know are on land where they'll find you." I'm desperate to help, because I know her loneliness and shame, because I love her as I love myself.

"Come with me. We'll hide in my room." She offers her hand, which I accept, and we walk into the water.

Her fingertips are shriveled like the frozen waves of lake water in winter. I take a deep breath, and we dive down to a house that was inundated when the government dammed the river to create this reservoir, our lake. An entire ghost town exists under the water, lovingly recreated above. Townsfolk whose families lived there for generations are haunted by the loss of their homes, their land, their identity. Everything was taken by the flood.

Ara and I arrive at her house, which looks like mine. I'm out of breath, but she insists on showing me her room from the outside, which is where my room is in my house above. My posters hang on her walls, my bed sits on her floor. This is too frightening to bear.

She holds me as I thrash to return to the surface. I slap and kick then tear at her flesh, excavating bones and tendons and bloodless muscle the lucent color and consistency of raw fowl. Sturgeons arrive in a frenzy over her disintegrating body, their immense forms coasting in and out of my view, emotionless as sharks.

I dig into Ara's hands and finally break free of her. When I reach the surface, I inhale profoundly. I worry I've hurt her, abandoned her, when I'm her only friend.

"What are you doing way out there?" my father calls to me from the shore where men are preparing a motorboat.

Ara's claws drag across my legs. Propelled by fear, I swim toward the dock.

My father arrives and pulls me into the boat. "The town has been searching for you all morning. We must prepare for the festival."

Winter

I ETCH THE frozen lake water with a ragged fingernail, and the ice ripples outward. Ara does the same from below. I can't see her because the ice is thick and clouded with air bubbles, but her scratches vibrate in my knees, my hands, my ear, the parts that touch the solid lake surface, and in my still-frozen heart. She's beckoning me away toward an ice fishing cabin.

The fisherman was here yesterday. The water he exposed will have frozen into a thin layer. She calls for me, but she needs her rest, to hibernate and rebuild her body.

## Spring

Slush floats on the water, and Ara emerges fresh and new. I comb her long hair snarled with ice crystals, then we walk along the river. She mourns the salmon, unable to return to their ancestral birthplaces to spawn after lifetimes exploring the sea. She weeps for the eels that mate in the sea and wend their way to live as adults in freshwater.

The fish ladders we made are ineffective. Trash is scattered everywhere. Ara's tears bring rain that floods the river until it washes the ugliness away. She knows it will all end up in her ghost town, but the resulting beauty of nature cheers her for a moment before she cries again.

The clouds unleash a downpour. Lake water flows over its confines, its momentum thrusting the underwater town and countless abandoned refrigerators and old cars toward the dam, rupturing it, returning the river to its natural course. Although no salmon have spawned this far north for decades, Ara assures me they'll return in the autumn.

She was born in the ocean, salty as her tears.

Summer

THE NAKED, mineral soil of the once-reservoir mocks the town. Despite Ara's spring deluge, summer's drought is extreme, the worst in generations. Snow in the mountains released its melt early on after an exceptionally dry winter. Diminishing glaciers supply little water. I haven't seen Ara for months and worry for us all.

∾

Fall

NO RAINS COME. The river trickles. At the place where it forks, I find Ara at last. Her back is to me. She is crouched, breaking bones and ripping flesh, feeding, and sucking marrow.

"Ara?" I approach warily.

She turns toward me, her face bloodied, her eyes those of a wild animal, and conceals her prey.

"What are you eating?" I move closer.

She growls and snaps her long teeth to scare me away.

I move closer still.

Naked flesh hangs off her skeleton. Rotting, fragmented salmon lie at her feet, but that is not what she's eating. It's a spotted fawn.

She slashes at me with her claws. I continue because I cannot imagine her hurting me. She shreds my face then surges upward to lap the blood from my wounds. I'm in her strong embrace, unable to move.

"Your blood is sweet as it smells." Her fangs tear at my flesh. "And your meat is ripe as a summer peach."

She caresses my hair as she licks my sliced face. No longer

in her arms, I'm free to escape and never return to her. Instead, I allow her to run her tongue along the bloody furrows made by her claws and teeth. Flesh rains from her until she is piercing me with the naked bones of her fingers.

Then her body smells like rainwater and her mouth like blackberries. She is herself again.

We lie on the fallen leaves, vegetal, clinging to the illusion of life. The sky closes and collapses on us, bringing the first precipitation in months. We laugh as we luxuriate in the rich mud, as the river swells and carries us away, past the valley that was once the reservoir, through the broken dam, and to the sea.

We are healed in the brackish water. My face has no scars, and her body is covered in healthy flesh. We lie on the beach. Now her fingers are again but bones she uses to force my head toward her until my mouth is on her neck. I open and bite. She extends her chin and groans, a sound like tall trees creaking and rubbing against each other in the wind. I close my fangs until I taste blood. She leans in for more. I bite harder, and she jerks her neck away leaving me with a piece of her flesh. It is tender and complex as wine, salty as the ocean.

Her eyes darken like a coming storm. She is again decaying, her body sinewy and rotten. I spit out the writhing, fetid mass. Ara scoops it up, pries open my mouth, and forces me to eat it, holding my nose and lower jaw until I swallow.

She rises and walks toward the forest beyond the beach, shafts of light passing through the wreckage of her body. Before the forest devours her, she turns to look at me, smiles while tearing a straight line onto her palm, and dissolves into darkness.

The creases of my palms no longer break into two branches.

I run, slipping in the sand until I reach the cathedral of

ancient trees. I follow the scent of rain but it's everywhere, and Ara is nowhere. When night comes, I lie on the duff, shivering, waiting for her to warm me. She doesn't come. I tunnel into the thick humus, covering my naked body with its compost warmth, and sleep.

In the deep night, Ara burrows into my arms. It is I who keeps us warm. Her breath is liquid on my face, her flesh putrefied. She is becoming the river, her heart echoing its sounds, the fluid fetal heartbeat of the headwaters. I pull back our blanket of forest floor. She is but a quicksilver puddle that shines in the moonlight as it writhes toward the sea.

WHEN I WAKE AGAIN, I am back where the river divides into two branches. Morning sunbeams slice the trees to warm my skin. Ara is not here. Although it will be cold, I wash myself in the swimming hole. For the first time, the water is more comforting than refreshing. It wraps itself around me like an endless silk scarf. I've never felt so alive, so much like myself. I float on my back, my long, black hair dredging the bottom of the hole, undulating in the current like underwater plants. My heart churns, falling and rising with each wave of the river, which carries echoes from its source in the highlands.

The sun rises above the mountains, blinding me momentarily. When my eyes adjust, I am surrounded by the town's men. They are holding hands in a large circle that is closing in.

My father breaks from the ring, which reforms as he approaches. I hide my body under the water. He speaks to me in a language I don't know, yet I understand. I move away from him. He calls me "Ara, she who brings the rain," and sings with the other men who are closed in around the swimming hole.

"Papa, it's me." Although they come from my mouth, the

sounds are not words I recognize. I can't remember my name. Falling leaves sigh "Ara" as they rasp and swirl on the wind.

The men bow their heads and kneel at my feet. Devin, the most recent boy to become a man, rises and moves closest to me. He holds a fine azure dress adorned with freshwater pearls, yellow oak leaves, and petrified wood that he passes to my father.

Devin reaches his trembling hand toward me. I dive to sit at the bottom of the hole. He hesitates, looks to the other men, removes his clothes, and follows, hugging a large rock on the river floor. Again, he offers his hand. I reject him. He waits, and I move closer.

He swims to the surface for air and returns. This time I let him touch my fluid hair. Then we're breathing air, and I know he's tricked me. The men pull us out, but I hold onto him so tightly that as the men try to separate us, Devin shrieks. Everyone stops struggling and leaves us in the river where we lie among the spawning and tattered salmon that have completed their life cycles. This delights me, and the rain showers upon us.

I lift my head so he can see my eyes, to show him the voids within, the universes they hide. Flesh hangs off me like rags. My body is rotting salmon.

The rain stops, and I am born anew. Devin bathes me and combs my long, black hair, kissing my neck when he hits a knot and I cry out. We leave the cove and other townsmen to dry in a sunny meadow, Devin pulled along in my slipstream as I run to a flattened patch where deer have slept then I sit.

"My queen." He sighs, lies down, and rests his head on a pillow of damp straw, the dress next to him.

As he dozes, women appear over the hill. I test the sharpness of my claws and wait. They approach with caution, carrying baskets. My vision is sharp. They bring fruit and bread and wine. One carries brushes and kohl powder for my eyes and red rose extract to add a flush to my cheeks and lips. Another woman—her hair shining like strands of golden silk in the autumn sun—holds gems and gold from my river.

I touch the arm of the woman with blonde hair. "Ara, why did you leave me?"

She kisses my cheeks. "I'm Gilda. We've all come to help you prepare for the festival."

Her voice rushes like a flow of sugar crystals. Then her head blocks the sun as she takes my hands in hers. The pits of her eyes consume all light and cast it throughout her body, which bleeds and falls off her bones in pieces. She releases my hands, moves her head, and she is a familiar young woman darkening my eyes and blushing my cheeks and lips.

Another woman passes the jewelry to her piece by piece—aquamarine earrings, turquoise rings, and necklaces made of white quartz cabochons with veins of pure gold racing through them like two-pronged lightning bolts. She pulls the dress over my head, latches it, and kisses me on the lips, coming away with rose red on her own. Fulfilled, I expand to become everything—a black sun. A fluff of cloud. Demon and god. River and sea. Beast and human. I conjure the rains, I quench the wildfires, I give life.

Gilda holds a mirror so I may admire her work. For a moment, its surface is transparent, and I see her smiling face. I blink and see myself, exquisite as a goddess. The women and I sweep out of the meadow toward the town where the men wait.

Dry grass flows in the wind that whispers, *"That which is above is from that which is below, and that which is below is from that which is above."* And I am the river that thunders white and black toward the ocean, for its life and mine are one and the same.

When I reach the fork, I forge onward along both trajectories, knowing I will recognize myself again where I meet the sea.

# SLEEP WELL AND DREAM OF DARK THINGS

## LAUREL HIGHTOWER

"Will it hurt?"

The boy's chin trembled, his lips pressed tight. Dark eyes begged her to tell him no, to gather him in her arms and protect him from what the world had become. Not as little as he once was, but young enough to believe his mother could keep him safe.

Wendy looked down, thankful her face was half in shadow. He wouldn't see her eyes, the tears that gathered at the corners and threatened to spill over. She wanted nothing more than to hold him close and tell him everything would be okay, that she would always stand in the way of anything that meant him harm.

She set her jaw and nodded. "Yeah. Probably hurt a lot. They're getting into your brain, after all."

He flinched, his mouth twisting as he clapped his hands over his ears. "Don't use that word," he said, his tone sharp and accusing. He knew she'd done it on purpose, and she felt his trust crumble away a little more. Shifting ground beneath their feet, a chasm opening between them.

She clenched her teeth and squeezed her eyes shut. Parenting was hard, but she'd never foreseen having to destroy her son in order to save him. "What word, *brain*?" she asked, hating herself even as she added emphasis to the last word.

Henry closed his eyes and turned from her, hands still tight over his ears. Not that it saved him from her penetrating tone. The "mom" voice had no mercy.

"No, stop it," he said, his small voice trembling. "It makes bad videos in my head."

"I know, sweetheart," she said in a softer voice, one that wouldn't break through the barriers he'd put between them. He was right to do so. In another life, she'd have condemned any parent who would exploit their kid's weakness like this.

Henry's intrusive thoughts manifested around age four, often triggered by certain words or sounds. Wendy was no stranger to the affliction and worked hard to help her son manage his misbehaving mind, making sure he understood the thoughts and images that roiled in his head didn't make him a bad person. Even when Josh told her to stop, that she was making it worse by drawing attention to it, she'd ignored her husband and concentrated on her son. She knew better than anyone, you can't just wish nightmares away. Now she wondered every day if she'd messed up. The intrusive thoughts were part of what had kept her son alive up to this point, and she worried that whatever progress they'd made in managing them could be his death sentence.

She shook her head, clearing it of regret. There was no way to change the past, and she'd done enough to keep him safe for a little longer. Henry crouched against the wall, pushing away from her body, her touch, his chapped lips moving silently while he suffered. She had little doubt those same torturous images would show up in his dreams, and took comfort from that.

Wendy sniffed back her own tears and looked away, down the candlelit hallway where the Machine waited. That was how she thought of it, a looming presence upon which so many lives depended. It might hurt for all she knew; she'd never been under, never felt the thing reach into her mind and stir her dreams. She had no shortage of nightmares—years of worst-case scenarios popping into her head without warning.

It had been like that as long as she could remember. If her gaze fell on a razor, her mind filled with an image of taking it to her eyeball. When she drove over a bridge, she'd picture losing control of the car and launching herself into nothing, crashing far below, jagged metal slicing her flesh, her body crushed between the weight of steel and stone. And motherhood came with fresh nightmares—of fucking up, leaving the baby on the roof of the car, hurting him in some way. SIDS, predators, poisons, choking—hideous injuries waited around every corner. After the dreamwalkers came, there were all new terrors.

Wendy's back teeth began to hum, a low-level vibration she felt through her bones. There was no sound associated with it, but she knew anyway. It was the Machine. They'd finally geared it up for the young woman who'd been waiting when they arrived, though it had been at least an hour since the silent man had taken her back. Wendy couldn't forget the way the girl's wild, desperate eyes met hers, as though she, too, wanted to believe Wendy could keep her safe. That she would intervene and save the girl, take them all away from this underground bunker that reeked of rat piss and mildew.

Henry moved close again, pressing himself to her side, his anger forgotten in fear. He felt it too, and knew what it meant. Worse than that, he knew he was next, and his little body shivered against hers. She wrapped an arm around him and pressed him close, biting her tongue against all the things she wanted to say and all the words she should. She couldn't bear to push him any further, and an inescapable feeling of impending loss pulled at her. She didn't know what kind of effect the Machine would have on her son—it was possible he'd never be the same, that she'd lose her sweet boy with his big heart. There were stories of that, too. Of treatment failures that left people drooling zombies, or clawing at their faces in a doomed attempt to escape from nightmares that followed them into the waking world.

The vibrations increased and buzzed in her ears. She pushed back a wave of nausea that rose from the hum through her chest, took a deep breath. Henry whimpered by her side but didn't make another sound until a sharp scream came from somewhere deeper in the building. A single shriek that cut off abruptly, and Wendy had no doubt it came from the young woman who'd been taken away. Was she screaming from the nightmares newly introduced into her fertile brain, or pain from the procedure? Or worst of all, had it been a failure and the dreamwalkers found her?

Josh hadn't sounded like that when they'd taken him. A lucid dreamer, he was always careful about what media he exposed himself to, what images he allowed to enter his consciousness. It was all too common for them to appear in vivid dreams from which he could never rouse himself. At least one night a week, Wendy would wake to his moans, the muddled tones of dream talk, and have to pull him out of it. It was why his solution to Henry's intrusive thoughts was to simply ignore them, not give them attention, and limit what the boy watched on television or read in the books he snuck from his mother's shelves.

The night the dreamwalkers took her husband, she hadn't been able to save him. Vivid though they were, his dreams that night were too benign to offer any protection. He didn't have a lifetime of anxiety to conjure dark protectors in his sleep the way Wendy did, and the dreamwalkers carved right through his mind like butter. She'd seen them once or twice by then, a lurking, staccato presence at the edges of her mind, like artifacts on a film reel just out of frame. She felt their wanting, watching her dream self through hungry eyes, but the hellscape of her mind was too much for them to cross, and they left her in favor of easier prey.

When they came for Josh, he'd sat straight up in bed beside her, eyes wide open though they were glassy, almost whitened. His lips peeled back so hard they split, oozing blood onto his teeth. And the sounds he made...grunts of pain, groans, keening cries of misery. He couldn't feel her shaking hands on him, or hear her attempts to wake him, to pull him from the grip of the dreamwalkers. Panicked tears streamed down her cheeks as she watched her husband die, powerless to help him, until at last he made a strange hissing sound, of air escaping his lungs for the last time. He died with his fingers curled into claws, his flesh torn and bleeding from the desperate scratching of his jagged nails.

"Mommy?" Henry's voice was thick with tears. "What kind of nightmares will it give me?"

Wendy squeezed him tighter, kept her eyes on the flickering candles. He'd given her another opening, one of many opportunities to fill his young mind with fear, equip him against the dreamwalkers. Whatever tales she told him now would visit him in sleep, when he was most vulnerable. She was tired, so tired, her resources depleted by a sleep deficit that was somehow worse than when Henry had been a colicky baby, screaming at all hours of the night.

Now, when he screamed, it comforted her.

"Mommy?"

Wendy cleared her throat, prepared to launch into a lurid

description of her last nightmare, one in which her husband died over and over, worse each time, a whole row of Joshuas sitting up in bed. Another line she would never have crossed in her former life, but before she could get far, the soft scrape of footsteps sounded from down the hall. Wendy fell silent, listening to the steps getting closer, tension building in her chest until she thought she might scream.

The man appeared in the doorway, dimly backlit by candles. He didn't say anything, instead stood waiting, until finally Wendy pushed to her feet, pulling Henry up with her. He shook violently against her, hands clutching tight to her waist as she moved them forward. When she reached the man, she saw he wore dark sunglasses, despite the dim lighting. She couldn't tell if he was looking at her, meeting her eyes, or if he could even see.

Her hands sweating, she thought suddenly of a book she'd once read, something about a birdhouse or the like. The protagonist had been a mother, keeping her children safe in a world where catching sight of a roaming monster would destroy them all. They'd worn blindfolds, hadn't they? Was that what this was? Did the people who operated the Machine know something about how to keep the dreamwalkers at bay? Had they ever used their own invention, or had they taken another, darker route? She wondered if there were even eyes behind those dark glasses, or just empty sockets.

They stood in silence until she spoke. "Is it time?"

The thin man nodded and turned back to the hallway, leading in silence.

"Mommy, I can't."

Wendy took hold of Henry's shoulders, pushing him in front, her tone steely, concealing her fear. "You can, and you will." God, she hated herself for this.

He whimpered as he walked, needing to be nudged

forward every few steps as they followed the silent man. There were closed doors as they moved down the hall, many of them still and quiet, but others with stirring or sobbing behind them. Wendy shuddered and tightened her grip on Henry's shoulders. She stumbled over him when they came to a stop at the threshold of a larger room as poorly lit as the rest of the labyrinth, though she could make out a looming shadow against the far wall.

A low moan came from Wendy's right, and she squinted into the darkness. Lying across a rusty metal bin was the young woman who'd just undergone the Machine. She lay on her side, hands limp in front of her, eyes rolled back in her head, mouth slack beneath that white, unnatural gaze. She spoke beneath her breath, too fast and soft for Wendy to make out.

"Do you have someone to care for him?" asked the man, no longer silent, his darkened gaze once more upon her.

Wendy tore her gaze from the young woman with effort. "What?"

"For after your treatment," he said. "You won't be in any shape to once we're done. Not for a long while."

"How long will she be like that?" she asked, feeling Henry's shoulders creep up to his ears beneath her hands.

"It varies," the man answered, unmoving. "Some recover quickly. Others stay for days."

Wendy cast a glance behind her. "Are they the ones behind the doors we passed?"

"Yes. So, like I said, you'll need someone to care for the kid. We're not babysitters."

"I'm not a baby," said Henry, his small voice trembling. "I can take care of myself."

The empty gaze fell on the boy, and the briefest of smiles broke the man's stone facade. "I'm sure you can, little man."

Wendy cleared her throat. "Anyway, the treatment isn't for me. It's for him."

The smile fell away from the man as though it had never been. He rubbed a hand against his jaw. "We don't do many kids."

Wendy looked around the room. "Why not? He's the one who needs it."

A high, reedy voice came from the shadowed corner by the Nightmare Machine. "It's not calibrated for them, for one thing."

Wendy stared into the dark but couldn't make out the voice's owner. "So re-calibrate it."

"Doesn't work that way," said the man beside her. "One size fits all. If you want to do it, that's up to you. But I can't recommend it."

She licked her lips, breathed to calm her climbing anxiety. Henry fell silent, too afraid to speak, she imagined. "What are the risks?"

A hissing laugh came from within the room. "Too many to name. Even with healthy adults, we can't guarantee the results. I'm sure you've heard the stories. I can assure you, they're all true. It might be that his age and size don't matter, or it might kill him outright. Impossible to predict."

Henry turned his gaze up to hers, silent tears streaming down his grimy cheeks. "Mommy. Please."

"Anyway, it's imperative the subject be still. Moving at the wrong time can be disastrous, so if he's going to fight it, you may as well forget it."

Christ, but she wanted to forget it. Grab Henry and leave this place, carve out a better life somewhere far from anyone else. But you couldn't run from the dreamwalkers; they would find you in your sleep, no matter how far you traveled.

She looked back at the man who'd led them in, sensing

more humanity in him than his partner in the shadows. "I have to keep him safe," she said softly.

He studied her in silence. Or maybe he didn't. It was impossible to tell what went on behind the dark glasses. After a minute or so, he looked back into the room. "What if they did it together?"

A hissing breath drew in, then the rhythmic click of the person's tongue against the roof of their mouth. "We've never done that before. It might not be enough, splitting the output like that."

The man beside her shrugged. "Less chance of it over-whelming the little dude."

Wendy put her arm around her son's shoulders, drew him closer. "What will that do, if we go together?"

He shrugged again. "No way to know. It seems logical the efficacy would be divided, so you'd both get a smaller dose than usual, which might not be enough to keep you safe. Or it could fail completely."

"Or fry your brains. This isn't something to mess around with." The voice from the shadows was harsh, grating.

Henry shuddered, hunched away from her, pressed his hands over his ears while he chanted something unintelligible under his breath. Anything to shut out the torturous images of gray meat sizzling in a pan. He didn't say what he saw, but Wendy could imagine.

Wendy sucked in a breath, nodded. "I'll do it."

Henry looked up at her, his hands slowly lowering. Hope lifted his voice. "You'll go with me?"

Wendy looked down at him and smiled, held her hand out to him. "Yeah. Don't I always?"

A smile trembled on his lips, and he slid his fingers into hers.

She squeezed his hand and set her shoulders. "Let's do this."

The man beside her put a hand at her back, guiding her forward to the unseen instrument. Henry didn't have to be prodded now, his fear ebbing. Wendy was surprised to find her breath coming easier, dread replaced by acceptance. If it killed them both, so be it. Neither would have to exist in a world without the other.

The operator never came far enough from the shadows for her to see their face, but grimy hands flitted around her, attaching leads to her forehead, directly beneath her hairline, and on the back of her neck. Henry kept his eyes closed, still squeezing her hand, and Wendy studied what she could see of the Machine. She'd expected something hideous, all snaking wires and hissing steam, a nightmare all its own, but it was nearly featureless. A large, steel rectangle stood on end, a bit like a coffin. Blank-faced, devoid of buttons or dials or blinking lights—there was nothing to tell what lurked behind the facade, what was coming for them.

The stone-faced man who'd led them in stopped in front of Henry, checked his connections, and briefly patted the boy's cheek. Then he turned to her, bent, and locked his dark, empty gaze on hers. She sensed him wanting to speak to her, tell her some truth or platitude, but instead he turned and gave his partner a thumbs up, backing up to stand in the door.

The operator moved behind them, unseen, and after a sharp click, that bone-shaking vibration rose again. It was much worse this time, the Machine holding them in its grip, setting Wendy's jaw aching, her chest rattling. Henry whimpered beside her, and she squeezed his hand tighter.

"Remember, baby, you've got to hold still. Just close your eyes, like at the doctor's office. It'll be over soon."

A second later sharp pain lanced from one electrode to the

next, a feeling like being burned before a jolt of excruciating lightning traveled along her body. She lost control, her brain sending aimless, flailing commands as pain became the only thing she knew. She couldn't hear her son over her screams, forced from her throat by jangling electricity. Henry's hand slipped from hers, and she surrendered to the pain.

WHEN WENDY next opened her eyes, Henry's slack face loomed above her. He gazed at nothing, his eyes cloudy, blood running from deep furrows he'd made across his cheeks and nose. She screamed his name, pushed herself up from the ground where she lay, and shook his still body.

"Henry, no," she moaned. "Please, please, no."

"That one's not me," came her son's flat tones from somewhere behind her.

Wendy scrambled to her feet, turned until she saw another Henry, just as dead as the last. His swollen purple tongue poked out between blue lips, eyes red with burst capillaries.

"Not that one, either," Henry said before she could scream again.

Wendy took a deep breath, closed her eyes. "Where are you, baby?"

A light touch on the back of her hand made her jump, but when her eyes flew open and she looked down, there was her son, alive and well, looking up at her, solemn but not afraid.

She pulled him into her arms and held him close, gritting her teeth against the images of his dead face that she knew would stick with her. "You're okay? Does anything hurt?"

Henry stayed in her hold, his chin propped on her shoulder as he stared behind them. "This is what you dream of?" he asked.

Wendy pulled away and followed his gaze, sucking in a breath. Nightmare vignettes blinked in and out of sight as though a spotlight traveled among them. In each one, her son was dead or dying, and always, always alone.

She took hold of Henry's shoulders and tore her gaze from death. "It's my worst nightmare. Always has been."

He nodded, turned in her hold, and pointed in the other direction. "Those are mine."

Wendy squinted into the darkness before her and saw another set of vignettes. But every figure here bore her face, some of them dead or dying, like a mirror image of her dreams. Others loomed over a quivering dream-Henry, sprouting claws in one instance, jaw cracking to reveal row upon row of sharp teeth in another.

She looked away, closed her eyes. She was Henry's nightmare, repeated mercilessly as far as she could see.

"Are we in a dream, Mommy?" he asked, looking up at her with the simple faith he'd always had in her.

Wendy breathed out. "I think so, baby."

"Will we ever wake up?"

She raised her gaze to the farthest spot she could, and saw them, the dreamwalkers. Hovering overhead, impossibly large and looming, but never coming closer. There were nightmares enough to keep them at bay. She sat on the featureless ground and pulled her son into her lap, pressing his head to her shoulder so he wouldn't have to see.

"It doesn't matter," she said on a sigh. "We're safe here in our nightmares."

# NOT EVERY LIVING THING WILL ROT AWAY

## ERIC LAROCCA

You die many times when a relationship comes to an end—little deaths, hardly unbearable but uncomfortable all the same.

There's no precise and flawless way to end things, especially after so long. Particularly when lives become intertwined like ivy and hemlock leeching across the side of a home, spiderwebbing together and knitting an unseemly patchwork of our most private tendencies.

Of course, there are skilled ways to peel a grape, to slice an avocado, to crack open even the most temperamental boiled lobster—but ending things, permanently concluding relations between two people once in love, remains a far more delicate matter.

"I think we should see other people," he tells me as his fork stabs the poached egg I've prepared for him. "It would be good for us."

"Is that so?" I ask, stirring my spoon in the cup of coffee I forgot to reheat.

Lukewarm at best. My face scrunches, tongue curling at the bitter taste.

"Why do you think that?" I ask.

"I've been thinking it for quite some time," Dimitri says, clearing the phlegm in his throat as if it were an invitation for me to shove my whole arm down his esophagus and squeeze his stomach until it's no more than the size of a grain of rice.

"That's what you really want?"

He looks at me with a question I'm obviously not supposed to answer. "You can't tell?"

I answer anyway. Just to annoy him. "I can tell you've been unhappy."

"It's not that I've been unhappy," Dimitri tells me, pushing the poached egg as far away from his reach as possible—as if he were pushing me toward oblivion, as if he were discarding a broken toy. "I've been seeing somebody else, Gavril."

I sense my fingers tighten around my cup of coffee, squeezing.

"Somebody else...?"

His face thaws with a warm smile—a look of pleasure so contrived that I expect skilled Italian artisans had labored for days on end to capture something so delicate, so refined, and yet beguiling.

Dimitri looks pleased I had asked, as if we were moving invisible chess pieces to hurt one another on a checkered board that separated us at the kitchen table.

"What's he like?" I ask.

It's not that I want to know. I would have been content to remain ignorant—to wonder why he wears a special cologne on certain nights, to imagine the things he was doing while out. There's safety in not knowing. There's a modicum of comfort when remaining ignorant about how well your lover can harm you.

"He makes a better poached egg than this," he tells me.

Before Dimitri can utter another word, I grab the egg from the dish and push it in his face. He resists, shouting at me as I smash the egg against his mouth again and again. Finally, he gives in, and I push the whole fucking thing down his throat until he's gagging, whimpering with tears beading in the corners of his eyes.

I ask him if it hurts, but he can't answer me.

He's far too busy choking on the egg I had prepared for him.

There's a part of me that realizes he deserves better—a better egg to eat. After all, what's more embarrassing than choking to death on an undercooked egg? He deserves better than that.

*A breath escapes Gavril as soon as he opens the door to what's supposed to be his dream.*

*Instead, it's a gruesome homecoming—a nightmare.*

*His husband, Dimitri—a limbless torso braced on a set of metallic pipe-cleaner stilts—greets him. Eyes glistening with a plea for pity, Dimitri's toothpick legs and arms buckle like a frightened insect. His head lowers as if in prayer.*

*Kangas, an imperious-looking officer dressed in an unusual uniform, flanks the poor thing. Outfitted in a flesh-colored jacket as shiny and as transparent as cellophane, Kangas's emblem-decorated shoulder shoves Dimitri across the threshold.*

*Dimitri obeys, lurching forward on all fours to crawl like a human spider.*

*Gavril shrinks, covering his mouth at the wretched sight.*

*Kangas, coughing, lordly sneers at Dimitri. "You still won't reconsider?"*

*Dimitri's head remains down. He won't answer.*

*Kangas leans in close to Gavril.*

*"Will you talk to him...?" he whispers to him. "For his sake."*

*Kangas's fingers flirt with Gavril's fur collar. His face crumples, nostrils wincing. "Smells old."*

*Gavril's cheeks heat red. "I...always wanted...one like yours."*

*"Care to touch it?"*

*With a gentleness as if he were about to touch the world's most expensive Fabergé egg, Gavril reaches out and gently rubs his fingers along Kangas's coat of flesh.*

*"It's...exquisite," Gavril says. "Beautiful skin. May I?"*

*Kangas obliges. Gavril pulls at the skin, cooing with delight.*

*Dimitri turns his back to the both of them.*

*"Dimitri remembers this gentleman," Kangas explains. "Another government employee. The one who was executed for burning those poor children in their school bus."*

*Kangas flexes his arms, his jacket of skin squealing as he stirs. "Good thing he was so fat. Dead celebrities are in high demand now. But not as much as living, convicted criminals."*

*Kangas hovers over Dimitri the way a master intimidates a dog. He leans in, waiting for an answer.*

*Dimitri merely shakes his head.*

*Kangas shrugs, returning to the door. His feet kick the small metal box set to the side of the entryway. "A delivery's due tomorrow. We'll be expecting the heart tomorrow night."*

*Dimitri's face whitens. His voice firms. "Tomorrow night?"*

*"Get to work," Kangas says, slamming the door shut.*

*Deafening silence fills the room for a moment. Gavril paces, unsure what to say, what to do.*

*"Something...to eat?" he gently asks his husband.*

*The two of them don't seem to notice the small honeybee scaling the wall beside the doorway, stirring while it watches them.*

Gavril rummages in the bedroom closet, ripping open dust-covered boxes of Dimitri's clothing that had been packed away for months.

"Were the potatoes burned?" Gavril asks his husband, surreptitiously hoping for a compliment.

Dimitri crawls into the room, his every movement unsure as if he were nothing more than an unwelcome animal—a horrible nuisance, a pest to be exterminated.

"They were fine, G," he says.

"Are you sure—?" Gavril asks again. "They tasted burnt."

Out of his peripheral vision, Gavril notices Dimitri glance at the nightstand beside the bed and see the wedding band Gavril had left there.

"Said they were fine," Dimitri says.

Gavril accepts he won't get anywhere with Dimitri.

"What did Kangas want you to reconsider?" he asks him.

"My punishment."

Gavril stares at his limbless husband, incredulous. "It's already done."

"He wants my skin," Dimitri tells him.

Gavril turns, face softening but attempting to hide his enchantment with the ghoulish idea.

"My heart especially," Dimitri says.

"For the Prime Minister?"

Dimitri's eyebrows wrinkle, bewildered.

"It's an honor," Gavril says to him. "How much?"

Dimitri turns away, clearly incensed. "Does it matter? Let the pig die."

Gavril can scarcely believe it. "You told them 'No?'"

"Why wouldn't I?"

Gavril does his best to conceal his disappointment, burying his *head in the closet of labeled boxes and trunks overflowing with clothing.*

*"I'll have to cut bigger holes in everything," he says and starts to laugh. But when he turns, he notices Dimitri is not amused.*

*"Sorry," he says, recoiling a little.*

*Then Gavril flips a box upside down and empties a pile of shirts and pants onto the bed.*

*"You packed everything of mine away?" Dimitri asks.*

*"I wasn't sure—" Gavril stops himself. "I didn't know when—"*

*Dimitri's lip pulls downward. His eyes lower, too.*

*"I know," he says. "Monsters aren't supposed to come home."*

As we undress for our morning shower, I tell Dimitri how I inherited an antique teapot from my grandmother when she died. He's never cared for drinking tea, and he insists only the most pretentious and pompous cock-sucking faggots prefer tea to coffee. Dimitri knows full well I keep loose-leaf tea in a jar in a cupboard—secreted behind jars of preserves simply because I know he'll lecture me, chastise me for the inclinations I have that he despises.

"I've been thinking about us," I tell him as I shrug off my shirt and begin to unbutton my pants. "I've been thinking about how things often feel unfinished when two people leave one another."

Dimitri doesn't seem too concerned. He's already skirted into the shower stall and is lathering his skin with a bar of lavender-scented soap.

"It's going to feel like an arm has been amputated when we eventually leave one another," I warn him, speaking over the sound of his humming. "We might as well peel all our skin off and hang them like tattered curtains in a doorway."

"What are you trying to tell me?" Dimitri asks, sliding the bar of soap into my hands as I inch into the shower stall with him. "Just say it."

"I've been having these dreams lately," I tell him. "I don't quite understand them. They frighten me sometimes and I wake up with my heart racing."

"You eat too much before bed," he says.

"I think they're trying to tell me something," I say to him.

Dimitri rolls his eyes and turns his back on me, the cool water blasting him all over and wilting his manhood until it's shy and completely shriveled. But I pull him back toward me until he's facing me once again.

"I think we need to punish ourselves," I tell him. "I don't think we'll be able to move on from one another unless we surrender to these punishments."

For once, the look on Dimitri's face resembles concern.

"You'll let me go if we do this?" he asks me. "You promise not to call or to write or to send for me if I agree to this?"

Of course, it nearly decimates me to think Dimitri wants so desperately to be rid of me. But I remind myself that I've already endured worse.

When Dimitri finally agrees, I tell him to remain in the shower. I skirt into the kitchen, throw a pot filled with tap water on the stove, and crank up the heat until the water finally begins to bubble after a few minutes. When I'm certain the water is scalding hot, I pour the water into the teapot and make my way back to the bathroom. Dimitri is there, waiting for me with both hands covering his manhood as if suddenly embarrassed.

"What are you going to do?" he asks me, twisting the faucet dial off until the shower water slows to a mere trickle.

"I'm going to cleanse the both of us," I tell him, brandishing the teapot filled with scalding hot water.

I notice him wince a little when I approach, and I find myself surprised at the sight. It's the first time I've noted him possess any kind of fear or hesitation.

"It's going to hurt," I warn him. "Anything that's worth it always does."

Before he can respond, I hold the teapot high above him and tilt the kettle until he's showered with scorching water. Dimitri screams hoarse while I pour the water over the both of us, our skin blistering and reddening hot.

When I'm finished, I let the teapot slip from my hands and shatter against the tiles, little bits and broken pieces skating across the bathroom floor. I grab hold of Dimitri and I pull him tight against me, the feeling of his sizzling skin against mine nearly unbearable, and part of me wonders if we'll finally melt into one another and slip away until we're completely and utterly lost like two storm-swept wanderers who are always eventually brought back together.

*DIMITRI LIES IN BED, limbless body propped up on a pile of pillows like a discarded rag doll.*

*Gavril slides under the sheets beside him, pecking his husband's neck with a kiss. Tongue circling his ear, Gavril's hands begin to wander down Dimitri's stomach and underneath the elastic band of his underwear.*

*But Dimitri pulls away.*

*"I...can't," he tells him.*

*Gavril winces, unsettled. After all, Dimitri had never turned down an opportunity for intimacy before. Had he really changed that much?*

*"You don't want to...?"*

*Dimitri hesitates slightly. "How much of the money is gone?"*

*Gavril straightens, sensing his face draining of all color. "Please. Don't ask me that."*

*"How much?"*

*Gavril's eyes avoid Dimitri at all costs. But Dimitri won't back down, staring at him intently.*

*Gavril deflates. "Most of it."*

*Dimitri's eyes close. He swallows hard.*

*"What was I supposed to do?" Gavril asks him, climbing out of bed and pacing the floor like a frightened animal. "Keep living off rations for another month? I...didn't know when you'd—"*

*"I know," Dimitri says gently. Then he kisses Gavril's hand. "I need your help."*

THE NUDE CORPSE *of an elderly gentleman lies on the operating table beneath a giant lamp.*

*Gavril, garbed in a blood-stained apron and face secreted with a mask, stands beside the tray of instruments and containers of fluids. Dimitri, crawling on all fours, hovers beside him to supervise.*

*"You've decided on the incision site?" Dimitri asks his husband.*

*Gavril, unsure, goes to mark the place on the cadaver where the lower jaw meets the throat.*

*"No. Don't," Dimitri says. "The slightest blemish, the skin's worth nothing. Now. Take the scalpel. Make the incision. Carefully. You've seen how I do it."*

*Gavril picks up the scalpel and presses the blade against the cadaver's neck.*

*"Have the tube ready to drain," Dimitri tells him.*

*Gavril is about to make an incision when his hand slips. He slices down the cadaver's throat. "Shit."*

*"What did you do?" Dimitri asks him, his voice trembling with concern.*

*Gavril prepares the tube for drainage, scrambling to grab a cloth to wipe down the blood pooling along the table. "I didn't mean to—"*

*Gavril's hand slips once more, and he drives the scalpel through the cadaver's chest.*

*"Fuck," Dimitri cries out.*

*With a squelching sound, Gavril pulls the scalpel out of the corpse's sternum.*

*"It's ruined," Dimitri says. "The heart's not even salvageable."*

*"I'm...sorry. I didn't—"*

*"It's ruined. Everything."*

*Before Gavril can say anything else, Dimitri crawls away and disappears out the door.*

*Just then, Gavril notices a small honeybee as it lands on the corpse's nose. A whispering dot of black and yellow, wings twitching little beads of blood.*

WHEN I AWAKEN from my dream, I find Dimitri's side of the bed has already been made and he's gone. I can't help but wonder if he's left for good this time.

I pull myself out of bed and make my way downstairs to the kitchen where I find him seated at the table. His eyes are vacant, listless. His breathing is ragged and hoarse, something whistling in the pit of his throat while he sits there and absent-mindedly stabs the table again and again with a small screwdriver.

"What are you doing?" I ask him, noticing how he's left gaping wounds across the table from the screwdriver's tip.

"It's my turn to hurt you," he says, his fingers tightening around the handle. "It's only fair."

Of course, I can't argue with him. I had suggested the

damned thing in the first place, and I know for certain the only way we'll be able to remove ourselves from one another's lives is if we hurt each other and make each other suffer.

He orders me to remove my clothing and spread myself out on the dining room table. I obey without hesitation, climbing on top of the table and exposing myself until I'm completely vulnerable.

Dimitri doesn't warn me what he's about to do. Instead, he just does it.

With one swift gesture that immediately decides the matter, Dimitri swipes the screwdriver between where my legs meet. I feel intense pressure and heat followed by a dull ache—an agonizing pain that seems relentless in its efforts to torture me. When I glance down at the gruesome work he's conjured from my manhood, I realize he's torn me open there and has summoned my blood from some secret wellspring hidden deep inside me—a geyser fountaining all over him until he greets me with a face that looks sticky like it's been hosed with motor oil.

I try to weep and call out to him, but my throat closes until I cannot speak. I glance down again at my exploded cock—more of my secrets undoing from me in a livid stream that promises to wash him clean—and I think to myself, *"This isn't fair. He's hurt me more than I could have ever possibly dreamed of hurting him."*

Then it occurs to me: Perhaps that's the point.

*G*AVRIL STANDS POSED LIKE TAXIDERMY, *elevated on a small wooden box. Dressed in a latex black-and-white French maid's uniform, a mask of human skin painted with exaggeratedly feminine features hides his entire head.*

*An elderly woman, Mademoiselle, kneels in front and attends to him. Her thinning crown of ashen gray hair is secreted by a black turban decorated with expensive jewelry.*

*She coughs, lovingly adjusting the wig of blonde curls over Gavril's bald cap.*

*Dimitri sits and merely watches the absurd ritual from across the room, eyes dimmed of any emotion. He eyes his metal legs and arms tucked in the corner—a permanent reminder of his captivity, his punishment.*

*Mademoiselle begins slipping Gavril's oiled arms into a pair of latex gloves.*

*Once finished, she steps back and admires her labor.*

*"Turn," she orders.*

*Mademoiselle spanks his rear with a leather paddle. Gavril turns until his white-frilled backside is facing her. She coos sweetly.*

*"There," she says. "You're not such a stupid whore after all. Très Bien. Now. Un petit cadeau. Touch yourself."*

*Gavril cups his left breast with one hand and shoves the other between his thighs. He heaves, panting.*

*"What a perfect little slut you are," Mademoiselle says. "How the men must fancy the whore maid. Especially when on hands and knees. Not only to clean."*

*Gavril nods.*

*Mademoiselle turns to Dimitri, bowing, as if addressing a sultan.*

*"The little bitch is ready for you," she says. "What would you like done, monsieur?"*

*But Dimitri doesn't answer. Gavril watches him from across the room. His husband's eyes are glued on the wall—a small honeybee crawling along the paneling.*

◞◟

DIMITRI LIES *naked in the half-filled, grime-rusted bathtub. Gavril kneels at his side and runs a warm cloth over his chest and neck.*

*He notices a small honeybee sitting on the leaking faucet. They both watch it pace until it flies away.*

"In my next life, I'm going to be a honeybee," Dimitri says tenderly. "A honeybee works to live. It doesn't live to work. A honeybee knows no misery."

*He closes his eyes.*

"It used to be quite comforting to think about," Dimitri says.

*Gavril merely looks at him with a soundless question.*

"Before we made a business out of skin, there was one certainty: every living thing will eventually rot away," Dimitri tells him, his voice softening a little. "But not anymore."

*Gavril says nothing. He merely dips the cloth into the bathwater and then lathers Dimitri's shoulders with a bar of soap.*

"You know we can't afford those appointments with her every week," he says. "Especially now."

"It's not much," Gavril says.

"Why do you even do it—?" Dimitri asks him.

*Gavril dips the cloth in the water once more and then begins scrubbing Dimitri's throat.* "Makes me feel beautiful."

"That's all?"

*Gavril hesitates.* "Helps me to forget. Especially now."

"Forget what?"

*Gavril closes his eyes, the word too hurtful to confess. Finally, he does.* "You."

*Dimitri's eyes burn holes through Gavril.* "You won't ever forgive me, will you?"

"What you've done can't be forgiven," Gavril says. "How could you let a man die because you couldn't take a dead boy's heart?"

"I told you. I couldn't."

"So, you burned the boy's body to ashes?"

*"Life had already used him enough," Dimitri says. "I'd never let them have him."*

*"Because you fucked him?" Gavril asked. "They should've taken your heart. They should've peeled your skin to make a three-piece suit for the Prime Minister. Every day, I wish they had."*

*Dimitri's eyes sparkle wet at his husband as he seems to understand what's to be done.*

~

I AWAKEN and find that Dimitri has fastened my crotch with what appears to be a makeshift tourniquet.

"I hurt you bad this time," he confesses, a little visibly maudlin. "I suppose I was...a little too zealous."

With trembling hands, I struggle to straighten myself until I'm sitting upright. It hurts to bend, and it isn't long before I sense that familiar dull ache heating the place between my thighs and coiling there as if it were a permanent reminder of all I had lost because of Dimitri.

"I'm going to make it so that it was like you never existed," he tells me, pushing me down until I'm spread out on the dining room table once more.

"It wasn't supposed to end like this," I tell him, clearing the catch in my throat. "We'll never be able to part now."

Just before I lose consciousness once more, out of the corner of my eye, I notice a pair of mud-caked boots and a shovel leaning against the door. I can't help but wonder if Dimitri has already been digging.

~

*DIMITRI, a limbless torso without his stilts, sits propped up in a leather armchair.*

*Kangas and a somber-faced entourage of government officials, all outfitted in various styles of skin-stitched jackets, surround him. An official, flanked by a notary recording longhand, recites from a document.*

*Gavril watches without expression from across the room.*

*"A verbal contract from the offender stating "Yes, I do" will be recorded as a measure of compliance in this codicil," the official says, eyeing Dimitri. "Do you understand?"*

*Dimitri clears the catch in his throat. Kangas leans in close to him.*

*"Yes," he says. "I do."*

Dimitri's *naked body lies on the table under the giant lamp. The excarnator, garbed in a priest-like latex apron and face hidden behind a rubber mask, stands over his body. Kangas supervises nearby with Gavril at his side.*

*The excarnator brandishes a hypodermic and inserts the needle into Dimitri's left side. Dimitri flinches, groaning.*

*Gavril, mesmerized, approaches the operating table as the excarnator prepares the scalpel.*

*Dimitri's and Gavril's eyes meet. Body deadening, Dimitri's mouth opens. His voice a pathetic murmur. "G—?"*

*Gavril leans in close to Dimitri's mouth. An inhuman gasp.*

*"The potatoes were burned," Dimitri says.*

*Gavril straightens, sensing his face hardening with anger.*

*Kangas merely folds his arms, smirking.*

*As if inviting red paint to canvas, the excarnator sweeps the blade across the bottom of Dimitri's lower jaw and opens him there until he spills out like whitewater blasting through a broken dam.*

*Transparent sheets of Dimitri's skin hang from black cables in the cellar workshop room. The table—a gruesome mess of crimson-colored ribbons and shiny flecks of bone soaking in a gentle current of blood that has slowed to a trickle after a few hours.*

*Kangas waits, holding a small metal box as if expecting a sacred offering. The excarnator approaches him, ceremoniously delivering a wrapped heart-shaped gift. Kangas closes the lid, locking it. He doesn't seem to notice the honeybee climbing along the side of the box.*

*Gavril salivates, waiting for an answer.* "The money— How soon?"

*Kangas says nothing. He merely glares at him with a look of pity. He coughs in his face. Then his blood-dotted fingers reach out, petting Gavril's cheek and smearing a wet line of red there.*

"Exquisite," *Kangas says.* "Beautiful skin."

*The excarnator stirs, brooding as he observes them. The scalpel glistens in his hand.*

"May I?" *Kangas asks.*

*Kangas, frowning, pinches Gavril's cheek. Gavril's face pales, eyes widening like a trapped animal.*

*The small honeybee—a velvet speck of black and yellow—lands on Kangas's fist.*

*Kangas pinches Gavril's skin harder this time, pulling.*

*Gavril, eyes wet and begging for an answer, draws a breath in sharply as he comes to understand the horrible truth of what's to become of him.*

I awaken again, my throat clogged with dirt. Spitting out bits of earth, I try to move my arms but find I cannot. They've been pinned underneath a mountain of muck and mud.

It's not long before I notice Dimitri towering above the

small grave he's dug for me in our backyard. As if I were a deceased pharaoh, he's already decorated my final resting place with various artifacts of our supposedly undying love for one another—the smashed bits of the egg I had once prepared for him, the broken teapot, the screwdriver he had used to disfigure my cock.

While he shovels more dirt on top of me until I'm completely covered—a shameful secret forever lost to the rest of the world—I notice a small honeybee circling his head and floating near his ear, as if the damned thing were telling him what to do and urging him to shovel faster.

It would be too much to wish for Dimitri to peel off all his skin for me, to wrap me in a dewy coat of his flesh and promise that he'll never abandon me again. Perhaps I've been wrong to yearn for something he could've never given me even if he had a mind to.

As the light blinks out from my vision and the mountain of dirt swallows me, I sense myself drifting off to the kind of permanent sleep that seems to claim all those who are keenly aware of the inevitable.

I think of how not every living thing will rot away.

I know for certain that I'm buried in the shallower pastures of Dimitri's mind, and if he were ever determined enough to rip me from the grave he's shoveled there, I wouldn't break apart like other poor things he's tossed aside.

Instead, I'd slither from beneath the filth, plucking out the maggots that circle like pearl beads inside the hollowed sockets of my eyes, and I would gently ask him, *"Darling, what took you so long?"*

# THE SEVEN-YEAR WAR

LEE MURRAY

**Bridget Brave:**
Hiya
I'm going to have to
pull out of D&D tonight

**Owen Warmaster:**
Nooo!
You've gotta be here Bridge!
I've been working on
this campaign for a month
It's epic

**Bridget Brave:**
Yeah sorry
I think I've got the flu
Might go and take a nap

**Owen Warmaster:**
That's fair

2LEE MURRAY

We'll miss you
Next time

BRIDGET WAS tired to the bone. The campaign had been brutal; long days in the saddle and even longer nights sleeping on the uneven ground. When they weren't moving, they were digging the trebuchets out of the muck. Whoever said war was glamourous had clearly been in his cups. It was an interminable cycle of setting up camp, brief hours of sleep, breaking camp, and moving out again, all while guarding their flanks against the enemy's raiding parties, which had been harrying them like hungry wolves since they stepped over the border. Sordid skirmishes which had weakened their lines, and their morale. The incessant rain and treacherous terrain hadn't helped. Nor had the whispers that the queen had made a mistake leaving the safety of her domain, murmurs bordering on traitorous. But now, the news had come that the queen's cousin was riding out with a host to join them, intending to wedge their enemy between the two armies. At last, they would have their battle.

As dawn neared and pink light blurred the horizon, Bridget's exhaustion dropped away, replaced by a surge of excitement. She gripped the reins as her war mount stamped its hooves, the beast snorting smoke in the morning chill. All around her, chainmail jangled and armour plating clanged, rattling her nerves.

On her left, Christian clamped down his helmet. Further down the line, Margot gave Bridget a salute. Owen chuckled as he gripped his axe. Brave companions ever since Bridget had entered the queen's service, she would live or die alongside them.

44

A distant susurration carried on the breeze—the archers with their longbows. The steed whinnied, impatient. Soon...

At long last, the trumpets blared.

Bridget drew her sword, savouring its slick glide, and then they were thundering down the hillock, their pennants flying, in a deadly maelstrom of hooves and haunches and heraldry, Bridget one rider among hundreds leading out the foot soldiers, and behind them, the peasants with their pitchforks and shovels.

All her childhood imaginings had been wrong. Experience had taught her that war was louder, faster, crueller, and more terrifying. Every moment lasted an eternity—or brought one. They were plunged into hell.

The battle raged in an explosion of flesh and fury, the armies meeting in a wall of iron and fire. Horses panicked and reared, their eyes rolling white with fear, and the air sang with swordplay as the queen's knights parried and struck home, pummelling shields and penetrating armour, in search of muscle, heart, and bone. Bridget closed her mind to the stench of sweat and piss, and the wails of the dying. Many more fell silently, their throats frothing with blood. Minutes passed into hours, dawn into morning. By now, Bridget was swooning with exhaustion. Her arm burned and her eyes stung.

"Where is that feckless coward?" Christian shouted over the clamour. The promised army had not come. They were outnumbered, outmanoeuvred.

How long could they hold out?

Bridget had no time to think. Owen was down, his mount's legs butchered beneath him. Bridget kicked her tired horse, urging it forward as the enemy swarmed over him, four stocky men with axes.

*Too slow!*

She would not make the distance in time. But in a flash of

colour, Margot wheeled, charging the melee in a flail of hoof and iron. She sailed over the lame horse, taking a man's head with her. The decapitated body crumbled where it stood, spraying gore, the sight of it sending Owen's attackers scrambling. He rolled to his feet.

Bridget saw her chance. Barrelling by, she thrust out a hand, caught him by the forearm, and swung him up behind her.

Her heart trilled with relief. No, not relief. Something else. Puzzled, she looked down, saw the arrow sticking from her side. "Owen," she said. And then she was falling...

Time slowed. She lay in the mud, while the battle roared around her, and stared at the clouds, their edges spooling in grey wisps. She was freezing. She wanted to rise, but her armour weighed her down. She didn't have the energy to even lift her head. She grasped for her sword to use as a crutch, but her fingers clutched at nothing.

Was she dying?

The trumpeter sounded the retreat.

From someplace far off, someone called her name.

"BRIDGET SAID she wasn't feeling well. A bit of a cold. Or the 'flu.'

"We didn't think anything of it. You have to understand, in the before-times, Bridget was really full-on. Into everything, you know? Summers, as a teen, she'd spend her weekdays putting together parcels at the food bank, and weekends, she'd be at the beach with the local surf lifesaving patrol. The rest of the year, she'd be juggling her university studies, swim training, tabletop gaming, not to mention a part-time job at Starbucks. And in between, she'd still find time for her friends.

That was Bridget for you. She just didn't know how to take a break. So when she got sick, Mike and I thought she'd been overdoing it, that she'd allowed herself to get run down. We figured a few days of R&R, some good naps and decent food, and she'd bounce back to her usual self. But the naps got longer and longer until eventually she was sleeping all the time. We had to shake her—hard—to wake her, and even then, she would often drift off again within minutes. It was all we could do to shovel food into her. Mike would sit her upright, and I would spoon the food into her mouth. I mashed it up because I worried that she'd gag and choke. It was like having a baby again. A twenty-two-year-old woman eating purée. She was just so tired.

"We wondered if it might be glandular fever. The nose-bleeds started somewhere in there. I can't recall exactly when. A few weeks in, I think. We knew then that whatever Bridget had, it wasn't just exhaustion."

I wake. At first, all I see is a blur, nebulous and cloudlike. Its edges spool with grey wisps. In my consciousness, touches of colour hover, and there's an undercurrent of sound, like the hum of wind or the distant roll of waves. I'm aware, of myself, of being alive, but who I am, and where, I have no idea. I focus on the blur and those swirls of pastel watercolour, and will the world into focus. My mind aches with concentration.

I drift off again before I can capture it.

In the doctor's surgery, Mrs. Brave stares at the window. There's nothing to see, the view outside blurred by the stark white Venetian blinds "We felt bad," she says, "not taking her in to see the doctors sooner, because when we finally did, they admitted her straight away, ran a whole heap of tests—TB, Parkinson's, Wilson's Disease, deficiencies." She nods at the computer. "I forget all the things they tested her for, but it'll be in her records somewhere. Poor Bridget was a human pincushion with all the blood they took. And despite the tests, despite all those brains working on her case, things were getting worse. Bridget was sleeping all the time. Shutting down. The rare times she was awake, she was vague and unresponsive. I called it the flop because that's when the floppiness set in. Soon, she could barely shift her limbs or lift her head, and afterwards she lost the ability to wiggle her fingers. Mike and I spent hours at the hospital pleading with her, begging her to acknowledge us. We just couldn't get through. She wouldn't even make eye contact. And then she lost her ability to speak.

"Eventually, after a year of indecision, the medics came back with a diagnosis. By then, Mike and I were a fixture at the hospital; it had gotten so all the staff knew our names. We even carried our toothbrushes around with us, so I think they had mixed feelings about telling us. On the one hand, they'd finally pinpointed the problem, but on the other, the news was, well... quite frankly, it was shite. Bridget had tested positive for cryptococcal meningitis.

"There was nothing anyone could do. The doctors were too PC to use the word vegetable, but that was the upshot. They told us to take her home and make her comfortable; she didn't have long."

"She's awake." It was Christian's voice.

Bridget opened her eyes and squinted her friends into focus. They were all here—Christian, Margot, and Owen. In a makeshift tent somewhere, judging from the hazy yellow light.

She winced. Her side ached. She lifted her fingers and felt the wadding circling her torso.

"It's not fatal," Margot assured her. She cupped her hand behind Bridget's head, offering her a beaker of water. "No sign of poison, and the healers insist the arrow missed your organs. Some rest and proper victuals and you'll be fine."

Bridget took a grateful gulp. Her throat was dry as parchment. "The battle?"

Christian shook his head. "Rupert abandoned us. We lost the day, and many friends."

Bridget's heart clenched. "Owen?"

Margot smiled. "He rode back for you, against the tide of the fleeing army, to pull you from the field."

Bridget couldn't see him, but at her side, she felt his hand clasp hers.

Mrs. Brave fiddles with the hem of her cardigan. "Life can be weird, can't it? What the doctors said might be weeks turned into months, and then years of care. Five years on and Bridget was a living, breathing ragdoll, her eyes as vacant as a pair of buttons.

"Our lives had become a constant cycle of care. Slaves to her care, Mike said. But who else was going to look after our baby girl? Nights were the worst. One of us had to get up every two hours to turn her over, so she didn't develop bedsores. We did it turnabout, Mike and I, one of us sleeping in her room each night, so the other could rest. Then we'd get up at five, get her dressed, shovel some mash into her, and load her into the car to take her to the special needs centre where she'd spend the day while her father and I were at work. That place is a godsend, and the nurses are terrific. Honestly, I don't know how I could have gone on without the respite.

"We probably would have been here much sooner."

I DON'T KNOW how much time has passed when I emerge into the no man's land between being truly awake and living in Mum's world, or truly asleep and living in my dreams.

I suspect I've been drifting in and out for a while now.

The first time I become fully aware, the moment I realise I am buried in the grave of my body, I scream into my head. I scream and scream and scream. Thrash limbs that refuse to move. Focus on my fingers. On my tongue. *Move! Move, dammit!* But I am powerless. Impotent. And entirely alone. The revelation is bone-shaking. Brutal. I can't even cry.

Mum is the only constant, my anchor in this half-life, but she isn't the mother I remember. She is floury and dried out, like a puckered apple. I listen to her shuffling about her day, I stare right at her whenever she passes, and she doesn't even acknowledge me. To her, I'm asleep.

I wonder about Dad. I guess he must be at work because I never see him. Sometimes there's a nurse who helps with my care. Well, I can't bathe myself. The humiliation is mortifying. I beg for an escape.

During these visits, I watch a lot of television. Mum leaves it on to keep me company. Not the news. Nothing to give me context. Instead, it's set to children's programming. *The Wiggles* mostly. Perhaps she hopes to fill the room with something cheery. Or maybe she believes my brain has devolved, and this is some kind of therapy. Whatever; the result is a mind-numbing purgatory. Grown men singing infantile ditties, telling Jeff to wake up and get his wiggle on. I'd give them the finger, if only I could move it.

I can't, though.

I can't even die.

Please, God, for the solace of my dreams.

OWEN YANKED hard on the straps of her cuirass, rousing Bridget from her strange daydream. The four of them were about to sneak out of the castle on behalf of the queen. They would take a tunnel under the moat and sneak through the enemy encampment, their mission two-fold: firstly, to entreat the queen's cousin for men and supplies, and secondly, to ensure Christian didn't kill the pernicious bastard before they could make the request.

Despite the peril, Bridget was keen to be away. At first, she'd been glad for their inaction, the time allowing her arrow-tip injury to knit. As the months passed, she chafed at hiding behind the ramparts, doing nothing while the people starved. Thankfully, the well was supplied by an underground source and impervious to the putrefying cattle the enemy had dumped in the river. But with the prolonged siege, coupled with last year's campaign, even the rats were hungry.

"We should get the queen away," Christian grumbled.

"And risk delivering her into the arms of the enemy?" Owen retorted.

Christian snapped on his sword belt. "She has kin to the south."

Owen scoffed. "So far away, it could take years to return with a force."

'It's of no matter," Margot interjected. "She wouldn't go, anyway. She would never abandon her people."

"But that's just the point," Christian said. "If the queen were to leave, surely the enemy would lift the siege."

"Or they might storm the castle and kill everyone," Bridget said quietly.

I'M AWAKE AGAIN. I know because the television is blaring. Fucking *Wiggles*. I am infused with technicolour rage. I will myself to sleep again, to disappear into another world where I can fight this tedium, but sleep evades me.

I check the angle of the sunlight on the curtains. *Damn.* Mid-morning. It could be hours until sleep takes hold again.

I become aware of Mum: she's flitting in and out of my field of vision, her cell phone lifted to her ear. I wish I could roll my eyes. *Honestly, Mum.* She never got the hang of holding it out in front of her like normal people.

She picks up the remote and mutes the TV, momentarily blocking out the tedium.

*Thank heavens.*

I focus my thoughts, straining to catch what she's saying, wondering if it's Dad.

"Owen, please, there's no need to apologise," Mum is saying. *Owen? I remember an Owen.* Strange images float through my mind.

"Seven years of this, and you've never missed her birthday..." *Wait? Did she just say seven years? I've been like this for seven years?*

"Really, I'll tell her you called... No, no, there's no change. I promise, I'd call you if there were. It means a lot; you checking in on her like this. Her other friends, well... People move on,

52

don't they? I don't blame them. Anyway, what about you? Tell me what you've been up to."

There's a pause, and I imagine I hear babbling on the other end of the phone. A tinny thin echo. Incoherent.

"Who bought it?" Mum goes on. Her back to me now, she's gazing out the window. Whatever she's looking at, it's too far for me to see. "Gamefight? Oh, Gameflyte. Are they a big brand? Really? That's fantastic, Owen. I'm so pleased... Yes, I know she'd be thrilled for you." Mum turns to face me, her face wet with tears. "So lovely of you to reach out."

"Mike left us at the end of the fifth year," Mrs. Brave says. She gives the doctor a weak smile. "I could see it coming. He hadn't really wanted kids in the first place. That was me. I nagged him into it. It was why we only had the one. Oh, he loves his daughter. Once Bridget arrived, she was his poppet, you know? Dads and their girls. And Bridget had him wrapped around her little finger. All dimples and ringlets, and the way she giggled. And later, he was so proud of her. But five years of sleep deprivation, of lifting her from the bed to the chair, from the chair to the car, into and out of day care, five years of moving her and massaging her: it takes a toll.

"And as far as we could tell, there was no end in sight.

"I probably should've put up more of a fight. For us. For me. But by then Mike and I hadn't shared a bed, hadn't had sex, since Bridget came home, and all we talked about was day care and drool, so there wasn't much left to fight for. Plus, it's hard for a father, isn't it? Having to wipe your grown daughter's vagina. When he wasn't with us, he was working.

"It's no life.

"When he told me he was leaving, I remember being more

53

annoyed than sad. Maybe a little jealous. After he'd moved out, I employed a nurse to help with all the lifting—"

The doctor interrupts, "But Mike's on board with all this? He agrees with your decision?"

"He signed the legal paperwork. It's there in the file. Well, he'd already left, hadn't he? Already, saw her as a lost cause."

THE MISSION WAS A LOST CAUSE. Bridget knew it the moment Rupert's knights confiscated their weapons at the door.

Christian was seething. Margot laid a hand on his sleeve. "We're here now. May as well parley," she murmured as Owen led them into the Great Hall.

But a child toddled from the crowd waving an enemy pennant, and Christian's ire boiled over. He snatched up the flag, and stormed to the dais, thrusting it in Rupert's face. "What did our enemy offer you to forsake her?" he raged. "A slice of her lands?"

Rupert smirked. He brushed away the flag, signalling to his guards, who surged around them.

"Not just a slice," Bridget said bitterly, "but the entire kingdom. And perhaps her body, too."

Guards seized them by the arms.

"We're the queen's envoys!" Christian shouted.

Rupert steepled his hands. "Four lowly knights? I think not. Perhaps you are spies. Some time in my custody would be prudent. Until we are sure..."

Bridget started. Rupert had never intended to send aid, however pretty the talk, and now he meant to stop them from warning the queen of his perfidy.

"Fool!" Owen spat. "You'll be their puppet, nothing more!"

But already, six guards were marching them from the chamber.

Margot twisted and called, "Who will come when the enemy turns on you?"

The doors thudded closed—and Christian whirled, snatching a sword from the knight at the entrance. He held it to a guard's neck while he stole a second blade, which he tossed to Owen. Bridget twisted free of her captor's grasp. Armed, Owen and Christian battled the six guards. Two others bundled Margot away. *No!*

Two men went down, injured at rib and knee, Owen and Christian still fighting, while Bridget grappled for a weapon.

"Go!" Christian screamed as a third man fell. "Warn the queen."

Bridget was torn. Leave Margot? Margot would tell her to do just that.

Bridget turned on her heel and sprinted down the alley. Next minute, Owen was with her, and Bridget knew Christian was buying them time. Holding off the guards.

They raced across the bailey. The outer gates were closed.

"This way!" Owen yelled, veering right.

Bridget took the stairs after him onto the allure. She pulled up. Looked over the parapet at the river surging below.

"Stop them!" someone bellowed.

Owen swept up her hand and they leapt.

Plunged...

Bridget kicked hard and spluttered to the surface. No sign of Owen, but she was still in range of Rupert's archers. Praying he was safe, she put her head down and swam.

She'd half-swum, half-drifted maybe a mile on the icy current when she found him floating face-down in the water. She flipped him over, relieved when he sucked in a breath, then hooked a hand under his chin and struck out for shore.

It took all her strength to drag him from the river and under an outcropping. He'd passed out from the pain, his leg skewed at an awkward angle. Likely broken when they jumped. Even if he were conscious, he couldn't walk, let alone run. Warning the queen, saving her friends—it was all up to her now. Bridget tore a strip from her tunic and splinted the bone. Then she carried water in a hollow piece of bark and left it beside him. There was nothing more she could do except stay with him, and she couldn't do that.

She touched his face gently. "Sorry, Owen," she whispered.

She got to her feet, checked the angle of the sun, and set off to the west, running hard, keeping to the shadows and the trees, out of sight, until she was almost dropping from fatigue. Still she ran. Hours and hours. She couldn't rest. She had to warn the queen. Owen was injured, and the others captured. There was no one else.

Delirious with exhaustion, Bridget didn't see the hole. She lurched forward, tumbling down a slope, Branches pricked and scraped her. She reached out, grasping for a handhold.

At last, her head clunked on a tree trunk.

When I come to, the light is blinding.

"Bridget, honey, you remember the neurologist?" Mum asks. "Mr. Thompson."

Who? My eyes hurt. Everything is white: the wall, the curtains, the ceiling. There's a squeak of linoleum and a broad man wearing a paper mask comes into view. He lifts my arm.

What's going on?

"So she's been squeezing your hand recently?"

"Not me. It was the nurse. Natasha. She comes in a few hours a day to give me some respite. She said she's felt it more than once. And that Bridget's eyes have been wobbling more."

The doctor squeezes my hand.

I want to snatch it away.

"She flinched," the doctor says. "It might be voluntary. Or, then again, it could be a reflex. We can run some tests. I see it's been some years since they were last done, so perhaps things have changed. I just don't want you to get your hopes up."

For fuck's sake. Stop talking! I haven't got time for tests. My friends need me. The queen's low-life cousin has captured Margot. Owen is alone and injured. Rupert's men might find him, or he could die of shock or thirst. And who knows what has happened to Christian? Plus, the queen's besieged in the castle waiting for aid when none is coming. Someone has to warn her.

I *have* to get back!

I tune the doctor out and race back to my dreams.

"WHAT DO you think Bridget would want?" Mr. Thompson asks now.

Mrs. Brave considers the question. "If she's in there, I hope she'd want to live, she says quietly. "I hope she believes something in this life is worth coming back to. I've spent seven years of dreaming of that moment, when she'd open her eyes and truly see me. I'd do anything to see her smile one last time. Bridget could light up a room with her smile. I know, I know; it's a fairy tale. A mother's desperate hope..." She looks at the slatted window again.

"But deep down, I know this isn't the life Bridget would choose, or she would have reached out to us by now. She would've fought harder. Maybe that's not fair. I don't know.

Perhaps she *is* in there fighting. Who knows how time works for her? How long am I supposed to wait for a sign?"

She slides the papers across the desk. "And the thing is, even if she were to wake, what kind of life would she have? A prisoner in her own body. Nobody wants that. So maybe this is kinder?"

I'm in the dreaded in-between again. Awake and immobile in the bleakness. Except today is different. The energy is different, and the TV is off. Something is happening. Dad! My dad is here. I'm sure I saw him flit past. He looked older and thinner, but it was definitely him. The nurse is back, too.

Wait. Why is Mum crying?

She leans in and pushes the hair off my forehead. "We're so sorry, Bridget."

What's happening? Are they getting a divorce?

Dad clasps my hand. I can't see his face, but I recognise the salty musk of his aftershave. "Bridget. I'm sorry I haven't been around much." His hand is warm in mine.

*That's okay, Dad. You're here now.*

"I want you to know that if I thought there was any chance..."

Chance of what? Is Dad dying?

Mum strokes my cheek. "The doctors say you'll never wake up, baby."

The words settle in my chest. I'll never wake. *Never wake.*

I see the nurse now, holding up an ampoule. Filling it with yellow liquid. At last, I understand. It's over. My parents intend to kill me.

I've been asleep for years. The rules must have changed.

And I remember the tests.

My mind somersaults. I've wanted this so much. Wanted to die. *Wished to die.* But now that it's happening, I don't want it. If I'm dead, what about my dreams? What about Owen? And Margot and Christian? They'll think I've abandoned them. No, I would never—

To get back to my life, *my real life*, I'll endure the half-life.

Mum drops a kiss on my forehead and pulls away.

*No, Mum. Don't do this. Please!*

As she turns away, I see her, *truly see her*. All these years, caring for me, waiting for me to wake. Hers has been a half-life, too.

*I can do this, Mum. I can do it. Please, give me another chance.*

The nurse is approaching now, the needle raised. Out of sight, Mum is sobbing.

I have to show them that I'm in here. An eye movement. A blink. The smallest squeeze of Dad's hand. Anything. Oh God, please. *Please.* I'm awake. I'm here...

The nurse closes in.

A bead of liquid drips off the needle.

# LABYRINTHINE

## MICHAEL BAILEY

We are stuck
in this waltz
of our mind

J osh sits at his red piano, paint on his hands. Some has congealed around and under his fingernails and he's high-strung on the chemicals that define him, as well as others introduced into his system. It's chaotic, this life, both beautiful and horrendous and fragile, he thinks, then says to the echoey room, "But it's all we had," the words dancing off the walls, and he sings, "that's why we shared it / couldn't kill you, love / so don't be scared of it."

Damn, that's good, the 'scared' in the final line stretched out long to offer weight. Catchy, sure; yes, it could work. Yes. Albeit generic, the phrases perhaps spoken enough times in common tongue to make it unplagiarizable (*Is that even a word? No*). He's about to write it all down, even scribble the made-up word. He needs to transcribe the lyrics before he forgets because some-times words overwrite words. He's about to ink a verse or two in his somehow-not-yet-falling-apart notebook, into which all flowy words go, when the pen hesitates, the way a paintbrush hesitates before stroking, the way the blade hesitates before cutting. *Paint, blood?* They can be fragile, thoughts. Then the pen goes back to where it was before, on top of the piano, although the words hang unwritten above the paper a moment and he thinks, like the last sung words, fading, No, '*don't be scared of it.*'

Someone sang something so similar, he muses, an acci-dental and clever alliteration, which makes him smile. "Shit, someone sang it. Before now. Before me. *Ante nosotros, mi amiga,*" he says and taps Amelia. Yes, she has a name—the piano—the way anything loved so long and so often should have a name. They'd been together ten years—his longest rela-tionship. He doesn't want to get any more red on her (*She's already red and gotta good* read *on her*) but wants to play her, badly. Wants his fingers on the white of her bones. *Te llamaré Amelia,* he'd told her long ago, *y te jugaré hasta la muerte.* She was complicated: an acoustic, keyboard, stringed percussion instrument. Yes, he'd play her 'til her last string gave out.

The clingy words had fallen too easily off the tongue to be original, to be *his,* and he knows this, though he wants the words as his anyway. They had to've been from a song heard a long time ago, on the radio, maybe, back when people used to listen to radios, nothing too recent; twenty, thirty years in the past. A friend of a friend of his back in New York would say it like that: *had to've.* And if that friend, or even friend of a friend, knew what he'd done...

Shouldn't've done it, Josh. *Shouldn't've* done it. Gotta come up with something new now to overwrite what happened. Have to write it out in a song, cover all this wet pain—

*—paint, blood?*

He admires the red on his hands, some of it like polish on his nails, which matches the high gloss of the instrument he's about to play—*strings in a coffin*—and cracks his knuckles; well, tries to but only one pops, quick as a sixteenth note. *Tenth notes*, he quips, *these fingers*—not the expected full measure, a segment of time defined by several beats.

*Bar*, it's also called in musical notation, used to trap all the notes together in a single cell, like a prison. No, a *bar*, and oh how a drink sounds like a terribly-wickedly-good idea to help finish the unfinished song and drown the rest of the haunting morning. Early morning, or very late night? The single-syllable *bar* and its many multi-meanings burn through him: like a metal rod, it burns; like a child's forgotten chocolate it melts; like a ray of sun- or moonlight it warms and cools; like a place where alcohol is served—*yes, the best of the bars*; or like a restriction—*no, honey, not another drink...you've had too many... please stop*; or like a lawyer's exam or the partition in a court-room, or as in 'to fasten,' or like to prohibit a person from doing something rash—*like stabbing, like murder, like another round after the 'last round'*—or like a counter to lean on when exhausted—*a drinking bar, yes*—or like a small segment of sheet music. That's a whole lotta *bars* and a whole lotta *likes*. Maybe that's the first line of the new song, something with a whole lotta hidden meaning behind a single, not-so-simple word.

"But what's the tune?" he says to the keys, out of tune, hands hovered over them, shaking, but only because of antici-pation. "What chords, what's the chorus, and what verses will tell this particular story of what shouldn't've happened? What's the *song?*"

It all starts with a note, followed by others strung together, some clinging like lovers to create a worth-repeating melody that doesn't mind sticking to the mind.

Sticky, these digits, but he wants to fingerpaint Amelia with them anyway. She won't mind. She's mostly red already. "No, you won't mind."

He knows he's onto something when he doesn't write the notes or the words down when he should, but they're suddenly there the next morning light after a long blacked-out night. And that's exactly how this song is writing itself. Had he blacked out from drink? This morning, last night? No, not this time, though the drink hides certain truths.

That could be a line, too, Josh *(talking to ourselves now, are we; yes, we believe so),* poetic and rhyming and whatnot, although probably a little too pushy on the purple prose. Gotta get out of this third-person stream of consciousness.

He tends to wake, middle of the night or middle of the morning, humming a tune, and when he returns to playing, the notes are still there, as welcome as a friend sharing round after round of Jack® & Coke®—those two words, of course *(better as one, making love to each other in a glass, glass after glass),* belong to Jack Daniel's from that good 'ol black$_{(out)}$ label *Old Time (Concierto) No. 7.* Yes, another drink. He makes another J&C, downs it because it tastes like familiar, and returns to Amelia before she leaves him.

The blood-red piano smiles flatly at his musings, her white teeth interrupted by the black toothless-like half-step interval ♭ s and ♯ s to compliment the A, B, C, D, E, F, G tones. Seven white notes and five blacks for each octave: a spine his fingers slide across.

He plays E ♭ B ♭ G, E ♭ ~B ♭ G, the second time holding the E ♭ throughout the B ♭ and holding the G-note a half-beat longer, then a quick E ♭ B ♭ before stepping down a bit and repeating the pattern with D ♭ B ♭ F... *Fuck,* that's just the first part of "Clocks" by Coldplay, he realizes, but holding the F since it sounds nice. Maybe he can do something with it, in time, 3:3 time (*No, that's not right*), still holding the F. Add a note here, blur the lines between other notes there, still holding the F. All music is inspired by music heard; the way all written stories are inspired by stories read. It's much like a waltz, this borrowed part of a song, a ticking clock, although it's a 4:4 time signature. 120 beats per minute. An excited heart. The F fades until gone.

Josh thinks of the heart, how it can beat consistently for so long on its own over the course of so many years and suddenly be stilled, or be slowed until still: *be* stilled and *be* slowed, until a person B $\flat$ -lined, opposed to doing so on its own; an ever-slowing metronome, tick-tick-tick-tick, then still. 4:4, no more. The musician: a god of the life of sound.

"*Held* until still," he says aloud, again admiring his hands. Those four syllables resonate the way a violinist carries her whole note, four beats on her bow. He imagines a fermata at the end of the measure—*the bar*—holding the note until someone shows her to let go, a conductor with his knife-baton until killing her last note. Then he remembers the rosin on her finger and the way she touched his face as though marking him before they parted ways.

An odd thing to do.

"A new song!" he sings, bringing the end up an octave.

He wears the hat, same one as always, both literal and figurative. It's a multifunction hat: pianist, composer, poet, writer of songs and all things literary: books, screenplays, playwrights. People recognize the literal hat. It's in every public picture, with his head cocked to the side, a little stubble, an expression teasing *I know something about this world that you don't, and I'll share little pieces with you through all my creations as the black mad wheel of time turns.*

Yes, a new song, a waltz for the three voices in his head, a simple yet purposeful arrangement of $B_3$ $A_4$ $D_5$, $B_3$ $A_4$ $D_5$, *one-two-three, two-two three*, "One lost voice, two crossed minds" then transitioning to B E ♭ D, "three parley" and then—

## 3:4 TIME SIGNATURE

*One*-two-three, round 'n' round; *two*-two-three, our thoughts spin; *three*-two-three, twirled and whirled. Never you, never me, what a thrill, always we. *One* lost voice, *two* crossed minds, *three* parley. One-two-three <sub>(four)</sub>. (*Wait-wait... Four?*), no don't stop; match the beats—one-two-three—*yet what's this— yes what's this*...hidden beat?

Ghost-like voice, distantly: "Dance that dance, *four*-ever, hand in hand, feet on feet, lest she die, once again," fading out, until gone.

One-two-three, *two*-two-three, *three*-two-three.

Spoken words. Foreign voice. New to us.

*What the fuck?*

1 of 3: "Who are you?"

2 of 3: "Let us be."

3 of 3: "Go away."

No response. Back to it. Focus now.

*One*-two-three— *yes let's dance—always dance—'ever-dance*, *two*-two-three, endlessly *three*-two-three. Ticking clock: second hand (slices time), *snick-snick-snick*; minute hand (hammers down), *tick-tick-tock*; then the hour, *click-tick-clang! click-tick-clang! click-tick-clang! click-tick-clang!* Clock strikes four, nothing more.

*Fuck was that?*

1 of 3, stern this time: "Who are you?"

Ghost-like voice, faraway: "Who am I?"

2 of 3, shakily: "Yes-yes, who?"

66

Ghost-like voice, still quite far: "Vanished twin."

3 of 3, lost in thought: "Vanished twin?"

Ghost-like voice, drawing near: "Three, but now (four)."

Stutter-step, *one*-two-three, slight slip-step, *two*-two-three, fluttering, *three*-two-three (misstep), palpitates, come on now, count them out, we shall dance, just us three—

TWO JOSHES WASH four hands in the sink until the last of her is gone. Can't write a damn song with her sticking around, no. Kool-Aid swirls of pink circle the drain—one-two-three-*fuck!* —translucent pink then clear. They look in the mirror, which is cliché to include in a narrative to describe character(s), he knows—yes, he knows this well—but the reflection has a smudge under his nose and so must the reflected. Could be coke dissolved under a slightly runny nose, for a cold still lingers; could be something else: *her,* third-chair violinist working her way up the ranks. While teaching Josh some basics, she'd improved, moved up a chair, then told him there wasn't enough time for lessons, though he pleaded. Oh, those eyes when he pleaded...

She slid that small finger of hers across the rosin that had fallen with her, touched the spot just under his nose: *boop.* The first and only time she'd touched him.

One Josh touches the same place with his right index finger, just as she had, and the other Josh with his left. Both bring it to their mouth to taste, although neither knows the taste of resin. The two Joshes separate, one going to the music room, the other disappearing, for now; *there,* but not. Perhaps when the door closes and the lights turn off, a third Josh keeps him company, the two of them talking, all private-like—a reflection of a reflection in the dark, sharing secrets.

A new door opens to instruments: a drum set, three functional guitars with varying numbers of strings, a broken bass, banjo, keyboards (*plural, always plural, other lovers*), xylophone, tambourine, flute, mandolin, and violin. He's played them all, same way he used to play with toys as a child, eyes filled with excitement. A yearning to learn. Some he's great at, like the guitars and keys, of course, and some just okay, and others... well, they make noises the way people do when putting hands and lips to them. There are others, but he goes to the violin.

Inside the case is a small container of rosin. It's hard as stone, so why had it left a smudge? He mimes the girl's final action (*first person instead of third*) but after his finger waits under his nose long enough to smell pine, he puts the tip to his tongue. *Well?* It tastes like tree sap, bitter yet *ancient*, how old age and convalescence might taste if placed into a tiny container to later strum notes on a string. It tastes like the remnants of what she'd smudged him with, so perhaps her rosin had reverted to resin in the hot morning sun.

She'd marked him, *boop*.

*You* did this, she'd said before silence.

He makes another drink a while later with a lot of J and a splash of C. One turns to two turns to three and then four. It's not yet noon, but there are no 'official' rules for drinking, just whatever feels right to the drinker, and *this* feels right. He drinks until the image of her finger reaching up to touch him is gone, until her glossy eyes fade, until he finds himself once again at his red piano, Amelia, this time pounding a lower-octave F key in 1:4. 60 beats per minute and willing his heart rate to match: *Fuck. Fuck. Fuck. Fuck.*

## 1:4 TIME SIGNATURE

One. Lone. Drunk. Down. Sad. Gloom. Cold. *Thoughts?* Some: lost, woe, death, harm, self, through, done, kill, soon. *Notes?* Yes, few: blue, sole. Dreams: dance, *two, three, four.*

THE SIGNATURE'S WRONG, all wrong. This new song can't be in 3:4 because there are more than three in the song, this story: Josh, his reflection, his reflection's reflection, and *her.*

Four notes are required, so he plays a 4:4 fourth- to fifth-octave sequence of $F_4$ $A_4$ $D_5$ $E_5$ on the whites, which sounds creepy as shit when played to match his slowed beat-per-second heart rate. He holds the fourth note another tick, tick, tick, tick, along with his breath—heart palpitating as though sick of the note, done with it—before repeating the pattern lest it drive him mad. F A D E. Yes, that's okay. Perfectly okay to fade. A start, anyway. How *all* songs begin, or *should:* by experimenting with order, with pace, or entirely by accident *(a misplaced hand, an ill-timed push; yes, that sometimes happens).* Sometimes what happens is only an accident, right? Or are accidents purposeful? The last note, it sounds so *wrong, wrong, wrong!*

He presses the F instead of swearing, three times, and holds it.

A last note can linger, can burrow into the mind, can haunt. Shouldn't've done it, Josh. *Shouldn't've* done it. He plays the first four notes again mostly to get rid of the lingering note and because repetition can often help determine what comes next. 60 beats per minute, nice and slow. F A D E, and when he plays the last note, it stays around far too long.

"The four of us are dying," Josh says aloud, and so he

switches back to 3:3 and the prior B A D, B A D, and sings, "Just us three / don't you see," transitioning to the original E ♭ B ♭ G, "labyrinthine?" And that could be the name of the song: "Labyrinthine," like the maze of his mind, with or without the punctuation. Could be a question or a statement. "Three sylla-bles, as it should be" *(Shit, those are both four)*. The G stretches out as he contemplates the possibilities. "All it needs," he sings in E ♭ B ♭ G. "Gee," he says, in the same tune as the note.

He imagines dancers matching the beat, *feeling* the song more than hearing it, circling round and round a ballroom in a swirling waltz. *One*-two-three, *two*-two-three, *three*-two three. Twirling round. Yes, that's it. Smooth, smooth, smooth. But the violinist and her delicate reaching hand adds a fourth unwanted note, and it shouldn't be there.

"Don't you *see* me?" he sings and plays, the words there on their own, *her* words, not his. *C?* Josh's finger slips on the next measure and plays F A C E, her face suddenly there, burned into him, which he shakes off and corrects to F A *D* E on the next go 'round, suddenly back to 4:4 with her last haunting note, and he shakes his head for not getting it right. A 'fad' without the last, he thinks, without *her*, without her gaze, and stabs D$_4$ hard near the middle of the piano to kill the persistent E and those ever-staring *eyes*. "Yes, I *see* you." Three notes plus one.

"Won't you bleed out," he says, his words this time, not a question but a statement. "Won't you stay still. Won't you just *fade*."

No, not until the fourth is gone can there be a waltz, he tells himself. She's still here...washed off his hands but still here, like the itch under his nose.

Another drink or two or three or four.

## 4:4 TIME SIGNATURE

Now this feels odd, the four of us, dancing like this. More like a march, or a box-step, than fluidity, than elegance; crossing the veil, toward our death. There's no finesse, no round and round, so what's the point? Who takes the lead? And who is led? Not much to it. Just one more beat. Does the fourth add? Does it subtract? A hiccup-waltz, one-two-three (four).

1 of the 4: "Why are you here?"

2 of the 4: "Why do you stay?"

3 of the 4: "Why won't you go?"

4 of the 4: "A final dance—you owe me that—'least you can do. Just *one* more note, *two* remember; you *three* took mine, and left me *four*—"

1 of the 4: "In each measure."

2 of the 4: "4:4 four beats."

3 of the 4: "We all get that."

4 of the 4: "Won't forgive you—"

Not that we care. A final dance, and then you leave. *One*-two-three (four). *Two*-two-three (four). *Three*-two-three (four). *Four*-two-three (four).

*(It's not so bad, what-what we did; no not so bad)*

4 of the 4: "Sing my sad song, don't forget me. Play my sad song, play it in key. The crime you've made, write that sad song, and don't let me—"

*FADE.*

Not enough words, not enough time, not enough keys, not enough rhyme. What are the lines? What is the pace? What are the notes? What is this place? In harmony, remember the—

*FACE.*

One-two- three (four).

*(We are dancing, the four of us, soon to be—)*

JOSH SITS at his red piano, blood no longer on his hands. Was it blood? He can't remember the details, only that a new song wants out of him. A waltz. Three notes per measure. Three syllables per line. *One*-two-three, *two*-two-tree, *three*-two-three. Yes, a waltz. He writes it all down: the notes, the ♭ s and ♯ s, even scribbles the title, and finally the lyrics into his somehow-not-yet-falling-apart notebook, when the pen hesitates, the way the hand hesitates before grabbing a blade. He wonders if four beats might be needed. So much can be buried in a fourth note. His thoughts bleed. They can be fragile, thoughts. Then the pen goes back to where it was before, on top of the red piano, Amelia. All he can think about is a single lost note—

1:4 TIME SIGNATURE

End.

# THANK YOU FOR PARTICIPATING

## TJ CIMFEL

**Hello. Thank you for participating in the Gardner Empirical Institute's Sleep Study (GEISS). This is the first in a series of brief daily online questionnaires. Please respond to every question in your own voice. Be as thorough and truthful as possible. Delayed, incomplete, or misleading responses may result in dismissal from the study and prorated remuneration. This is a real-time study. GEISS Researchers will review your responses each evening and may tailor questions in subsequent portions of the study. Please think of this as a conversation. And have fun!**

In your own words, please provide a baseline description of a typical 24-hour period in your life. Be specific.

*I usually get up around six to record, but I struggle to get going, so a lot of times I read my phone and drink coffee until I wake up, which sometimes means I'm not really laying down any tracks at all before I have to shower and get the day going. My wife is a stay-at-home mom, but she suffers from severe depression, so I'm usually the one to make the kids' lunches and get them ready and take them to school. I'm usually late to work because of that, but no one really cares about that stuff anymore especially because it's a given that I'll be working late. I spend most of the day coding, but we have occasional meetings. I usually get home in time to make dinner for the fam, do bath time, clean up, put the kids to bed, maybe watch TV if my wife is feeling up for it. If I'm lucky, I have the motivation to get back in the studio for a couple of hours, but lately I just lie in bed and stare at my screen until my eyes close. It might be the side effects of my other meds, so I'm curious to see what will happen with this whole thing.*

How much sleep do you get on average?

*I typically sleep five or six hours a night. I know it's not healthy and that the average is supposed to be something like eight or maybe even more, but there's just too much on my plate.*

On a scale of 1-5 (with 1 being poor and 5 being excellent), how would you rate your ability to fall asleep?

*Two. I normally can't fall asleep without trazodone.*

On the same scale, how would you rate your ability to remain asleep?

*Three. I'll sometimes toss and turn in the middle of the night and wonder why I can't fall back asleep, and then I realize after a while that it's just because I have to pee. I'd say about 50% of the time I fall back asleep without issue. The rest of the time, I just stare into the dark and twirl about whatever's going on in my life. It's a hopeless feeling.*

On the same scale, how would you rate your ability to wake up in the morning?

*One. I've started setting multiple alarms because I don't trust myself with the snooze button. And like I said before, even after I wake up, I'm basically a zombie for the first hour of the day. Which sucks because that's the only time I have for myself.*

Do you ever get sleepy during the day?

*Hahaha. That's an affirmative. Mornings are fine. Caffeine is a helluva drug. But after lunch, it's all downhill. I have trouble paying attention in meetings, and there are times at my desk when I prop my chin on my hand and zonk out for a few minutes. There's a corner of my cube where no one can see me. It's frustrating because I never feel that way at night when I am supposed to fall asleep.*

Do you ever feel your daily functioning is compromised due to challenges with sleep?

*I guess I'd say no. I'm still able to do everything I do. I guess I'm just not doing everything I want to. Does that make sense? Although I'm not sure if that's a sleep issue or a "my life" issue.*

What do you hope to get out of this study?

*Better sleep. Better energy. More time to focus on my true passion.*

Have you discontinued and destroyed all other medications you are currently taking?

*I have.*

**Please take one capsule now and submit.**

**Hello. Please complete the following questionnaire as thoroughly and truthfully as possible.**

On a scale of 1-5, (with 1 being poor and 5 being excellent), how did you sleep last night?

*One. I got in bed at the same time I usually do and read my phone. I thought I might be getting drowsy, but my oldest had a nightmare, so I had to talk him down because my wife was already asleep. I guess that's one of the good things about her depression, she doesn't have any issues with sleeping. Anyway, I probably drifted off around one, but I couldn't really regulate my temperature during the night. I kept taking my pajamas off and then putting them back on. I'd be sweating my ass off (Hope it's okay that I use colorful language. You did say I should answer in my own voice.), then I'd kick off the covers and immediately get the chills. I figured it was a fever, but when I took my temperature, it was normal. When I did eventually fall asleep asleep, it was probably after three. I woke up groggy, too, and it took me longer to clear my morning brain fog.*

Did you experience any somnambulism (sleepwalking) or somniloquy (talking in your sleep)?

*No.*

Did you dream? If so, what about?

*No.*

What are the names of your wife and children?

*I put this in the release form already, but my wife's name is Jennifer, and my sons are Abe and Phineas.*

**Please take one capsule now and submit.**

⤳

**Hello. Please complete the following questionnaire as thoroughly and truthfully as possible.**

On a scale of 1-5, (with 1 being poor and 5 being excellent), how did you sleep last night?

*Okay, so this was interesting. Like, the quality of my sleep was actually a four or five, but the duration of my sleep was a hard two. Early on, I had the same issues as the previous night. Temperature and all that. I probably wasn't out until three in the morning or so. My mind was racing about my wife. She's really not doing well. But this time, once I fell asleep, I was down for the count. When my alarm went off, that was the best part. My eyes popped open, and it was like there was no grog whatsoever. I went downstairs, brewed a pot of coffee, and worked on some overdubs. Stuff sounds great!*

Did you experience any somnambulism (sleepwalking) or somniloquy (talking in your sleep)?

*No.*

Did you dream? If so, what about?

*I think I did, but I can't remember what it was about. I just remember being outside.*

What are the names of your wife and children?

*Is this a copy/paste from yesterday? Jennifer, Abe, and Phineas.*

**Please take one capsule now and submit.**

**Hello. Please complete the following questionnaire as thoroughly and truthfully as possible.**

On a scale of 1-5, (with 1 being poor and 5 being excellent), how did you sleep last night?

*Ten! Holy shit. I closed my eyes at one and opened them at six.*

*No temperature issues, no nothing. It was amazing—like I blinked and woke up. I know it was only five hours, but if I could sleep like this all the time, I wouldn't even care!*

Did you experience any somnambulism (sleepwalking) or somniloquy (talking in your sleep)?

*No sleepwalking. But my wife did complain that I was mumbling some stuff in the middle of the night. Like nonsense babble. I have no recollection of this. By the way, I am totally going to name one of my songs "Somniloquy."*

Did you dream? If so, what about?

*Yes! I was in my backyard. It was a beautiful day. All the colors were super saturated—our house, the grass, the trees. I don't know that I've ever noticed color in a dream before. Are you dosing me with LSD? If so, keep it up! I was playing my Strat. It wasn't hooked up to an amp, but it was loud and clear and I could change its tone just by thinking about it. The thing was, I could only play in tritones. No matter what I tried, how I placed my fingers on the frets, it was always tritones. It was super weird too, because even though tritones are one of the gnarliest chords in music, it was beautiful. Like, the most beautiful progression I'd ever played before. There were a bunch of little blackbirds with yellow eyes. They were next to me on the ground, and it was like they were watching me play. I don't think they were crows. They were smaller. Hold on, going to Google. Grackles. I think they were grackles. After a while, I noticed the ground in front of me would shift based on the dynamics of my playing. If I played quietly, it would ripple a little. But when I let it rip, it was almost like the ocean. The birds bounced when I played. It was hilarious.*

What are the names of your wife and children?

*Jennifer, Abe, and Luke Skywalker.*

**Please take one capsule now and submit.**

∾

**Hello. Participant is reminded to answer all questions as thoroughly and truthfully as possible. Failure to comply could lead to loss of remuneration and/or revised study parameters.**

On a scale of 1-5, (with 1 being poor and 5 being excellent), how did you sleep last night?

*Five for quality, one for duration. I think I'm getting less sleep each night, not more, which is weird. I maybe got two, two and a half hours. This drug is supposed to help me sleep, isn't it? Don't get me wrong, I feel rested, I feel sharp. I'm drinking less coffee, too. I'm not nodding off in the afternoon. But this can't actually be healthy, right?*

Did you experience any somnambulism (sleepwalking) or somniloquy (talking in your sleep)?

*My wife told me I was out of bed for a half hour. I asked her why she didn't come get me, and she said she just thought it was more insomnia. I have no recollection of being up, and like I said, I felt like I slept like a baby.*

Did you dream? If so, what about?

*I did. I was in my backyard again, and I was playing that same song on my guitar. The grackles weren't on the ground anymore. They were hovering in midair like hummingbirds, only their wings weren't moving. The ground rippled each time I played a chord (tritones only still), and after a while I realized the grass was actually folding in on itself little by little, like there was a sinkhole opening up and my guitar was making it happen. Eventually, there was a hole big enough to drive a car into. The grackles started moving in a circle above it—not flying, just kind of rotating through the air. Bizarre stuff.*

Did you look in the hole?
   *WTF?*

What are the names of your wife and children?
   *Jennifer, Abe, and Phineas.*

**Please take one capsule now and submit.**

**Hello. Participant is reminded to answer all questions as thoroughly and truthfully as possible. Failure to comply could lead to loss of remuneration and/or revised study parameters.**

On a scale of 1-5, (with 1 being poor and 5 being excellent), how did you sleep last night?
   *I've been trying to get ahold of you. I tried calling the study hotline and the Gardner main line and only got automated responses. No one replied to my emails, and your chatbot was a joke. How did you know I dreamt about a hole? How did you know that I dreamt at all? Or even slept? I sat there staring at my computer screen yesterday worried I was losing my mind. And it's not helping that I can't reach a single human being at your facility. Could someone please get in contact with me immediately? I slept an hour. I don't understand why I'm not tired. Rank that however you want.*

Did you experience any somnambulism (sleepwalking) or somniloquy (talking in your sleep)?

*I babbled. I walked around. And that was* during *an* hour *of* sleep.

Did you dream? If so, what about?
*Yes, about the field and the song and the grackles and the hole. And no, I didn't look in the hole.*

Did you look in the hole?
*What is this bullshit?*

Do you love your wife and children?
*Jennifer, Abe, and Phineas.*

**Please take one capsule now and submit.**

**Hello. Participant is reminded to pay close attention to all questions to ensure the most thorough and truthful responses. Participant is reminded to not use the study questionnaire as a means to communicate information outside the purview of the study. Should assistance be needed, please contact the study administrator via the provided hotline.**

On a scale of 1-5, (with 1 being poor and 5 being excellent), how did you sleep last night?
*I didn't. And I called the damn hotline is what I'm trying to tell you! All freaking day. You get sent through this lunatic audio maze and wind up at the same place every damn time. I know you're supposed to be some cutting-edge scientific institution or whatever, but that won't mean shit if you can't understand the basic rules of customer service.*

Did you experience any somnambulism (sleepwalking) or somniloquy (talking in your sleep)?

*No. That would require actual sleep.*

Did you dream? If so, what about?

*Your drug doesn't work.*

Did you look in the hole?

*I'll give you a hole to look at, fuckface.*

Do you love your wife and children?

*What the FUCK is that supposed to mean? Why the FUCK do you keep asking me about them and how is it relevant to this study? I'm not taking another capsule until I talk to a live human being. FUCK YOU.*

**Please take one capsule now and submit.**

**Hello. Please complete the following questionnaire as thoroughly and truthfully as possible.**

Are you aware of the risks of not participating?

*Yes.*

Would you like us to schedule a follow-up from yesterday's one-on-one with our outpatient administrator?

*No.*

Do you love your wife and children?

*Please don't hurt them.*

**Please take one capsule now and submit.**

$\sim$

**Hello. Please complete the following questionnaire as thoroughly and truthfully as possible.**

When was the last time you slept?

*I believe it has been about 72 hours now. I swear to God I will remain compliant with the study as long as required, but please understand that the stress and anxiety (and now physical pain) I am dealing with as a result of my participation may be skewing the results for you. I would like to discuss a safe way to withdraw from the study. I'll make a healthy donation to your foundation. I'll recruit others to take my place. Anything.*

Did you experience any somnambulism (sleepwalking) or somniloquy (talking in your sleep)?

*No, but I am experiencing constant anxiety and pain from the extraction site. My hands are trembling really bad. I've been getting light headaches the past few nights, but that may be because of caffeine withdrawal. I haven't had a cup of coffee in at least two days. I feel scatterbrained, like I can't hold any one thought for too long. Or maybe that's wrong. I can hold a thought, but others crowd in around it, like I'm having multiple thoughts simultaneously. How is it that my brain can operate without sleep? What are you guys giving me? Like, at work, I'm performing better than ever. I squashed a bug that had been stumping the team for weeks, and I'm processing code twice as fast as before. I've been recording at night while everyone else sleeps because it calms down my brain and it's something to do and I always used to complain about not having enough time or energy to do what I really love. The thing is, now that I'm doing it, it's like all my old songs don't sound good to me anymore. They feel juvenile, overly simplistic. I went back into one of them and started tinkering and realized what was wrong. I started re-recording some tracks with just tritones and it was like something clicked. It's so fucking good. So fucking beautiful. My oldest came in and interrupted me last night, and I shouted at him. I felt terrible, but also a little good. I'm so goddamn tired of bottling things up.*

Did you dream? If so, what about?
*I didn't sleep.*

Did you look in the hole?
*No dream, no hole.*

Where are your wife and children?
*I WILL KEEP TAKING THE MEDS.*

**Please take one capsule now and submit.**

∼

**Hello. Please complete the following questionnaire as thoroughly and truthfully as possible.**

When was the last time you slept?
*Tuesday. I really wish someone would reach out to me.*

Did you experience any somnambulism (sleepwalking) or somniloquy (talking in your sleep)?
*My headaches are worse. I'm really irritable. I called into work, but that was a mistake because I can't really be alone at home.*

Did you dream? If so, what about?

*I don't know how, but I think so. I was in the studio, middle of the night, working on a new song. It's the only thing that helps with my head. I was playing this beautiful progression of tritones and layering them onto other tritones, and I started copying and pasting them over and over, just making this wall of sound in Logic Pro, and I felt this euphoria I've never felt before and suddenly I was in the backyard. Like, I was literally standing in the backyard. There was a grackle floating next to my right shoulder, and I swear it turned its head and looked at me with its yellow eyes and said, "What's your true passion?" Only it was my voice that came out of the bird. I could tell the birds were waiting, so I played my guitar and was playing all of the tritones at once, like in my recording. Like, I would strike two fucking strings, two fucking notes, that's all, but all of the notes played and when they did, the air kind of vibrated, or the birds vibrated in the air and they started moving in a circle above the ground like before, not flying though. And I kept playing and the ground fell in on itself and the birds moved in the circle faster until the hole appeared. And then the birds flew in. The next thing I remember I'm back in the studio playing music, only I notice there's dirt and grass on my guitar. What is happening to me?*

Did you look in the hole?
*If I do, can I be done with this?*

Where are your wife and children?
*Why are you doing this? Are you doing this to others or is it just me? My new therapist told me this was a specialized study, but I'm scared. Is this because of what I told her? I didn't mean it. It's just how I feel sometimes. I'm a good person. Can we be done now? Please?*

**Please take one capsule now and submit.**

**Hello. Please complete the following questionnaire as thoroughly and truthfully as possible.**

When was the last time you slept?
*120 hours ago.*

Did you experience any somnambulism (sleepwalking) or somniloquy (talking in your sleep)?
*I can't stop shaking.*

Did you dream? If so, what about?
*I went to clean off my guitar and found blood and hair on it.*

**Thank you for participating in the Gardner Empirical Institute's Sleep Study (GEISS). As a participant in Cohort B, you have been receiving an inactive formulation that includes starch and sugar. You may now return to your previous medication regimen.**

# THE LOOKING GLASS PILLOW

## ANGELA LIU

E veryone wanted one after they were featured on The Grinning Mannequin Show with everyone's favorite android, Arthur Z, hooking himself up to the Looking Glass Screen just so the audience could see what kind of dreams a man with a mechanical brain could have.

LOOKING GLASS PILLOWS™: DON'T WASTE YOUR SLEEPING HOURS.

*See your better life on the other side.*

"It says 'Designed by an insomniac, for insomniacs,'" my best friend, Liza, says, pointing at the train ad of a woman blinking through different iterations of herself: chef, dancer, sea otter, comet-catcher. The background music is poppy and soulless. "Maybe you should get one."

"Sounds scammy," I reply. We'd all seen the pillow cafés that had opened all over town the past few months, the rows of cots visible from the windows as people popped pills to dream for days.

The woman steps out of the ad like a ghost, translucent enough for us to see the residential towers sliding past the windows behind her. She smiles, eyes closed, blowing us each a holo-ad with the Looking Glass' red rabbit logo and a one-month free trial coupon code.

INSOMNIA RUNS in the family like high blood sugar and the inability to ever be on time. My mom likes to pretend she's the responsible adult, doing her night charade of brushing her teeth, slipping into her pajama gown, and switching off all the lights before 11:00 p.m. But I always catch her sneaking into the kitchen after midnight. She'll pick out some leftovers from the fridge and bring the plate back to her room to eat while she binge-watches romance dramas on mute with the subtitles on. Sometimes I can hear her laughter through the paper-thin walls all night long.

I'm less active. I just stare at the ceiling and fold out stories in the darkness. I become the people I want to be, travel through the cities I want to see, devour foods I'll never have the chance to try in real life. In a way, my insomnia lets me lead a double life. When we were still kids, I used to call Liza during the night when I couldn't sleep, and she'd tell me about the books she was reading or how her mother's new boyfriend would send her weird messages or how she wished we were both cats because cats can come and go whenever they please.

"We could just sneak out the window now and meet up at

THE LOOKING GLASS PILLOW

the all-night café and pick through the leftover donuts the old lady leaves after midnight," she'd say and then laugh.

"We're gonna have to battle the rats for that honor," I'd reply, tracing the neon sign of the café onto my ceiling, the familiar vinyl upholstery booths inside, the perfect disc shape of Liza's face.

I both loved and hated my insomnia.

When I show my mother the free trial coupon, she's the one who goes to the shop to pick up the sample Looking Glass pillow. She says it'll be good for me, that I won't stay young forever.

"They even threw in free insurance," she says, looking proud of herself.

"Insurance for what?" I ask, helping her bring the oversized box in.

The Looking Glass pillow looks and feels like your average department store showroom pillow except for the colorful embroidered symbols sewed into the casing that look more Takashi Murakami than Martha Stewart.

"It says each marking sends different signals to your brain, like some kind of neural mesh," I answer, flipping through the small manual that came with the pillow. There are drawings of people lying down and splintered diagrams of brain parts matched with the embroidery patterns. I lie down and mimic the position of the mannequin-like woman on the page, pressing my head firmly into the pillow to start the setup.

"How does it feel?" my mom asks.

"Like a cheap hotel—" I wince. Finger-like projections dig into my scalp. I try not to move my head as instructed.

"Something wrong?" my mom asks, leaning in to inspect the pillow, but I hold up a hand.

I scoot up, still feeling the fingers. This is new, but not necessarily bad.

THE FIRST NIGHT, I dream of school. *What a rip-off*, I think, but it's my deepest sleep in weeks, so I can't complain.

My Looking Glass self has longer hair and a more adventurous wardrobe: denim distressed to the point of no return, more shimmery tassels than zippers. I have a boyfriend that my Looking Glass friends adore and my Looking Glass mom is ecstatic to meet. His face is too perfect, his got-it-togetherness at professional levels. I feel small and insignificant in his golden shadow, but still, I swell with pride as strangers watch him longingly, as if I've inched closer to perfection by association. He's mine, at least inside the Looking Glass.

"I'll protect you," he likes to say, holding my hand with this intense look like some beast might tear through the walls of our school and devour us.

Our virtual neighborhood is filled with nothing but perpetually sunny gardens, ever-blooming azaleas, and buses that guzzle out muffin-scented smoke. I don't know what he needs to protect me from, but I let him believe what he needs. I do this for both our sakes—to keep our compatibility high.

"I love you," I type on our private channel as we listen to the teacher lecture about crumbling ocean ecosystems.

Our eyes meet across the virtual classroom. I smile and glance down at my screen, but he doesn't type anything back.

"SO, HOW'S THE NEW PILLOW?" Liza asks as we share a basket of waffle fries at the all-night café and do our math homework. Her mother offered to buy her a Looking Glass Pillow for her birthday, but she asked for a new scooter instead.

"It's all right," I say, not wanting to talk about how my

imaginary boyfriend's been ghosting me on the communicator.

Outside the window, the same woman from the train ad smiles on the billboard, her eyes closed. *Looking Glass Pillows - The top-selling gift of 2045. Give a loved one the gift of another life.*

"Just all right? My mom used the free trial coupon and won't talk about anything else now. Reality's apparently offensive to her now."

I snicker on cue so she doesn't think I've turned into one of those people obsessed with their Looking Glass world, the ones we used to gawk at in front of the pillow cafés.

"It's just like a really interactive TV. You find a character you like, and you can go frolic off with them," I say dismissively, connecting dots, tracing the u-shape of a parabola on my graphing paper. There's something relaxing about mirror-symmetry, how a single point splits and infinitely diverges from itself. "And when you get bored, you dump them and switch to a new one."

"Doesn't sound so different from real life," she shrugs, peeking over at my graph and copying my coordinates. "You find a hot boyfriend in there already?"

THE FIFTH NIGHT, I'm a house cat. I claw at a cactus-shaped scratching post my owner has bought for me in the living room and watch a red-headed woodpecker in the tree in our backyard with predator eyes. At twilight, I leave through a small kitchen door and sharpen my claws on live rats.

My neighbor is a heterochromic cat named Liza. Sometimes we pass each other in the narrow alley behind my house, tails tangling and untangling. Sometimes she leaves bird heads for me by the recycling bins which could be either an invitation to friendship or a vicious warning. My owner shoos her away whenever she paws at the window.

I press my face against the glass, pretending to bask in the sun, waiting for her to return.

THE NEXT NIGHT, my perfect boyfriend asks to meet me at a lake a few train stops from our Looking Glass school. It's a quiet place where our classmate, Looking Glass Calvin, drowned the summer before during an incident no one talks about. Long thin nets hang over the deadly water like the ribs of a god-sized beast.

"You're so beautiful," he says, his hands lingering on the crook of my neck. "You're the only one I want."

We stand at the edge of the suicide lake as his hand cradles the back of my head and he leans in for a kiss. The thought of cats and bird heads fade like ripples on the water.

*You're the only one I want to be inside.*

I shake the voice from my head. Woody reeds sway as the fireflies pulse to life, burning out the last few hours of their Looking Glass lives. His hand moves lower.

Days of unanswered messages disappear. It's easy to forgive in the Looking Glass, even easier to forget. I hold my breath, waiting for his hand to go lower, for him to scratch that unreachable itch.

"SET IT UP FOR ME," my mom says, pointing at the pillow on my bed.

"It might hurt your neck," I say calmly, smoothing lotion on my face, hoping she can't read through my lie.

"Liza's mom said she's dating Arthur Z in there," she responds, her competitive streak uglier than over. "I'm gonna find that heap of metal and have him serenade the meaning of life to me."

I can't tell if she's serious. Our moms have been friends for so long, they argue like they're still the children they were when they first met.

I bring the pillow to her room after her bath. As I put it down on the bed, fluffing it the way she likes, a sharp pain shoots through the back of my left eye, followed by trails of white floaters—the beginnings of a monster migraine.

"Go ahead, lie down," I say to my mom, closing my left eye, but the floaters keep swimming.

"What do I need to do?" she asks, getting on the bed, smelling of the menthol pain relief patches on her neck.

"Just sleep. The pillow will do the rest."

"How do I know it's working?"'

"You don't," I say, the pain behind my eye sharpening into focus. "But you should have the most vivid dreams you've had in a long time. Like the ones you had when you were a kid."

"Like...ice cream and talking dinosaurs?" she sounds doubtful.

"Just lie down," I snap, feeling a wave of nausea.

She winces as she presses her head back into the pillow. "Is it supposed to sting?"

I can only see the hazy outline of her face through the pulsing floaters. "It's just in your head." I swallow back acid. "Just go to sleep, and you'll feel better. The secret meaning of life's waiting, isn't it?"

THE PAIN in my head radiates down my neck and arms. I feel the invisible fingers even without the pillow. I stare up at the ceiling and try to count sheep, teeth, sharks in the ocean, but I feel eyes on me instead. Hundreds of them, tiny, begging me to let them in. *Please, please, please.*

～

MOM'S SCREAMS pierce through my dreamless sleep like thunder.

I scan my room for the closest weapon, pick up the sharp pen-shaped award statue for Student of the Month from 3rd grade, and head toward her room.

The hall lights flicker on around my feet, following me silently like deep sea wrasses.

Mom's door is ajar. I peek in, holding the award statue like a hunting knife at my side. It's dark inside, except for a faint glow on the bed. My mom's face is grotesque in the green light, eyes clocking around under closed eyelids, mouth hanging open in a whimper-scream.

I shake her awake.

"You were having a nightmare," I say when her eyes fly open. Her arms are covered in sweat.

"No, no, no," she says, looking at me like she's seen a ghost. "Start it again."

"But you were screaming—"

"Start it again." Her eyes are wild. "I need to go back. I need to get it back."

"Get what back?" I look down at the embroidered symbols on the pillow casing, the circles and lines almost like a grinning face, as if they've played a joke on her. "It was just a dream, mom."

I take the pillow before she can argue.

THE USER MANUAL has at least ten pages of warnings:

- *Do not use if pregnant.*
- *Do not use if you suffer from seizures.*
- *May experience disorientation and nausea.*
- *May experience short-term memory loss.*
- *May experience distortion of reality.*
- *Consult with your doctor if experiencing depression.*
- *Discontinue immediately if you develop a rash.*
- *Discontinue immediately if nightmares persist for more than one week.*
- *Use it.*
- *Use it.*
- *Use it.*
- *Don't even think about leaving.*

I blink, but the last several sentences are gone.

IN THE MORNING, my pillow is missing. My head is pressed against the comforter of the bed, a still-wet drool stain on the cream-colored fabric.

I peel myself off the bed.

The sound of drilling outside is corked by the double-glass windows, but I see the cranes telescoping out. Smoke and steam rise from orange chimneys below and above, the entire city trying to detox itself in the morning.

My mother is pulling out ruby flesh from a freshly peeled grapefruit, a coffee mug next to the cutting board. Her eyes looked bruised from lack of sleep, her body almost bone-frail. She hasn't slept since the nightmare.

"I took your pillow while you were sleeping," she says, not looking at me.

"Is that safe?"

"I don't know."

"Why did you do that then?" I ask, barely hiding my annoyance now.

"You were screaming."

"Why didn't you just wake me up then?"

"Because the soul eater would have just snuck into your brain and hid there," she answers.

"Right, the soul eater."

She hasn't stopped talking about the "soul eater" since the day I let her try the pillow. He haunts her conversations more than my deadbeat father and all the problems he left behind.

We watch the cleaning drones hover in front of our windows with their pre-programmed LED grins, spraying soapy water and squeegeeing the glass clean.

"You think I'm crazy," my mom says.

"No, I think you're tired." I watch her drop another fleshy grapefruit wedge into her mouth.

"I need to kill the soul eater. That's the only way you'll be free," she says, chewing slowly. "That's a mother's job."

I CALL the help number in the back of the manual.

"Hello. You have reached the Looking Glass Company. I'm afraid you have contacted us outside of our usual business hours. Please leave your name and number and we will get back to you as soon as possible."

I wait for the beep.

"Hello. My name is Mary..." I hesitate to give my full name. "My mother has been having persistent paranoid episodes since using the pillow. She thinks something is trying to—"

*Beeeep beeeep beeeep.* The line suddenly disconnects.

"I HEARD THE PILLOWS' AI can get jealous," Liza says as we share a basket of waffle fries at the all-night café and plot out sines and cosines.

"Jealous of what?" I ask, the words like ripples of water in the cold café. My graphs extend in all directions, spilling over the paper, zipping across the walls and floor like airplane flight paths. I haven't slept since my mom hid the pillow.

"They love their owners," Liza says. "The ones they first bond with. They want to be with them forever."

"That's pretty creepy." I finish a fry and lick the salt off my fingers, still remembering the feel of my perfect boyfriend's hand on my neck.

"Really? I don't think it's that weird," she says, motioning for the waitress to refill her coffee. "If you were the only person who knew everything about a person, wouldn't you get possessive, too?"

My MOM ISN'T in the kitchen in the morning. No stripped grapefruit skins on the countertop or coffee dregs in the sink. The drones are still at work drilling and cleaning outside. I knock on her door but there's no answer.

I float back to the kitchen alone. My body feels like a husk without a brain. The hollow-cheeked face reflected in the window is a stranger. I try to smile; it smiles back. How many hours had it been since I last slept? I've lost track.

I head to one of the pillow cafés. I don't even care anymore. In the window, strangers lie on black cots, their pillows glowing red in the dim light. Attendees stand against the padded walls like statues awaiting activation. Liza and I used to joke about how the end of the world could be happening outside and the people inside would never even know.

The doorbell chimes as I enter. The air smells stiflingly of prawns and dried urine. Each sleeping guest has a browning patch on their left arm, a crinkled blue one on their right—nutrient and hydration patches designed by the Looking Glass Company's parent company, Living Inc. Self-cleaning adult pads cover the lower halves of some guests to ensure a call to mother nature doesn't interrupt the perfect dream. They've got everything you could need nowadays to avoid reality.

"A two-night plan, please," I say, handing the attendee behind the register my credit card. Behind her is a floor-to-ceiling screen displaying all the phases of the moon.

"Certainly. Would you like to add on a deep tissue massage to your package?" the attendee smiles on cue, robotically professional. "We find our guests feel significantly more rested afterwards."

I watch one of the attendees roll a sleeping customer onto her side and run a muscle stimulator over her arms and legs for a few seconds each, then rolls her onto her other side and repeats.

"Not this time," I say with a weak smile. I'm not rolling around in enough cash to afford comfort, too.

"Of course. Please proceed to bed #27."

I'm DRIFTING in the ocean. I lick salty water from my lips, squeezing a strange sea creature in my hand.

"Is this the thing they told us would save the world?" Liza asks in her golden swimming cap.

Our rescue ship, like a massive black whale, honks in the distance.

When we return to shore, my mom is waiting with her new lover, a man named Fins who looks like an anthropomorphized shark with a bald head and grinning teeth sharp enough for tearing flesh. I find myself wondering if he knows my perfect boyfriend. If Looking Glass boyfriends ever get together in the cloud and gossip.

"The Coast Guard came when we were doing...something." My mom sighs, but Fin's grin widens, knife-like. "There's nothing out there. You're old enough not to be so stupid."

"But we found the way out of here. You can come with us," I say, raising my arm to show her the sea creature, but my hand is empty. When I turn around, Liza's gone too, the ocean now a dust-choked black field.

I JOLT AWAKE. My neck hurts, my ears ringing like a tuning fork. I reach for the back of my head, but there's nothing there. I close my eyes again, still seeing the silver light, the fingers still...

Someone clears their throat loudly. My eyes open again. The attendee from the register stands over my cot, blocking the overhead lamp.

"You've got a call," she says, handing me the headset, and gestures silently toward the bathroom in the back. Can't disturb the rest of the sleeping beauties, after all.

The bathroom light twitches on as I enter, washing everything in blue light.

"Hello?" I say, my voice echoing against the tiles.

"Thank you for contacting The Looking Glass Company. We are following up about your mother."

"How did you know where I'd be?"

"All our pillow systems are connected through a neural mesh," the representative says mundanely. "Your mother has been brought in for further evaluation."

The bathroom door swings open and a frazzled woman in an adult pad waddles into one of the stalls with a handful of clothes, mouthing an apology.

I lower my voice to a whisper. "She agreed to that?"

"Yes. She was most cooperative. She was eager to understand how our technology may assist in alleviating her worsening symptoms."

"Symptoms?"

"The chronic insomnia," the representative replies. Something pings from her side like an old microwave, followed by mumbling voices. "She asked us to call you so you wouldn't get worried."

"Is she okay? When is she coming back?"

The woman in the stall flushes the toilet. I can't hear the representative's response. "—nothing to worry about—"

The woman throws open the stall door, wincing at the sound when it slams into the wall.

"Your mom is—"

Water gushes out of the faucet. Hand soap buzzes out of the auto-dispenser. The woman finally turns off the water, flinging water off her wet hands into the sink.

"—additional aberrant cases. We are looking into potential software issues—"

The hand dryer blasts on.

I shake my head. "I'm sorry, I can't—"

"Thank you for choosing The Looking Glass Company."

"Hey, wait—"

*Beep. Beep. Beep.*

∽

LIZA IS WAITING outside the café, licking a strawberry snow cone.

"I saw you in the window," she says. "Something happen to your pillow?"

I can see the judgment in her eyes without another word. "It's complicated."

"Complicated enough to lie on a possibly urine-stained cot for a good night's rest?" she asks, the snow cone melting, sticky red water dribbling down her fingers.

"It's been hard getting to sleep," I say, the dream still fresh in my mind. I can still taste the salt water on my tongue. "Even harder than usual."

"You've hated sleeping for as long as I've known you. Why're you so desperate to do it now?"

Twilight smears orange and pink in the valley of sky between the skyscrapers. Silence stretches between us.

"It was on the news," she says.

"What was?"

"The Looking Glass Pillows. It took an assload of convincing, by my mom just went to drop off her pillow at the Recall Center."

"Recall Center?"

"A global recall was announced last night. There've been a lot of bad cases recently. Worsening insomnia, overdependence, persistent night terrors. Apparently, there's a whole group of customers from New York to Beijing that claim they keep seeing the same dream."

"What dream?"

"Something to do with a soul eater."

Liza was never a fan of conspiracy theories. Her mother once gave away half a year's salary to a man she'd met in a French cooking class who claimed to be from the future and was trying to stop World War III.

"They say the soul eater promises them anything they want. Who the fuck knows?" she says and motions toward the pillow café entrance. "This place'll be closed down by the end of the week, along with all the others."

Children pour out of the karate school next door donning sweaty white robes and different colored belts, their parents holding out juice boxes and snacks like human vending machines.

"Did you ever use your mom's pillow?" I ask.

"A few times," Liza admits.

I hesitate, watching her finish her strawberry icy.

"Were we friends inside your Looking Glass?" I ask finally.

"'Rule #25 in the manual: Don't ask your friends and family about your relationship in the Looking Glass.'"

"That isn't written in there."

Liza smiles, holding her hands up. *Guilty as charged.*

"I think we were in love," she says, licking her sticky fingers, not looking at me. "And then you left."

"I—"

"We were also feral cats and played catch with bird heads and tried killing each other a few times, so try not to think too much about it." She laughs in a way that makes me feel like I've done something terrible.

"I'm sorry."

"It was just a dream. Buuuut..." She finally looks at me and bumps me lightly with her elbow. The gesture leaves a warm swelling in my chest. "If you still feel bad, I'll gladly take waffles and your math homework answers as payment."

"Deal," I say, stuffing my hands into my pockets. A white floater trickles into my left eye like a firefly. "But I gotta go return the pillow before a lawyer breaks into my house for the evidence. Meet you at the all-night café at 8:00 p.m.?"

"Sure. Hey, I..." Liza scratches her forehead, hesitating.

Cleaning drones buzz across the windows of the massive mall behind the pillow café, their headlamps beaming to life as the sun dips below the lowest building. I wonder if they dream, too.

"You remember when we were kids?" Liza asks.

I nod, but my head aches, the floaters swelling.

"I kind of miss that, how you used to call me when you couldn't sleep at night. Remember how I terrorized your first quasi-boyfriend in middle school after he broke up with you over some stupid thing about leg hair?" she continues.

I nod, wanting to bury myself with embarrassment.

"I know I look like an ice queen most of the time," she says, "but I pay more attention than you think. I'll always be here when you need me, okay?"

"I know," I say.

Behind her, the streetlights flicker to life one after the other like a domino line of tiny suns, the floaters swirling around them like fireflies.

THE CURTAINS ARE DRAWN in my mom's room, the air purifier set to max, the fan whirring in the corner.

"Mom?"

Someone's unlocked the door in my absence, but they've left no trace of themselves.

I turn on the television, unmuting it to fill the silence.

"Ten board executives at Looking Glass Inc. have been arrested in one of the biggest dream tech scams in the past fifty years," a reporter buzzes with the breaking news. "One million Looking Glass pillows have been recalled due to a defect which has affected customers' ability to sleep. Thousands have reported paranoid episodes, feeling a faceless presence when trying to sleep, hands reaching into their skulls... Several customers have not woken up. It is believed the developers were instructed to—"

I open the closet and find my Looking Glass pillow at the back, packed in its original box next to my mom's old books. I pick up the box, my fingers tightening around it. Music spills from the television outside—the catchy, awful theme song to one of my mother's romance dramas. Something aches in my head, almost like begging. My body moves on its own.

*I missed you so much,* the voice says. *Let me in, please.*

Okay, just one more time, I decide, before I bring it to the Recall Center.

# PERMANENT INK

## MICHELLE TANG

You'd been missing for eighteen months when the first tattoo appeared. I'd fallen asleep clasping your tattoo machine as if it was your hand, the long cord intertwined between my fingers as if it were a lock of your dark hair. My gin-soaked nightmares were more painful than any needle could ever be—your carefully-chosen tattoos, manifestations of your personality, disappearing forever as their canvas crumbled to dust in a hastily dug grave.

The black-stemmed cherry tree adorning your left shoulder blade, the twin dragons on your hips, and the tiny siu bao above your ankle disintegrated as I reached for you, like the dried-up ink in your old studio. Like the love you once felt for me.

My wrist throbbed when I awoke, and I glanced at your name, faded with the years. Emmy. I'd let you place it on me in your careful way, small enough to hide under my watch band. As a way to mark myself as yours. But this morning, a small Chinese character was traced beside it, the skin beneath still pink and raised. The symbol, jī, meaning "nearly."

I picked up your machine, its tip glinting red, warm to the touch despite being unplugged. "Emmy?" I called out into the darkness of our room. "Are you here?" My voice cracked, some unnamed emotion making it high as a young boy's.

Only silence called back, a ringing emptiness that carved me hollow for daring to hope. That this life was the real dream I was waking from, that you had somehow evaded death to return to me.

What did you mean by this character? You'd taught me that the meaning of words changed depending on the other characters around it. Had I woken too early, before you'd had time to finish your message?

I settled against sweat-dampened sheets and gripped your most treasured object exactly the same way, a hangover squeezing my guts and screaming up the base of my skull. My head throbbed in time with my wrist, heartbeats synchronized —linked—despite their distance apart. Despite my discomfort and the lamp I kept on for you, burning like a vigil candle, sleep claimed me once again.

THERE WAS nothing new on my skin when sunlight next seared my eyes open, but the character gleamed blood-drop red. It was the color of your lipstick, the one that stained the starched collars of all my work shirts yet never your teeth, and it caught my eye every time I moved my arm.

I should cover the tattoo before work—wrap gauze and clear film over it, the way I'd seen you do. You used to place such care in dressing your clients' new art, hands gentle but quick, a mother placing a diaper on her baby. You hated that comparison, shied away from the maternal instinct I was so sure raged inside you. I was a fool to push, to scream, until you'd burst into tears.

My wrist stung as if in response, and I tried to imagine what you'd say. *Stop berating yourself, John. I forgive you. Will you forgive me?* I've lost the sound of your voice. Some things couldn't be preserved with ink.

I wanted to show you the world, point to the tiny sign you've given me as proof of life. Maybe then the suspicious stares, the malicious whispers, would stop. It must have been you here last night. Who else could it have been? Only you had a key to our place, an old apartment I can't leave because it feels like leaving you. Only you knew how to write in your exotic symbols, a secret language I forced you to teach me so there could be no secrets between us. But...how could it be you? That would be impossible.

I scrawled a message to you on a sheet of paper: "Emmy, are you here?" The paper looked too white against our dark kitchen counter—a glare of sunlight, a gleam of hope.

My sleeve cuff scratched at the sensitive spot. I really should cover it, but to do so felt as if I were denying you all over again. Hiding you away from my colleagues and friends, instead of displaying you as something to be admired. Believe me, if you were here, alive and forgiving, I'd give you any body part of mine you wanted, professional appearance be damned.

God, I shouldn't have thought of body parts. You're fine. You're fine. You're living somewhere near the ocean, healthy and happy and free. Just like you always threatened, just like if I hadn't caught you with your car half-packed.

But you wouldn't have left without your tattoo machine. You always called it your baby, right before you'd flash your gorgeous brown eyes at me. "Don't you start, John."

"You're the one who brought up babies," I'd always say. Always you, starting the fights.

You wouldn't have left without your tattoo machine, which was why I always kept it with me.

AFTER THREE DAYS, my note on the counter stayed unanswered, and the lop-sided character on my wrist scabbed. Your machine came everywhere with me, even to get the mail, as if it was a phone that might ring. I drank gin I had no taste for, twined my fingers around the cord once again, and tried to dream of you. I chased even the nightmares now, just for a glimpse of your face. For answers I couldn't find while awake.

Tonight, I had a terrible, brilliant idea. In my drunken state, it was logical that you could only answer me through the machine, through the tattoo. Maybe, wherever you were, you could only see messages inscribed into my skin.

I clattered through your studio boxes, grabbed the first ink vial I found, and poured it into one of the plastic wells you used for clients. Purple. Purple as the roses I first brought you. Purple as your bruises after our spats.

I plugged in the machine and turned it on, the mechanical vibration in my palm soothing and ticklish at once.

Beneath your name, on the inside of my wrist, I pressed the needle against flesh. Sharp pain seared through me, my skin a piece of linen shoved beneath a sewing machine. Sweat dripped from my face onto the fresh wounds, burning like acid, mixing with blood and ink. But I pretended it was you holding your machine, you scrawling "Why are you here?" in crude, childish print. The pain was my punishment, my absolution. The days of wanting to hide tattoos have long since passed, eighteen months gone, and I needed answers more. I needed *you* more, Emmy.

I finished the Tanqueray, held your machine in my grip, and let oblivion take me to you.

A BUZZING CHASED me into consciousness, metal bees stinging my wrist. I searched the ravaged ruin of my forearm, still caked with ink and blood. Beside your faded name you wrote more. Your writing was dainty compared to mine, a surgeon's blade to a woodcutter's, but no less lethal. You'd added a character beside the other, forming a new word. A crucifix wearing a skirt—the word for "machine."

I tossed the damned device onto the blood- and sweat-stained sheets and tried to breathe. It was your spirit, your soul, coming back to reclaim your most prized possession.

When my heart slowed to normal and my fear abated, a jealousy stole over me. No matter what I did to you, in a fit of anger and hurt, you never bothered coming back. But for this... inanimate object... you returned? But what use would a spirit have for such things?

I smiled. You were ever the coy one, Emmy. Using excuses instead of being forthright. Surely, you returned for me, as a sign of your forgiveness. I would keep you here if I could.

"What do you want?" I scrawled, clumsily, the machine slipping in my damp, shaking grip. My left thigh was sensitive from shaving the hair to ensure a smooth surface, but it still hurt less than my wrist. "I'll do anything for you," I added, speaking into the tattoo machine as if it was a microphone.

I pictured what your reaction might be, the quirk of your red lips trying to hide a smile, your dark eyes glinting with laughter. Even in this strange, unbelievable way, communicating with you made you more alive to me.

This time there was no need for gin—though there was

more than enough still raging through my veins—or sleep. I brought the needle back to my thigh, moving without my control, like you were guiding my hand. It was more painful. You pressed deeper, went over the lines again and again until I squirmed.

Finally, another character emerged. Another word coupled with "nearly," a backward checkmark wearing a lowercase h like a hat—the character for "hungry," written in a demure pink.

I wasn't sure what powered your tattoo device, why it needed neither electricity nor ink. And by some dark power, the more the needle penetrated my skin, the more I was infused with you. I understood what you were asking from me. Perhaps with a few drops of blood, a little ink, and some death magic, you could return to life. To me.

"Take whatever you need," I wrote into my skin.

You owned me since the day we met. My biggest regret was losing my temper after I caught you at my night table drawer, trying to steal this same tattoo machine that was now reuniting us. I'd been racked with grief ever since. And guilt, of course. It took two people to fight, but only one to murder.

Its handle burned hot against my palm, as if I was touching your blushing cheek. And then you moved the machine towards my bare feet.

Hours later, the machine fell still. I headed for our full-length mirror feeling lightheaded and dreamy. I ached. I burned.

The bones of you were etched onto newly shaven skin, a lined skeleton superimposed on my own frame. "I thought I'd see the real you. The way you were, I mean. Not just bones."

You didn't reply, and I stared at my reflection in disappointment. I'd forgotten how tall you were, part of what made you stand out among the other Chinese women. We were a perfect fit, and I saw that even more now. While your bones were smaller, your ribcage thinner, your clavicles were traced right over mine. I could almost hear you humming again, the way you used to after our fights, a similar sound to your machine's monotonous drone.

I wondered about your real bones, what state they were in now, if an animal had found them in their shallow grave. "The tattoo's bigger than I expected, but it isn't so bad," I said instead, because I worried you would feel the sick pleasure that flared inside me at the memory of your corpse. "I can still hide this under my clothes. What's left to do before you can come back?"

We were joined so closely, I no longer needed to inscribe my question into my skin. Somehow, you heard me. You guided my aching hand, blistered and cramped from holding the machine for so long, towards my thigh. The tattoo needle scraped. Stabbed.

I read the Chinese character for "flesh" before my arm brought the machine higher.

Towards my face.

This time, I couldn't help but scream.

YOUR TATTOOS on me catalyzed a metamorphosis. Was this pain-filled meditation what a caterpillar felt as it dissolved into nothingness in its cocoon? My wounds wept tears of osseous grey and cartilage yellow from our pores before they scabbed over—a fragile, furious layer, as if you grew your own epidermis. As we healed, our thoughts were colorful, confusing things—memories that were both familiar and strange flashing beneath my closed and crusted eyes. I was a young man, playing in my yard; I was a small girl, washing rice with cold hands. I realized your thoughts and emotions were bleeding into mine, like mixing dyes.

Truths I never knew and now couldn't escape sliced into me, leaving scars. How much I hurt you when I hit you, when I hid you away. How you tried to flee me, so afraid I'd catch you but unable to leave your precious machine, given to you by your long-dead mentor.

By the third week of our transformation, we were fired from work for non-attendance, and our body itched like a lizard eager to molt. Patches of skin lifted and peeled away from us, ephemeral as ashes, eager to crumble into dust. And finally, as if you were a new butterfly emerging, you were reborn.

We slipped off the bed, scattering large sheets of dried skin onto the floor, and faced the full-length mirror. Your twin dragons rode my hip bones, the black-stemmed cherry tree slashed across one scapula like a guillotine blade. There was no siu bao though—this new Emmy had no room for cute playfulness. You'd drawn in your breasts, even the scars you carried from past injuries colored paler against the light brown tint of your skin. I gasped when I saw our face, your features tattooed right over mine, from the bright red lips down to the elegant slant of your eyes. It was disturbing and stunning, a blurred 3D image. It ensured we would be stared at wherever we went, a prison within our own flesh.

"What have you done?" I cried out, but my mouth was no longer my own, and no sound emerged. Again, I tried to speak, to scream. "How can I live my life like this, Emmy?"

I grabbed your tattoo machine while I still could, while my body was still mine. I smashed it on the floor so hard that pieces skidded across the tile. A deep satisfaction filled me, destroying the damned thing was something I'd long wanted to do.

You made no effort to stop me.

Your rage thrummed through our veins, thick as blood, as you showered and dressed. All the while, you hummed with your stolen mouth. I learned that you hummed to hide your hatred of me, that you pressed your lips together instead of cursing. The conversations I'd imagined between us, where you granted me forgiveness and begged for mine, were scoured away by this relentless, furious drone. The sound vibrated over our tongue, down our throat, to rattle in our chest. The same feeling as your precious machine tattooing against bone.

"When this is over, you'll leave?" I asked in the silence of our mind. Maybe I begged. "I'll be rid of you?"

You smiled with our lips, and you spoke in the voice I hadn't heard in eighteen months. "No, John. Unlike death, tattoos are meant to last forever."

# CAREFUL ON THE ICE

## JARA NASSAR

There she is again. You avert your eyes, staring instead at the expensive but ugly linoleum under your feet. Not that she would have noticed; she never looks at you, which makes not looking at her even harder.

You throw another glance. Today she's wearing her usual studded black fingerless gloves and a black skirt with a white spider web pattern. It's the first time you've seen her wear anything other than black, except for those dark red boots that lace halfway up her shins and add an extra five centimeters to her already tall height. Maybe she wears the boots to impress somebody. It's definitely working on you, even if you most definitely are not the intended audience.

You wonder what kind of person she might be attracted to. Tall hulking figures in long black cloaks? Punks with ripped pants and spiked blue hair? Or maybe men in suits, living boring lives she enjoys disrupting, having her fun for a while and then disappearing, leaving behind broken hearts and homes.

You blink. Someone is calling you.

Stepping past her, you carefully keep your eyes on the ground.

Inside, your mind wanders. You try to concentrate, try to listen to the therapist listing off symptoms and firing questions at you. You wonder if maybe she is sitting next door, lazily answering the same questions. The thought gives you a rushing sensation that fills your ears.

The therapist is not impressed by your lack of attention, but puts it down as another symptom, one of many.

Fifty minutes later, you finally leave the stuffy, overheated building. You have talked just enough to keep him satisfied. He tells you to come for a dozen sessions, your boss is happy, the HR mandate is fulfilled, all is good. Maybe if the therapist would say you needed a holiday, you could get one. A proper holiday—not two boring days just outside the city, staring at cows and crows, but two weeks... Hell, a whole month even, at the seaside. You'd go climbing and swimming and eat fresh olives for every meal.

While swimming, you'd impress some stupid teenagers with your aptitude in the cold water, calmly practicing your butterfly while they triple-dog dare each other to dive fully into the freezing waves, throwing jealous glances at you the entire time.

But one day there would be a sudden storm, and you'd be the only one at the waterside—the only one except for a lifeguard in a red bathing suit running up to you, telling you to get out of harm's way. And because you don't have a car, she'd offer to take you back to the lifeguard's cabin, where you share stories over tea with rum while outside, the storm rages...

You blink.

You're standing at a traffic light. A child next to you whispers—not very quietly—to his mother, "Mommy, why is that person just standing there? Can I press the button instead?"

You give the kid a smile that is supposed to look completely sane, but fails. He hides behind his mother's legs, staring at you with wide eyes. You decide you never liked kids anyway.

As you glance across the street, a small jolt goes through your body. There she is, walking briskly along the pavement. Her hair is dusted with the light snow you hadn't noticed before. She is walking away from you, not strictly in the direction you need to go to get back to your gray, lonely apartment but not really not in it either. You teeter on the edge of a decision. As the light turns green, you hurry across the street. You aren't following her, just taking a different route home for once. Walking is healthy, isn't that what they say? You're just taking a walk.

Her long black coat almost reaches the end of her skirt. She is wearing thin ripped tights, not enough by far for the cold that teases clouds from your breath, but she doesn't seem bothered. Maybe she is a vampire, coldblooded like the night. She doesn't mind the cold because the blood running through her veins is as hot as the snow falling from the sky. She lives in the ruined house blocks by the canal, coming out at night to hunt her human prey.

But she doesn't bite just anyone—oh no, she chases down rapists and murderers, following them 'til they kneel before her, with nowhere more to flee. They beg for mercy, but she just laughs and opens her mouth, revealing glistening pearly white teeth that grow sharper the longer you look. Then she strikes, biting deep into the victim's neck, relishing their screams as she drains them dry...

You blink.

You are on a traffic island in the middle of a different street, yellow winter grass underneath you, cars rushing by on both sides. She is standing on the other side of the road, straight ahead, and for the first time she turns her head towards you.

Locking eyes on your shoes, you pretend to retie them, and when you look up, she is gone. Wait, you think feverishly. But you weren't following her, so it doesn't matter that she is gone, right? You were just taking a walk. A different route home.

You peer from left to right, your eyes taking in the almost empty sidewalk. The only figures are hooded and wrapped in shawls against the icy cold. You realize you are freezing, your teeth chattering slightly, your fingers tinged blue and numb. You stick them in your pockets while straining your neck to see what is happening on the other side of the road.

There, she is walking far down the street to your right. How did she get there in such a short amount of time? She is by no means hurrying, instead strolling along at leisure, the opposite of everyone around her.

The light turns green, and you cross the street, head bent against the wind. You turn right and look up. She is only a few paces away, smiling. You stumble, taken aback by her apparent ability to bend space however she likes. Why is she smiling?

You flash your eyes around and see a tall figure, also dressed completely in black. She is smiling at him. He is her boyfriend, and they live together in a trailer on a supermarket parking lot. Sometimes they steal jewelry from department stores and sell it on the streets to earn some money they use to buy food for their scroungy but loveable dog. He keeps them safe at night, guarding the door while they dance and have sex to death metal so loud it knocks the air from your lungs.

You blink.

The stranger passed her without a sign of recognition. You stare after him. It has become so cold your nose starts dripping. You search in your pockets for a tissue. While wiping your nose, you glance up. She is still standing there. Her jacket is opened lazily, as if to say, "What's this winter you're talking about? Where I come from, that's real cold. You'd have to be careful with those pretty eyelashes of yours, they'd freeze right off. Come here, and I'll keep them warm for you. We have a special trick, let me show you..."

You blink.

You are walking along a different street—one you don't recognize. Looking around, none of the houses ring a bell in your memory, even though you have lived in this city all your life. The street is quiet, only a car with a broken window making its way down the road, leaving gray exhaust clouds in the air behind it. There are no other pedestrians. The houses appear closed off, the curtains drawn, the windows dirty. You realize your arm is linked with someone else's.

Her face is smiling that same lazy smile. You stare, flustered, your mouth slightly open, your mind reeling for something to say. You weren't following her, but somehow she noticed you. Chose you. Or was it you who walked up to her? No, surely not. You don't just approach strangers on the street. Definitely not.

Her eyes are dark—a deep, rich brown—and seem to peer right through your skin. Red heat creeps up your cheeks, a welcome change to the icy cold. The two of you are walking at a quick pace down the street. You do not know where you are going. Wasn't there a part of town where people say the doors just stand open and anyone can make themselves at home?

Some of the houses must be used by all sorts of people, for all sorts of things... Heat burns your cheeks even more at the thought. It is impossible to tell what she wants, that lazy smile playing around her lips, her eyes hungrily taking in your face and body. You aren't the one leading; she is. She has a plan for you. A plan she has been harboring for a long time, intricately made in the small hours of the night. She has been planning this day since before you met, maybe since before you were born. You are only a cog in a great machine, and this is the day that will define your life forever.

"What is your name," you ask.

"Samantha," she answers.

Has her hair always been this sleek? Even in the low light, it carries an irresistible sheen. You are drawn to touch it, your hand extending, but you catch yourself. Flustered, you brush your own hair behind your ears.

When did the sun start setting, anyway?

"So," you say. "What next?"

Samantha smiles. "Whatever you want." Her lips are painted dark red, matte and alluring.

"Whatever I want?"

Samantha keeps on smiling, and you feel a hard knot forming in the pit of your stomach. You push the feeling away and try to concentrate on what's happening in the here and now.

"Stop dreaming," your therapist said. "Stop dreaming and start taking control."

You blink.

A last feeble ray of sunshine is streaming through a skylight, illuminating a dusty hallway. You stand leaned against a wall, your jacket open. You gape down at your hands, which are tingling inexplicably, as if you just touched something burning. At your feet, you notice Samantha's coat, discarded.

She's walking down the hall. Her steps are all swaying hips and studded boots. Her sweater slipped down, exposing one round shoulder. You stare.

"Hey, your jacket..."

She doesn't turn.

You pick up the coat. It is threadbare, but you can tell it was expensive and thick once. You wonder where she got it and why she left it, but she didn't bat an eyelash at the cold outside, so why would she be bothered by it in here? The temperature has dropped another couple degrees. You see your breath in front of your face. You really should bring her the coat back. She will need it. You are just bringing her back what she needs. And anyway, she was smiling when she looked over her shoulder, making sure to draw your attention to her naked skin. She wants you to follow her. You are just doing her bidding.

The door she vanished through leads to a staircase. You clunk down the stairs, wondering if this might be a boiler room. Your boots have long since stopped warming your feet, which now are clumsy from the cold, your toes completely numb. You have to pull your head in as you descend to not hit the ceiling. Inside your stomach, the gush of excitement starts building.

At the bottom of the stairs, a hall leads to the left. A single naked lightbulb dangles overhead, illuminating the dirty floor. You follow the hall in big steps, trying to catch up with Samantha. You pass boarded-up doors that hide dark secrets behind them. A whisper emanates from them, telling you about lovers once held, now bound, meat slowly dissolving from their bones, ropes chewing through their skin and soon yours, devouring you, dissolving you...

You blink.

You are in a dimly lit rectangular room. The walls are filled with pictures, nailed directly to the wall, rising all the way to the ceiling. You see a laughing boy no older than ten on one of them, along with a smiling older woman who could be his grandmother. Another shows a middle-aged man with a scraggly beard, and yet another reveals a young woman with lines tattooed along her chin. Each picture holds a different person, some smiling in exuberance, others stern or stoic or angry, hundreds or even thousands of people in every shade of human emotion trapped forever on scraps of paper nailed to this cellar wall, and every eye is trained on you.

You are lying on a soft sofa, a spring drilling into your back. You cast a look around for Samantha and almost miss her silhouette in the low light. She is standing several feet away with her back to you, busying herself with something you cannot see. You feel a sharp jolt in your stomach, as if the spring has drilled through the remaining fabric right into your body. You suddenly realize she is standing between you and the door. The only escape is beyond her.

She turns around and smiles. "Ah, you're awake. I was afraid for a moment I was going to lose you. You're slippery, you know. Hard to grasp. But it's okay. I like a little challenge."

She is holding two glasses filled with a dark liquid. The color is impossible to tell, but you see little bubbles clinging to the sides. She covers the distance between you in a few strides and sinks into the sofa. Her hip presses against your thigh as the sofa sags under the additional weight. Your cheeks turn pink. You try to sit up. She laughs and puts her bare hand against your chest, holding you down with the slightest touch. As her fingers press there, you feel their warmth against your cold skin. Your jacket is gone, and your exposed neck is lined with goosebumps. You sink back, careful not to disappear completely into the sofa's depths, even though it would welcome you with a soft, warm embrace.

Samantha hands you a glass. Up close the liquid bubbles happily. "Cheers." She raises the glass to her lips.

You follow suit. The contents taste of drunken nights and high school kisses in dark hallways and soured fruit, and yet it is not wine you have been given. It is instead a truth serum, rendering you incapable to utter a single falsehood as Samantha leans over you.

Never once losing her friendly manner, she asks, "Who are you? Where do you come from? Why did you follow me? Who sent you? What do you know?" Her face is inches from yours, her hands planted next to your shoulders, touching your freezing skin. Her teeth flash in the low light, coming ever closer.

You blink.

Samantha is sitting on your lap. The touch of her body on yours is driving all thought from your brain. The sofa is so soft you can feel her weight pushing you down into its depths.

"Take off your shirt." She trails her warm fingers over your arms.

You follow her instructions.

She watches hungrily as you pull your shirt over your head, barely noticing the freezing cold. She caresses your chest, running her fingers up and down your body, leaving red-hot traces. You stare into her face, the eyeliner smudged, her eyes large and never leaving yours.

You unbutton your pants as well.

She leans forward and digs her hand deep between your thighs. You moan as she kisses your neck, her body the only source of warmth in the freezing room. She kisses up and down between your jaw and collarbone, softly at first, then hungrily, digging her teeth into your neck 'til you feel the skin break and utter a gasp of pain, loud and clear in the silent room of watching photographs.

She jerks her head upwards. A trickle of your blood shines on her lips. She stands up abruptly, turns, and walks the length of the room. She comes to stand at the other side, her back to you, her head bowed.

You blink.

You are sitting upright, your naked torso freezing in the merciless cold. Samantha is seated across from you in an old, worn armchair, the leather breaking open at the seams, spilling stuffing onto the bare floor. Her smile is still there, as if glued to her face. She stares at your naked chest. You feel goosebumps of shame and cold covering your entire body. She tricked you. She lured you with false promises and that fake smile, designed specifically to catch the innocent, and now she has locked you inside a cellar with who knows what kind of plans.

Still she smiles, she dares to flaunt that smug face. You know she has something hidden in her hands, clasped in her lap. A knife, razor-sharp and glinting? A dagger, encrusted with rubies? A rusty corkscrew that long since hasn't been used to open wine bottles? You can't let her fulfill her plan. You must take control.

In a flash, you jump up and bound towards her. Your foot connects with something you didn't see, and the sound of breaking glass fills your ears as you leap onto her, determined to wipe her face blank once and for all. Your force knocks the armchair backwards, tumbling her onto the floor and into the shards of dancing glass. You wrestle to get hold of her arms. You grin triumphantly as the smile is replaced by shock and... Could it be fear? It better be.

You blink.

Samantha is standing across the room from you. You see her bending over, taking off her boots and tights. She turns to face you. Slowly, she pulls off her shirt. She is wearing nothing underneath. A shiver of longing runs down your back. She lets her skirt drop to the ground. Now completely naked, she walks towards you.

You have never wanted anything as badly as you want to dig your fingers into her body. Her eyes drip with hunger. She straddles you, pushing her round cheeks against your hipbones. You touch her smooth skin, the curve of her waist, the firmness of her hips. Her wet lips are on your neck, her hands traveling down your chest, rubbing your nipples. She takes your hands and presses them against her breasts. You caress them softly at first, then more firmly. She lays her head back and lets out a strangled sound as you slip your hand down her back and dig your fingers into her flesh. You press her hips against your body and bite the soft skin as her moans become louder.

You blink.

You are on top of her, wrestling her against the floor. She fights, knocking you off for a brief second. She rises, but you know better than to allow her to reach out and sedate you into a helpless pile of flesh with whatever she has hidden. The icy air sears your lungs as you lunge for her, wrapping your arms around her waist. This time you push her down with your entire body weight, your knees pressing into the side of her hips. Her sleeve falls up to reveal a long gash running the length of her forearm as you grasp her right arm, pinning it to the floor. She tricked you. She must pay the price. You just want to teach her a lesson. You *need* to teach her a lesson, just for her own good. With some people, words aren't enough.

You blink.

You are lying on your back. She is on top of you, her body hot and heavy on your freezing skin. One of your hands is holding her around the waist, the other one is wedged underneath you. You try to shift your weight to free it, but she laughs and pushes you deeper into the sofa. She takes your free hand with her own and presses it down above your head, while her other hand travels across your waist, chest, collarbone, until it comes to rest around your neck.

You blink.

You are pinning her down. From all over the walls, pictures stare as blood gushes from her arm, hot on your sweaty skin.

Her shirt is ripped, as if someone had clawed until the old buttons gave way. It reveals smooth, naked, seductress skin.

You blink.

She is on top of you, her fingers curled around your neck. The loose spring is boring into your back as you struggle, trying to free your other arm to push her off, but her legs are locked around your body, clenched so tightly you can't extract your arm no matter how hard you try. Her smile however stays in place.

You blink.

She whimpers as you press your forearm into her chin. Her shirt is unbuttoned and wide open, exposing soft skin that is impossibly warm in the freezing room. You kiss her neck softly, biting at the smooth skin as your hands travel downwards. Her body feels limp underneath yours. You dig your fingernails into her flesh until she lets out a sharp gasp. You grin. You knew she likes it. It's all a game, and you are about to win the main prize.

You blink.

She is grinning more maniacally than ever, teeth bared and stained red. You feel her hot breath on your face as you struggle fruitlessly against her grip. Your hands have lost all feeling in a mixture of cold and obstructed blood flow. Your breath billows in huge white clouds in the still air.

You turn your head to the side as she leans in ever closer, and as you do, you lock eyes with the old woman in the picture you saw before. You swear she shakes her head at you, as if to say, "What is all this fuss about?"

Before you can answer, Samantha's lips graze your ear and a rush of excitement and terror washes over you as she whispers, "No need to fight. Just be good now..."

You blink.

You are in a dimly lit room you don't recognize. Pictures are nailed to the wall, hundreds of faces looming from all sides.

Every last one of them is staring at you with expressions of horror and disgust. The largest picture is one you almost recall, hanging in the middle of the wall, a snarl on cracked lips, a smear of blood across the round cheek. The face is horrifying to see, but its anger doesn't seem to reach you. It is like seeing an old childhood bully, a danger from another world, another life.

Slowly, you look down. Your trembling hands are covered in blood. A glistening shard of glass is wedged into one of them. You try to grasp it. Your fingers fail at first, but finally you pull it out. As you turn it over, long and curved, you catch a glimpse of a face reflected in it. You have seen this face before but can't remember where.

You blink.

Who is that person staring at you?

You blink.

# FEAST OF THE DREAMER

## PEDRO INIGUEZ

urelio Treviño swatted the blowflies hovering ravenously over his face as he spotted the patch of loose earth. The ravine was nestled at the end of a beaten dirt road, hours from the nearest town. Amidst the dimming afternoon light, he looked around one last time to see if there had been any stray hikers lingering in the distance to bear witness to his transgressions.

Satisfied with his solitude, he speared the shovel into the mound of black soil and the ground beneath his mud-crusted shoes broke seamlessly. It wasn't long before the stench found him, the fetid scent of rot and sulfur burning his nostrils. He hawked a wad of phlegm, spit it out, and grimaced.

*It will be worth it*, he reminded himself. *The dreams will come.*

Staring back at him from the pit was the countenance of what might have once been a middle-aged woman, her patchy green-blue face sunken and gaunt, her brown eyes frozen into a thousand-meter stare. She was beautiful in her own way, despite the onset of decomposition. Many were. Beauty remained long after death, he'd found. He rattled off the thought and continued to sift through the earth until he caught sight of her naked torso, her bruised skin swollen, puffy like a balloon.

As he strapped on a pair of latex gloves, he thought about the woman, lifeless under his shadow. For years, the local cartel had used this plot of land as a dumping ground and there was no telling who she may have been: A sicario's trifling ex-girlfriend, a rival boss's wife, a food vendor who refused to pay her dues.

On occasion Aurelio used to make up stories about the people he buried, anonymous in their solitude. It gave them, in his mind, a semblance of a new life, imbuing them with a soul. It was the least he could do. Sometimes it helped repress the guilt. Most times, it didn't. This one, he decided, had been a vocal activist waging a righteous war against the narcos and the string of missing women in the state. A cause worthy of a crusader like her.

Before he'd given up that life, he'd had to put down many like her, nabbing them in narrow alleys, whisking them away in the dead of night, never to be seen again. He'd bring them here, of course, or to any one of the dozens of clandestine death houses seeding the state. He dwelled on all the torments he'd inflicted on them over the years as they squirmed and gasped and pleaded for pity, their shrieks powerless to change a thing.

He stooped his head and closed his eyes as he felt the familiar tug at his heart, the old feelings starting to consume him, gnawing away at him like an infestation of fleas on a mangy dog. And much like a dog, after some mild discomfort, he shook off the feeling and went about his business.

Aurelio unclipped a box cutter from his belt, knelt beside the woman, and sliced her open from sternum to navel. He counted himself lucky; he'd found her before decomposition had liquified her organs. Like fruit, the bodies couldn't be overly ripe.

He quickly flinched at the swell of putrid air and buried his face in the crook of his elbow, stifling a hacking cough. He wished it didn't have to be this way, lurking like a ghoul atop a shallow grave, watching as the maggots feasted on her organs. But this was the only way to traverse the chasm between worlds.

Soon, the dreams would come. Soon.

Reciting the Lord's Prayer never really helped much to cope with the ugliness of it all, but he did it anyway before he shoved a gloved hand into the cavity in her belly. He scooped out a moist lump of cold, viscous entrail—much like the innards of a carved pumpkin—and rattled off a few larvae, shoving his prize into his mouth.

Like fruit, he reminded himself. Nothing more.

Aurelio ended his feast alongside the flies and maggots just as the sun sank below the world.

THERE WERE eyes all around this dusty country, watching, waiting eagerly to report to their masters sitting on golden thrones in fortified palaces. When Aurelio was convinced he hadn't been trailed, he entered his room and fastened the latch behind him.

The roadside motel was small, tucked out of the way and far from anywhere important. It would only be a matter of time before they found him and executed him for his delinquencies. He knew he couldn't outrun his pursuers forever, nor could he shut out the voices. Unless, of course, he fled where no one could follow—not even the ghosts of those he'd wronged. And there had been legions of ghosts, always skulking deep in the dark corners of his mind, murmuring amongst themselves, recounting his sins like bedtime stories.

Aurelio covered his ears with trembling hands until the voices faded into the ether.

The waiting was torment, the incubation period a drag through pain and sorrow-filled thoughts. In that time, he undressed, sat on the edge of his bed, and flipped through a bevy of scrambled television channels. Telenovelas, the local news, badly dubbed American films. Sometimes he would approach the window and peek through the blinds in bouts of boredom, the moon bathing the road in its pale blue light. A few times, he'd crack the door open and inhale the sweet summer air in anticipation of the ritual.

By midnight Aurelio felt the nausea form in the pit of his belly and quickly radiate up into his brain. As his head throbbed and his vision blurred, he flicked off the lights and rushed to light the candles on the nightstand. The sacrament brought him comfort. There was, after all, a sanctity to the process.

A fire flared throughout his face and his stomach churned in vile ways. Aurelio lunged into the bathroom, knelt at the gape of the toilet bowl, and expelled the contents of his toxic meal. The retch of gray chunks, bile, and blood stained the porcelain, pooling together to form a repugnant stew.

After he'd expelled the contents of his stomach for what seemed to be an agonizing stretch of time, he pushed himself up and peered in the mirror. Red eyes looked upon the raspberry blotches pocking his once-handsome face where the blood vessels had ruptured. He lay a hand on his head and felt the warmth of the fever running its course.

Every journey required self-sacrifice: The wrenching of his insides, the blemishing of his face, the scorching fevers. But it had always been worth the pain. Always. It brought him that much closer to the dream world.

Leaning against the bathroom doorway, arms wrapped around his chest, he broke into a sweat. Soon, the wonders would come to him once more.

Aurelio inhaled the stuffy air, shut his eyes, and saw the vague landscapes again, the eccentric orbits of dozens of moons dotting the night sky. He grasped out in front of him, as if the sights were tangible. Though nebulous, the images from the dreamscape had burned themselves deep into his brain, ingrained into his eyeballs like the lingering ghost images from an old television set. But the visions were incomplete, fragmented, like peering through a shattered stained-glass window.

He needed to venture further. All the way.

What was clear though, was the voice echoing in his mind as it had in his dreams, beckoning Aurelio deeper into that darkness. A darkness tinged with pleasure. Yes. The Apostle of Bloat awaited. His voice had been deep like pools of black water, yet soothing like an aloe balm upon seared flesh.

The sound of tires rolling over gravel spurred Aurelio toward the window. "No, no, no," he muttered under his breath. A blue sedan wheeled slowly down the road until it merged with the darkness on the horizon. He could never be too sure if his pursuers had found him. When his heart settled, he sighed and sat on the edge of the bed, his eyes feeling heavier by the second. Almost.

Aurelio remembered vividly how he'd first stumbled upon that dreamscape after gorging himself on a meal of spoiled beef. The spell of violent vomiting had left him bedridden and at the mercy of fevered dreams. Dreams that allowed him to leave the pain behind forever. Dreams where he knew peace and pleasure and the stains of guilt had washed off his soul at last. But he knew better now. They weren't delusions but temporary traverses into another reality. A place beyond human understanding. The dreams were gateways.

After that mind-altering experience, Aurelio had sought to relive his voyage—craved it day and night like an addict. But to venture farther into that realm, he needed to sacrifice more of himself, to grow dire in illness, close to death. He spent months experimenting with rotten foods, psychoactive drugs, his body exposed to varying stages of bacterial malady and self-induced fevers. During his explorations, he had discovered the secret lay in the ingestion of the deceased—the mortal fruit of the gods.

It began with roadkill, feasting on the burst intestines of small rodents on lonely stretches of highway. Then, it progressed to the rotten brain matter of mutilated cattle. All had wrecked his insides, his mind, carrying him further into that occulted realm. Tonight, he'd sampled the true fruit—the festering remains of a human corpse.

"Soon," Aurelio said, his voice coarse, his throat raw with flaring pain.

He crawled under the bedsheets, anticipating the sensory wonders, the splendors that awaited, where there existed a world of miracles and ecstasy and the sorrow that had eaten away at his insides like a brood of maggots would cease to exist.

AURELIO BLINKED AND, from one moment to another, he had traversed into a different world. Sleep became a tether to another reality. Like a deep-sea diver plunging into unfathomable depths, he waded deep into an ethereal realm not meant for mortal beings. He stood, naked and cold, before a world of vast obsidian mesas and spiraling peaks. Chasms plunged into infinite darkness, blacker than any shade known to man. The endless sky appeared like a mottled watercolor painting, its dark blue light bleeding into the volcanic land below. The air itself was charged with an electric current that stimulated the nerve endings on his flesh, causing his skin to erupt with goosebumps.

He suddenly dropped to the hot, rocky ground and writhed in ecstasy under the gaze of a dozen heavenly spheres, the scarlet satellites looping around the horizon until the sensations brought him to orgasm. He wiped tears of pleasure from his eyes, got back to his feet, and carried onward.

As he trekked further into the dreamscape, the soot at his feet grew hot until the skin on his soles burned and peeled away. His soul was so filled with elation, he scantly noticed the pain, nor the faceless souls of those he'd wronged, watching his every step.

Again, he heard the familiar voice, powerful and soothing, as it called to him from beyond the void. The words carried on the howling wind, undecipherable at first, but becoming increasingly clearer as he waded through the dream. "Aurelio," the words echoed repeatedly.

Deep into the dreamscape, Aurelio came upon an ashen man sitting on a marble throne, every inch of his skin covered by swarming flies. The man smiled crookedly, his arching brows shifting a crown of severed fingers atop his head.

"Do you know who I am?" the man said, his voice carrying forcefully across the air.

Aurelio knelt. "You are the Apostle of Bloat. I have heard your voice in my dreams."

The Apostle smiled, flashing a set of yellow teeth embedded inside tar-colored gums.

"I've been looking for you for a long time."

The Apostle curled his index finger, beckoning Aurelio forth. "Where do you come from?"

Aurelio shuffled toward the Apostle. The buzzing of the flies grew into an angry frenzy. "I come from a world of grief and death. Of decay and finality."

"I see," said the Apostle. "And what do you seek?"

"I don't have much time before our link is severed," Aurelio pleaded. "Soon, I will awake to a world of sadness. I wish to stay here with you forever in everlasting peace and joy."

The Apostle leaned back in his throne and nodded. "Come closer and I shall impart upon you grand wisdom."

Nervously, Aurelio approached the Apostle. Flies scattered from the king's head, revealing a man that looked eerily like Aurelio, save for his blue, gaunt flesh and the hollowed-out pits where his eyes should have been. Aurelio trembled at the terrible visage before him.

"Do not fear," the Apostle said as the flies settled back on his face. "Your days of running are at an end. A world of love and peace awaits." The Apostle leaned forward, his cracked blue lips nearly touching Aurelio's earlobe. "The way to bridge the gap between worlds is to taste one's own fruit."

Aurelio's own lips quivered. "One's own fruit?"

The Apostle of Bloat stood and placed a hand on Aurelio's shoulder, clamping sharp-nailed fingers into his flesh.

Aurelio jolted awake to the summer heat circulating inside his motel room, the fire of the candles spitting his flickering shadow on the wall. The light of the moon pierced the broken slats on the window, painting his torso blue. His bedsheets stuck to his sodden body, the sweat pungent with the contaminated waste circulating through his blood.

Aurelio's arms shuddered as he sat up against the headboard. He reached for the nightstand and unclipped the box cutter from his jeans.

His glistening belly rose and fell as he labored to breathe, his lungs filling with fluid. The fire in his head had spread through every limb and muscle and every movement felt like a miniscule torture. Aurelio licked his dry lips and dragged the blade across his abdomen, wincing as the wound split open and wept its warm syrup into his lap.

Like fruit.

The bedsheets readily accepted his body's scarlet offering, soaking up the blood like a canvas. His face contorted as he reached inside the gash, his fingers probing past the layers of flesh and fat. A wave of numbing coldness began to sweep through the fibers in his stomach, quenching the flaring pain. Black spots began to fill his vision as the blood stains expanded on the bed. Aurelio fought to keep his eyelids open as his trembling hand pulled out a meaty strand of intestine and brought the piece of himself to his lips. He began to gnaw slowly, his teeth chattering as the taste of warm copper filled his mouth. The juices of life seeped down his gullet and chin, branching off and meeting again on his chest like tributaries flowing into a river.

Once he'd had his fill, Aurelio settled back into a supine position and shut his eyes. The candle at his side began to flicker out as he awaited his final journey to a world where pain and suffering and ghosts were only things of make-believe.

# ARMINGRAABER

JOE KOCH

W e walked the escape route linked like a chain, arm in arm, heads bowed, hands clasped, elbows locked against the residual grit from the blast. Particles too small to elude stung our eyes, rendering us blind. The landscape of swirling ash offered nothing left to go back to. Our knees and necks ached like unoiled gears. The wind tore through every pore and shouldered roughly between us, but we held together, heaving forward, lurching on as one many-legged beast. When finally we hit the outer wall of the unexpected structure, we cried out in relief.

Kincaid nearly lost hold and broke from my grasp. My arm sagged with her weight.

"Stay focused," Eterin yelled over the roaring wind. "Now's not the time to give in to hysterics."

Later I'd explain his poor choice of words insulted rather than encouraged the sole woman in our group. I was the only recruit with a bare modicum of sensitivity to Kincaid's unique plight, thus I often took it upon myself to speak up. I reinforced my grip, cinched our elbows tight, and bolstered her up.

"We're almost safe. Must be a door near. Let's search the adjacent wall."

"Must be a door near." Eterin didn't echo as much as he spoke over me. "Let's search the adjacent wall." Perhaps my voice was lost in the gale of detritus. We struggled to reach the interior of the massive structure, fighting against the gusts to seal the entryway behind us.

Inside, we fell asunder coughing and gasping, chucking down our packs and blast jackets. The slap of flesh and leather on concrete sounded akin to silence after days of cacophony. Some recruits settled in the entry chamber. Others more resilient, such as Eterin and I, immediately set out to explore.

High ceilings accommodated a multi-storied loft with corridors well-lit once we found the main switch. The heart of the building we accessed easily despite a blinking security panel. The bolting mechanism on the door appeared broken. Not physically dismantled or worn out but beaten into malfunction as evidenced by surrounding gouges exposing dented metal below the surface paint. The door hung half-open.

Beyond, the bulk of the structure housed a huge machine room. We'd come in through the rear. Following circuitous paths through the bowels of inactive piping, boilers, and ductwork, we sought the front end of operations and branched out to locate survivors. Isolated with Eterin, I broached the subject of his misogyny. He listened as we walked.

When we approached the anterior face of the machinery, he finally replied. "Kincaid isn't a psych recruit like you. She doesn't know all that history. It's just a word. Don't sweat it, buddy." He clapped my shoulder and circled the control room, inspecting the equipment and stopping to pick grit from his teeth. He gazed up at the etching above a tall metal chute that ran downward from the highest rafters.

"*Armingraaber*," Eterin read out loud as the others caught up with us and gathered. "What is that, German? Dutch?" He looked expectantly around the group.

Kincaid was our translator. She remained absent. No one answered.

Such quiet in the large and presumably echoing space set me wondering why we didn't hear the violent gusts, the whirlwinds of particles chipping at the external walls and battering the roof of the towering loft. No windows gave a glimpse outside. Nothing rattled in response to the gale. That the blast might die down without us knowing disturbed me more than the impossibly insulated calm.

Steele spoke, never one to be silenced by a lack of expertise. "If it's German, something to do with poverty? Grave-digging? Might just be the manufacturer's name or a company logo. What sort of facility is this, chief?"

Eterin shook his head. "Damned if I know. Anyone's guess."

One of the engineers—Calandra, I think—paged through a black binder he'd retrieved from a podium at a foreman's desk. The binder was secured to the desk by a chain long enough to allow the reader to work controls near the base of the chute while referencing it. Calandra's free hand rested on a lever.

"Well, I can get it working, but I don't know what it'll do," he said.

"Hold on there." Several voices raised a dissenting chorus.

I came forward, followed by others. We looked through the binder, took it from Calandra, and passed it around. We murmured the words on the title page and spine: "*The Last MMRMX.*" With repetition the letters blended into a hum of invocation.

"Roman numerals?" one of the chemists asked. "A year or date?"

"No, probably a serial number," an engineer said. "Meaningless out of context. Look at the rest of this gibberish."

Next to Calandra, the engineer displayed the instructions page by page, flipping through twenty double-sided sleeves. "It just gets worse as you go further, doesn't it?"

Diagrams were interspersed with arrows, circles, numbers, and long strings of capitalized consonants similar to the title. Some lines of text ended irregularly, truncated to accommodate the drawings. Others spanned multiple pages with no break. The quality deteriorated toward the end, as if the latter pages had been copied from outdated technology.

I thought we should await Kincaid, who still lagged behind. I couldn't blame her. Later, perhaps, I'd confess my feelings to her in private. I hoped my behavior had spoken well enough and loud enough to set the stage. Not that I expected payment for doing what's right. I'd help anyone who needed an advocate. But Kincaid was special to me. I hoped she'd noticed I was different from the other men.

Before I had a chance to speak, Eterin nodded at Calandra. "Okay. Get her up and running."

With a unified gasp, we flew into protest. I yelled, lurched at Calandra, and landed hard on the concrete as the machinery rumbled into motion.

Calandra shoved another man off of him, but it was already too late. The switch had been thrown. One more leapt forward, and Calandra swung at him. He dodged the blow, and Calandra shouted, "What the fuck, man?"

Humming, throbbing, watery sounds erupted, making the air around us tremble. We froze, our scuffle frivolous in the grinding tension of sound and smell, of some perpetual movement now progressing through the huge operations room. From deep within the twisted bowels of unseen pipes arose hissing, smoke.

The sensation emanated from hidden recesses of vigorous pumping and immense heat, as though the machinery breathed fire. I couldn't help imagining we'd awakened a pregnant dragon.

Calandra backed away, cowering like the rest of us as the chute beside him shook with warning of an imminent deposit. Twisting and squinting, daring to break from the rest and crawl closer, I looked for the top of the chute, driven to locate the aperture from which it inclined. I couldn't see it, but in my mind it was like an eye peering down at me, a single orb assessing my contortions with the patience of a reptile and the wrath of a god. If it blinked, I wondered, would its tears fall to soothe our thirst, or would fire shoot from the top of the shaft and blaze away the sweet flesh of every human thing in its path?

The chute vibrated with our shared anticipation of what it might hatch. A man beside me howled with a feral madness I'd never encountered or envisioned, not even in my most severe untreatable cases in my time at the prison ward; a howling scream of pain too much akin to celebration not to trigger an ecstatic response in any living brain tissue. I fought to repress it, yet the organic message of the scream came from us all as we writhed. And the edges of my vision grew black as the metal tongue of the chute quivered. I no longer heard or saw the other men.

Then there were no screams. And there were no men.

I was alone.

And then I was not.

Silence again descended over all the men. Light oozed from the top of the chute. The light was not fire as I'd feared. It was fruit.

As if in slow motion and without any accompanying clamor, several bushels of green apples barreled soundlessly down the incline in a delirious vision. They landed in the reservoir at our feet.

Wonder stayed our hands. Starved as we were, we lusted to grab and devour them, but the oddity of their manifestation defied belief. Dare we trust our eyes? Dumbstruck, we gawked at the impossibility of a fresh harvest before us after the devastation of the blast and the barrenness of our long trek, not trusting the ripe and brilliant gleam on the surface of the food.

Steele broke the spell. Smirking, shrugging, he clasped a smooth chartreuse gem between both palms. Caressing and sniffing the shiny skin, he smiled and then opened wide to take a bite. The inside of his mouth was a darkened pit behind the sharp white teeth that cut clean into the crisp ivory flesh.

Grinning as he chewed, green flecks disintegrating into the pulpy mash inside his mouth, he said, "I am become death, eh? Am I right, fellas?"

Some of us may have laughed.

We ate. Our lips were cracked. The juice stung. Ravenous greedy animals, yet still human enough that we feared both the inexplicable manna and its source. I saw the questions in furtive eyes after our initial satiation, before stomachs churned with the ache of surprise nourishment after so long empty. Though the pangs were brief, some feared we'd been poisoned.

"Look," said Calandra through clenched teeth. "Whatever happens, it was either this or cannibalism. I know what I would have done."

Nothing in his demeanor or tone revealed what that was. I stood over him as he hunched in pain and my nausea came and went in waves. By the time it was gone, Calandra still failed to elaborate. Steele had slumped, muttering beside him, blocking further inquiry. Recovering men encamped in every nook. Few apples survived our feasting.

I gathered the fruit and nodded toward the pulsating corridors. "Better check on Kincaid."

Everyone was silent. Oddly so.

I stepped into the exit. Dizzy from the mechanical hum, I paused. Eterin approached and placed a hand on my shoulder. "I'm sorry, son. I thought you knew. We lost Kincaid in the blast."

"No," I said.

"It's hard on all of us. It was chaos back there."

"No, she's not missing; she's here." I gestured toward the depths of the machine room. A thin veil of smoke accumulated in the air between knotted piping and ductwork. I licked the sweetness of evaporating juice off my lips. "I'm taking this to her."

"Look, son, I'm sorry. But you have to get a grip. She's dead."

As I spun to argue, it hit me. Some of us were missing.

My confidence ruptured. Of course I hadn't counted our number earlier during the chaos and flight after the blast. I couldn't be sure my impression was right. Out in the fray, we'd barely been able to hold onto one another and make headway through the debris much less execute a roll call. I tried to remember all the faces.

"*Armengrueller*," said a man gazing up into the empty chute. His name was Omar or Oscar, I believe. He was one of a group of recruits with light-toned hair and unusual accents who had arrived together from across the border. Yet now, as he drew my attention amid our tense gathering, he was the only one I saw who fit that physical description.

"That's not the same," he said. "What was it before, *Armingruuber*?"

"Doesn't really matter," said Eterin. "Either way, it means nothing to us."

"We're safe here inside," said Calandra. "That's all that counts."

Reflexively, I looked to Steele to weigh in with his pithy sarcasm, but he was no longer there.

I scanned the room. The chamber offered no egress other than the machine corridors that my body blocked. I thought that earlier there had been external doors. "Shouldn't there be an entrance if this is the front?" I asked. "Where did Steele go? How did he get out?"

Eterin's forehead wrinkled. His eyebrows arched. As his head shook back and forth with troubled concern, Calandra watched him closely. I held my ground in the thrumming exit on the edge of the corridors.

"Steele, your buddy Steele," I begged Calandra. "Where is he? Did anyone see him leave?" The panic in my voice surprised me.

"Who the fuck is Steele?" a man said.

"This motherfucker gone crazy?" another asked.

Omar—or Oscar—pointed to the top of the empty chute. "This place is what's gone crazy. Look at that: *Armengruuber*. It changed again."

Men arose in outrage, others on the defense.

"That's what it always said," a bearded recruit said, clenching his fists and circling Oscar/Omar. He followed the bearded recruit with a steady gaze, meeting the challenge. Others chose sides as the two circled. I tried to count how many of us were left as the yelling and posturing escalated, but it was impossible. My focus jerked from one man to another involuntarily. My vision grew incapable of discerning who was present or distinguishing who was who due to the spasmodic flood of rapid eye movement.

A fight broke out. I ran.

Or I think a fight broke out. The threat of violence shook

my core and dulled my senses, like a sleepwalker unable to awaken. I believe a fight would have broken out soon if it had not yet.

Through the fog of hot steam, encased by vibrating metal surfaces, I stumbled. My legs fought me, still sore from our endless trek. I felt I might have been made of stiff alloy like my surroundings, overheated, stubborn and unwilling to bend, lurching forward in pain with the irregular thrusts of a neglected engine.

Convinced I had retraced my steps, I turned instead astray down a wrong path sheathed throughout with complicated transparent pipes. They circled me in a maddening pattern of vertical and horizontal array. Large tanks intersected or over-lapped, and in what direction the fluid inside them was meant to flow, I had no clue. Bubbles percolated within. The fluid grew deeper green in hue the further I went.

Lost, nearing the fulcrum of the next hopeless turn, the speeding bubbles slowed and grew larger, somehow more solid in appearance. They spun in a languid dance as though to tempt me, mimicking the green apples saved for Kincaid that I clutched in my pockets and hands. The scent of ripening fruit grew stronger. I salivated. Forcing myself forward against the hypnotic curiosity that stalled my steps among the fertile pipes, I veered around the corner and glanced back but once before I screamed.

Within the tanks, the green skins peeled away. Apple flesh bruised into a brown-tinged assimilation of human facial features, and the tainted fluid bubbled merrily with puckered, floating heads. I remembered their faces.

I darted away from the cavalcade of dead eyes. The sweet smell of fruit soured into a sickening mash. Ammonia and fecal fragrances stung my nose. Pressing through the tightening depths of the machine room, I wished in spite of myself for the familiar stress of the storm outside, for a disaster I understood how to navigate instead of a way forward that had no human anatomy or access in mind for its design. I struggled through the winding mesh of hostile surfaces, climbing, then crawling, and then losing sight of the ground entirely. Fearful of hot metal searing my skin when I mounted another transparent pipe, my palms met instead the unexpected sensation of a warm pulse.

Over the hum and hiss of the workings, I heard a high-pitched voice.

"I have to know how tall he is in order to lock him up?"

Statement ending on a lilt like a question: it was unmistakable—Kincaid's tone and tenuous manner of speech. I took a quick breath to cry out and then stopped. Suspicious of the unknown entity with whom she conversed, I whispered her name.

I crawled closer.

The throbbing of the walls was like skin. The surfaces of the pipes I touched responded more and more like palpated veins. Rubbery, collapsed, or rolling under my fingers, the reactive flow inside the transparent conduits clogged as the machinery expanded and contracted with living anatomical action.

Rotting faces strained against containment. Heads turned. Their shrunken apple flesh oxidized into dark brown in every crevice, a folk-carved pastiche of old age. Obstructed, the crashing bobbing heads split apart in a dance of macerating fiber. They re-conjoined into obscene corruptions with too many faces amassed on one head, too many identities, too many mouths and teeth and eyes. The constant motion of the putrid clog in the pipe throbbed like a phallus under my weight. I thrust against the tangled machinery to worm my way free and slid out of control.

I landed in the chamber where we'd originally entered the unexpected structure in a puddle of viscous liquid several steps behind Kincaid. She was alone, facing the wall. I called her name.

A membrane flexed between us, absorbing the sound. It resisted trespass and cordoned me off from Kincaid like some criminal or an animal caged for the community's safety, a thing too dangerous to approach without a weapon or a tranquilizer gun.

But I was not like the other men. I brought her food while they left her for dead. Infuriated by the inequity, I screamed against the barrier. "I'm here now. Let me help you."

Unarmed and alone, she looked so vulnerable. I shouldn't have left her side, even for a few minutes to allow her to rest. The worst might have already happened. I wanted to take her in my arms and keep her safe and make up for my callous negligence.

I beat against the thick membrane with my fists to get her attention. No response.

It was then I remembered I held a jagged piece of metal instead of an apple in my dominant hand. The scrap appeared gouged out of the machinery, formed into a weapon with a furled handle that prevented my fingers from sliding forward onto the sharpened tip of the blade. Heavy layers of duct tape gave the handle a good grip. I recognized its crafting as my own concept, yet wondered that a project so honed could exist since finishing it would have taken me several days.

As I studied the tool trying to understand how it had come to be, I recovered detailed mental images that were like implanted false memories of the deliberate steps I could have taken to create the makeshift knife. I was sure I could accomplish the task over time in secret, only alerting my peers when it became necessary to use it in my defense.

I felt a strong fondness for the knife. Regardless of origin, it was now mine.

I cut a gash in the membranous barrier with the makeshift knife. As I sliced, a miniature and identical gash opened up simultaneously in the back of my head. When I peeled apart the thick edges of the machine-grown membrane, I felt the edges of the inside of my scalp peel apart and roll back and graze against the razor stubble behind my ears.

The stench of rotten fruit wafted behind me as I stepped through, and through me something also stepped, crossing the barrier to reach Kincaid. I filled my lungs with fresh air. The hole in the back of my head likewise breathed. It exhaled afterward with intense pleasure, leaking the gentlest of sophisticated poisons. Oil from the slit tickled the back of my neck. My uniform collar grew damp. My knife hand twitched.

"I'm here, my love. I'll take care of you now."

Kincaid's neck and shoulders moved with the false certainty of a somnambulist, twisting toward all potential angles except the true direction of my whispers. She beat the wall. She searched the chamber's concrete block with the obsessive persistence of a dog.

Louder this time, I begged her to turn and acknowledge my presence. Her pale arms flapped. Limp and insistent, she punched and scraped and tore at the concrete block. Her knuckles oozed with old scabs that broke open with fresh poundings. Her stunted breath seethed with depleted tears. I realized then what she searched for. Though we'd entered here to escape the storm, the chamber no longer had an exit door.

My voice came then as violent thunder, the voice of a god, for I was weary of being ignored. "Look upon me," I bellowed loudly, and she did.

Her mouth hung open, whether in idiocy or hunger I could not say. Her gaunt cheeks spoke of long starvation. Her bulging eyes bent with disgusted malice upon my generous gift. Slowly, carefully, for she seemed less like a woman and more like a frightened animal.

I held out the scavenged apple to feed her.

Her breath seized. I followed her frozen gaze to the thing in my hand. It was not like the juicy green apples upon which we'd feasted, except in similar shape and size. Rather, it was like the floating shrunken heads with conjoined rotting faces blocking the machinery's throbbing transparent pipes.

One might have made such an abomination by peeling the face and scalp from the skulls of several men, folding layer upon layer of eye and hair and ear in overlapping patterns, and then fusing the seams of heretofore unrelated flesh with cauterizing heat from the convenient metal surfaces of nearby ducts. One might fuse each Omar, Oscar, Steele, or Calandra into one symbolic man. In fact, by the shape and texture of the thing in my hand, it appeared that was exactly what had been done.

Still, I held my gift out to Kincaid.

She slid sideways along the wall to evade me. Perhaps she was confused or driven mad with hunger. I came closer and forced it up to her mouth for her own good, backing her up against the concrete blocks. My blade pressed her neck with an encouraging glint, though I noticed with slight shame the metal retained a few unfortunate stains.

When I spoke to her, it was not I that spoke but the gash newly blooming in the back of my head. The voice slurred with fragrant liquids and the clumsiness of its inexperienced lips. "There is no way out, only a reverse orifice we must continually re-enter in order to gestate together. In this place dwells a god gone mad with feeding and being fed, for we have lost control of the machine and entered its lucid death."

As my fingers pressed harder upon the abomination I

forced into her mouth, I felt the conjoined lips and teeth of Omar or Oscar or Steele move in uncanny unison, speaking the same strings of consonants like a chant. I knew the proclamations to be true, for my every cell burned with the same godly hunger.

Ah, but my desire for her love was stronger, at least in that moment as I finally held her close. I would not kill Kincaid like the others and reorganize her to feed the machine. I would become the machine, and she would become me. A whole greater than its parts. The gestalt psychologists theorize you are every person, every place, and every thing in your nightmares, and once you realize this, you have no nightmares. There is nothing to fear.

My fists dropped. The knife clattered. The abomination squealed as it cracked open with a hard splat. I forced my undreaming mouth to speak, but just barely. "Please, darling. Run."

"You can stop this," she said without cowardice. "For once, this time around, you can really just stop."

My heart on hers like a vice, I realized Kincaid was right.

But the collar of my uniform was damp. The poison had set us in motion again. Or perhaps I was simply a poor excuse for a psychoanalyst and in denial of some obvious pattern. I turned around to face her with my vocal cloaca moistened and fully unfurled, ready to suck another Kincaid inside to gestate. It slavered at her and said, "In the wake of Orion's drowning, the pregnant dragon and husband of storms. You are an egg of what may become, planted tender in the belly of another, and another, and another you."

Lunging blind and backward toward Kincaid, my soft new orifice met with sharp pain. The knife shredded my cloaca and stirred the brain tissue within. She pushed it deep and wrenched the blade in furious circles. Some part of me approved. What better place than in the back of my head for her to build a bloody nest of tattered neurons and poison remains?

I collapsed. My nose broke when it hit the floor. I only knew from the sound of the snap.

"Feed me," I begged her with my human mouth. "Feed me to the machine."

Her tone no longer tenuous but forceful and clear, she said, "You picked the wrong person to fuck with." She crouched down close enough to make eye contact, the knife raised between us. "I don't even know your name or rank or what it is you're supposed to do around here. Just that you went psycho after the test blast, and it has been one long fucking night. So if you'll excuse me, I've got an appointment outside with the sunrise. Sweet dreams, loser."

She stood and kicked my ribs to make sure I stayed inert.

What more could I say to prove my love?

She disappeared with my knife into the rumbling bowels of the machine where pipes twist and new membranes hatch. She had heeded my advice to run, and I hers to wake up. As the drooling gash in the back of my head screamed with the death throes of the coma exploding its lucid state, another mind within me awoke to the realization that the hunt would begin for both of us anon. Perhaps it would be endless, for in my desire to hold her close and keep her safe, I had long ago dreamed away all the doors.

# MEMORY DIPPED IN SEPIA

### ANAEA LAY

I have it right this time. I'm certain of it.

My cheek presses into the fibers of the carpet, long and scratchy, twisted together and fraying like a synthetic grove of tiny tree trunks sprouting from the rigid loam of the living room floor. I grasp the fibers between my fingers, draw deep, dusty breaths. It smells like the rubber from the vacuum cleaner's hose, slightly burnt, and the tread of hundreds of feet. I am soaking the carpet with my tears, my arms and back raw and stinging with the thin red welts left behind by the phone wire my mother ripped from the wall. It was over in a flash, almost too quickly to feel it. What lingers is her anger, her lasting frustration. Welts are rising and growing warm across my bare skin, but what I feel is the chasm of terror that comes with learning that you've done something so terrible your mother doesn't love you anymore.

I've got it all put together now. I'm certain. This never happened.

This is what they meant when they told me not to use the memory box.

I remember so much. So much of it isn't real. But you are. I know you are. And I can't remember you at all.

That's why I need the box.

MEMORY IS A FLIMSY, unreliable thing. It shifts like water and changes like sunlight. If we're careful with our memories, pulling them out when we're free of influence and rehearse them to ourselves exactly as they were when we first put them away in the wardrobe of our mind, they become stronger. Never safe, but more secure. It's terrifying, to realize how fragile the substance of our memories is. What are we but our bodies and the memories that reside in them? I am the slight outward turn of my foot, learned when I broke my fourth toe, and my quickened pulse when I smell molasses and think of January blizzards, and the anxious tendency to rub hands over biceps. I am the conviction that you are real, that as I lay in bed on countless lonely nights, you wrapped your arms around me and promised love and safety and the assurance that I deserved them both. What am I without these things?

The box is to memory what a projector is to a film reel, unspooling it in order to shine a light from behind and put it all on display. With the normal settings, when it works, the memories are painted in sepia, clearly marked as artificial, separate things. Memory is what makes us, and the box fixes a thing meant to be fluid. That isn't safe, they said. We must be cautious, they warned.

At first, it was just for therapy—the box. A way to share the seeds and roots and cores of the thing that must be understood or altered or adapted to. A way to confront the demons lurking in your memory on ground more stable than the shifting landscape of your mind. Therapy and false memory have a long and intimate history. Where better are we equipped to face and mitigate the risks? Where better to reap the reward of the risky, tricksy box?

I miss you so much.

Who are you?

ANOTHER MEMORY. This one is real. It is definitely real. I'm crossing the school lobby, arriving at school two hours late and eager to escape the empty corridors for the familiar claustro-phobia of my classroom. My shoes scuffle across heavy tiles that are dingy with decades of wear and my backpack pulls on my shoulders. My fractions homework is in there, half-finished and waiting to shame me. My arms are covered by a sweater, welts and abrasions safely out of sight.

No. There was no sweater. My arms were bare and smooth.

Mr. Harker, the principal, comes out of the office, on his way somewhere, and spots me. He wears navy blue slacks and a gold sweater over his shirt and tie. His hair is gray like the thin rim of his spectacles. "You're too young to look so glum. You should smile."

I smile, my left foot pivoting on my toe as my breath catches in my chest. I don't have a note or a pass. Will he want to know why I'm not in class yet, demand to know why I'm late? I show crooked teeth and chapped lips.

"See. You have such a pretty smile." Then he goes on, disappearing into the gym that is also the cafeteria that is also the auditorium.

I run to my classroom and a phone wire doesn't chase me because that part isn't real. But I felt chased. I felt a near miss.

Smile. I had to remember to smile.

I must have already met you by then.

I WAITED. I heard about the boxes, but I ignored them. Pretended I wasn't interested. When you can't win, you run. And when you run, you must forget or ignore or erase the thing chasing you. If you don't, how can you ever stop? I ignored the memory boxes because I didn't need them because there was nothing wrong because I was fine. I missed you and longed for you and wrote long letters to you in my mind, but I'd long since moved past you. I ran, and I left everything, and that meant you, too. Whoever you were. Whatever you were. You were part of all that.

But I couldn't stop thinking about you anymore. I couldn't stop remembering nights alone in bed, clutching my pillow and counting over decades of beads and praying with salt damp breaths that if I couldn't find a way to make it change, that I could at least understand. And if I couldn't understand, that it would at least become something I could share. I was so small, so alone. So very afraid.

I left the rosary behind when I ran—silver links connected opalescent beads. It's so small in my memory, but I don't think it seemed so then. I kept it in the white plastic case it came in, hidden in my nightstand drawer where I could find it by fumbling in the dark.

The beads between the decades were different.

They must have been.

I don't remember what they looked like.

They were black—matte black between the shimmering white. Yes, I can see it now. The rosary I clung to and left behind and which never brought me answers or salvation despite years of desperate, tearful faith and countless circuits over the decades.

I'll just fold that detail in with the rest. I've lost so much. I deserve to keep that.

THE BOXES DON'T WORK. The boxes are dangerous. The boxes tear us apart and put us back together as something different. The boxes are going away. The difference between not now and not ever is vast, and I couldn't bridge it. They began talking about banning the boxes, and I couldn't ignore them anymore. I'm still fine. I still don't need them. Nothing is wrong. But I had to look for you. I had to find you.

Each box is custom-made for you, filled with the substance you spill into it during a short procedure. Not you. Me. They made it just for me. I went to the clinic and changed into their gown with the scratchy ties and made the joke about how they were unlikely to find my pulse because I don't have a heart. And they asked me if I'm prone to motion sickness, and am I sure I'm not prone to motion sickness, and here, take this, just in case. Then I'm lying on a table and they've told me I'll feel something cold through the tube in my wrist and before I reach the count of ten I'll be unconscious.

When I wake, they'll have my box ready.

I count to ten. There's a clock on the wall in front of me, hands circling and ticking away seconds. I'm still awake. Maybe I hadn't felt the cold yet. Maybe this is a mistake. Maybe I've done this all wrong and suddenly I'm afraid because I won't know what happens, I won't be able to stop it, and everything is already going wrong. The tube in my wrist coils around me, tan rubbery plastic that always took on rounded kinks when you folded it behind the phone on the wall, hiding it out of place.

I smile.

NOTHING HAPPENED and I didn't do anything because nothing was wrong and there was nothing to do. You know. You were there with me, whispering assurances when I snatched the cord.

No. Not the cord. Something sharper.

Everything was dry. Static. Glistening crimson drying to rusty brown. I don't understand what happened. I never understood any of it.

There was nothing to understand.

You held me and whispered in my ear and promised me everything was fine, and I trembled and I listened and when the moment came, the way it always came, I was braced for it. I reached for the phone.

THERE'S A PARK. A stretch of grassy field with a dotting of trees, their branches reaching wide and casting dappled shadows. Sculptures stand in the open spaces between the trees, worn stone and twisting metal. Circles mounted on pillars and displaced petals in steel and gray and copper green. The grass is scratchy against my bare skin, burnt brown in the summer heat. I fold my arms over my knees, numb. This is shock. This is regret. This is knowing I've lost you and already wondering who you are. Remembering how small you are. How vulnerable. I sit in the shade of a tree and let my eyes loop endlessly over the twisting curve of a Möbius strip, going inside and out and in again but never escaping. I look over it again and again like a circle of beads, like a twisting coil of wire. I don't have the moment before this, but I have hours here. Alone. Alone for the first time? No. Alone for years and freshly aware.

I don't...
I can't...
You left me. I did something and you left me.
This didn't happen.
Nothing happened.
I'm fine.

THE PROCEDURE WENT WRONG, they told me. Failures like this are too common. That's why they're banning the boxes. Some memories refuse to remain fixed. They won't be pinned down, plucked away from their context, coated in sepia and made safe. Too much is already unreal, and the box can't hold it. The film is too twisted to fit on the roll. It snags and tears when they try to unspool it. My box is broken, and it can't help.

I kept it anyway.

You're in there. You have to be.

Once, I knew what I was, and I didn't mind. I accepted it. Because you were there. As long as I had you, it didn't matter how many chasms opened around me. It didn't matter how much I didn't understand and couldn't share. You held me and loved me and the white and black beads slipped through my fingers like water and nothing was good but everything was fine. It's fine. I will find you because you have always been there and I can't have lost you. I will know who you are. You're in there. I have the box and you're in there and I'll pull you out and I'll hold you and I'll whisper all the things you need to hear. Wire will bind us together and no matter how far you run, how much you change, no matter how many times we wash your sepia-stained clothes, I will always be there. I am a part of you.

Like the outward turn of your foot.

# P IS FOR PHANTASIES

## STEVE RASNIC TEM

Six months following his death I began having my father's dreams. I hadn't seen him in years, but to my surprise he left his house to me. It's an understatement to say we were estranged. My father was a monster.

The house was a small bungalow built sometime between the world wars on Alphabet Row, where the homes are lettered rather than numbered. Twenty-six of them. I thought it peculiar, but quaint. Some displayed a large wooden letter by the front door. Dad's place was #P. His P was a couple of feet tall and several inches thick, covered in cracked and peeling yellow paint. The fat loop on the P recalled the potbelly he had when I was young. I used to imagine he stored his considerable anger there.

When I first arrived, I heard the peeps and chirps coming from that letter, begging calls from a nest of fledglings stuffed inside the loop. No sign of the mother. The letter was an ugly, rotting thing, but I chose to leave it alone because of those innocent beings.

The first thing I did upon taking possession was to check

the backyard for holes, cavities wide and deep enough to trap a little boy inside. Rotting squares of plywood were scattered across the ground, and I looked under each one. Thank God I didn't find a single pit, or a body.

I had never lived here, but for the first few weeks I experienced this discomfiting sensation of déjà vu. Maybe it was Dad's familiar old furniture, or the way he'd arranged things, or the clear evidence of violence in the damaged walls, doors, and woodwork. I could feel his presence, and his absence, his abuse, everywhere. He bought this house after I left high school and moved away. We never spoke after that.

I didn't want this place, but money was tight, and I had no home of my own. He owed me for everything he'd done to me. The house was filthy and full of trash, rotten food, ragged clothing, broken glass, disintegrating furnishings. But it was a small structure, and it didn't take long to make it more or less presentable. I threw a rug over the spot where they found his body.

The first few nights I didn't sleep well. It was still a stranger's home, and even after all that cleaning an unpleasant smell lingered. But eventually fatigue dragged me down into slumber, and then into dream. Normally, I don't remember my dreams, but to my surprise this was about to change.

I'm a young boy in the nightmare, but I don't feel much like myself. My body is naggingly different. My shoulders hurt, and there are burns on my arms and hands. That much is familiar. He used cigarettes, or sometimes just a lighter to toughen me up.

But I also have a limp. I never had a limp before. I remember my dad had a limp from a bad break which never healed. He never told me how he got it, just that it happened when he was a kid. So I'm like his twin in this dream, a notion which disgusts me.

In the dream I'm walking these dogs, two hulking, snarling brutes. They are so huge I can't control them. They drag me wherever they go. Sometimes they stop, turn their heads and snap at me. Their massive teeth get a little closer to my face each time. I'm terrified. But my father makes me walk them every night. This has become both my chore and my punishment, although I have no idea why I'm being punished. He loves these monsters more than anything, far more than he loves me.

The path is dark and there are few lights. I rely on the full moon and these beasts' sense of direction to guide me through the neighborhood.

Three mountain lions block our path. They have descended from the ridges high above us. They are even larger than my father's dogs who begin to mewl and back up against me as if I might be able to protect them. I don't know what to do, so I drop their leashes and run. Behind me, I hear their human-like screams and the sounds of rending meat.

Later that night, I sneak back into the house. I don't know what my father will do to me, but I'm afraid it will be worse than what the lions did to his dogs. I stop in the hallway and look at myself in the mirror. I've seen that face among the pictures on the mantle. It is my father as a young boy. He is alarmingly skinny and nothing like the big man I remember. His face is so pale it glows.

A large bald man staggers out of the bathroom. I am frozen and cannot move. He is looking my way, but I don't believe he sees me. This is my father, I think, even though I do not recognize him.

THE NEXT MORNING, I could hardly move. I felt as if I'd been beaten. I realized the large bald man in the dream had been my grandfather—I'd seen photos of him with those same ferocious-looking dogs. I couldn't make sense of it. Bad enough my father turned my childhood into a nightmare, but now his nightmares had become my dreams.

But I didn't want to read too much into it. Dreams are mysterious, their rules illogical, and they're ultimately beyond interpretation as far as I'm concerned, despite all the books purporting to explain them. I was living in my father's house. Echoes from his life were bound to appear.

That afternoon, I was up on a ladder on the front porch examining an area where the roof had leaked into the porch ceiling. I carefully peeled away some rotting beadboard, hoping it was something I could fix myself. I heard a distant rumble and then a nearby growl. I got off the ladder and looked around, keeping the prybar in front of me in case I needed to protect myself. The growling continued, and I looked out at the yard and checked the bushes on each side. The noise stopped. I waited, then climbed the ladder again.

The prybar slipped easily between the worst of the rotting boards. I exposed a discolored joist, but it appeared to be merely stained. I pulled down another section, and a large volume of dust exploded in my face. Or was it smoke? It was hot and smelled like smoke.

Wisps of vapor gathered into whiskers, then teeth, then huge milky eyes. The hound's head jerked forward, snapping, and sent me flying off the ladder. I lay on my back, the wind knocked out of me, feeling for pain. I gathered myself and stood up again. I saw the yawning cavity above my head, with nothing protruding, not even smoke. But still I knew I was done for the day.

I heard the growling, or rumbling noise several times over the next week, but I never found a source, and of course I knew there was no vicious dog hiding behind my porch ceiling. Sometimes when you're anxious you see things, and I'd understandably been anxious since moving into my father's house. But it was my house now, wasn't it? My house.

I knew I was spending too much time alone. I hadn't planned it that way. I just hadn't made any friends in the neighborhood yet. I'd gotten a new job working from home. The company required me to come in once a month for in-person meetings. Most people would envy me, but spending too much time alone, you get a little panicky. You lose confidence in your ability to hear or see things accurately.

THE BOY who is not me is in the pit again. Or I am. I can't always tell the difference. But of course, I've been here before. I know what the inside of one of my father's pits looks like. I know this setting so well: the slick muddy sides of the pit, that disgusting liquid texture impossible to climb. When it rains, even with the plywood cover my father drops over the opening, a few inches of water get in, and I shake uncontrollably, especially when he leaves me in here overnight. I don't know what we've done to deserve such a punishment—probably nothing at all. I scream and scream, but no one comes. I don't know whether they can't hear me, or if they don't care.

A flagstone covers the bottom of the pit. This is my father's version of kindness. I can crouch on the stone and avoid most of the standing water. The boy who is not me is even skinnier than me, able to fold himself into a small, inconsequential package, where he can sleep and dream his dreams within dreams.

I know something which most do not: dirt has its own distinctive voice. If you know how to listen, you can hear its laments: how we bury our secrets here, how no one knows all the mysteries dirt contains, how weary the dirt is of our cruelty and murder.

Sometimes I answer and the dirt answers back. But it offers no sympathy. The dirt doesn't care.

In the morning, the plywood is lifted, and I stare up into the face of my grandfather: his hairless head, his small dark eyes, his brutish jowls. Now I understand where my father got the idea for the pit.

IN THE DAYS which followed I found small, muddy footprints on the back porch and in the kitchen, and once in a staggered trail leading to my bed. Muddy handprints, or paw prints, splattered the edges of my sheets. I thought it was possible they belonged to some animal, although I could find no other signs of the creature. It seemed unlikely they belonged to a little boy. But I still re-examined the backyard anyway looking for holes. Every morning a milky mist rose from the ground and filled the backyard. The bordering trees appeared as no more than streaks of charcoal on a white canvas.

Several mornings in a row I was awakened by a distinctive, sharp barking in my left ear. I received a reprimand for consistently not signing in to work on time. I had no idea what I'd been doing all those mornings. I hadn't been sleeping. Or had I?

The growling returned sporadically. I tried to ignore it. Maybe there was some rational explanation for the sound I hadn't yet discovered: air in the pipes, some loose boards, a mechanical issue with the refrigerator's compressor. At least it gave me an excuse for continuing repairs and improvements— I figured during the course of the work I'd stumble upon an answer. Every spare moment I wasn't on the computer for work I was doing something around the house: painting walls, replacing carpet, prying up boards, installing new flooring, tearing into plaster.

At the end of the day, I'd fall into bed exhausted, but sleep was fitful and full of stories. I never felt rested the next day. The dreams were more exhausting than my labors had been.

At some point the growling morphed into a kind of loud snoring, like some giant was sleeping fitfully in the next room. The hissing and the throat sounds were extended, and troubling to hear, as if this unseen behemoth were in a desperate struggle to breathe.

I always thought of the house I grew up in as a kind of cave, a man's house, a manspace. A man cave. This place felt much the same, my father's final burrow, a hole suitable for animals to live in, where some growls were to be expected. Missing a woman's softness, a woman's touch. I never knew my mother. If she had lived a little longer maybe things would have been different. If I could have seen her at least once, maybe I'd have some memories of her now. My father would never talk about her. He didn't keep any photographs of her as far as I know. Was that why I was being punished? Because my birth had killed her?

Even on nights I couldn't sleep, I lay unprotected from his dreams. In the dark, the dreams walked and wept. They filled the house and spilled over into the yard. Yet they brought me no closer to understanding him. He had been like the weather, elemental and unreliable. The smallest things would set him off: a dirty dish, a misplaced jacket, a Sunday newspaper left out of order. I failed him in every way imaginable, at least in his eyes. More than once he'd described his punishments as his "duty as a father."

A FOREST HAS TAKEN over the living room. A white vapor passes slowly through the trees. Deep within these woods, I hear a monster snarling, but I cannot find the creature responsible. I sweep up the pinecones and leaves and needles and the other debris the trees drop and take them out to the trash. This house will never be entirely clean, completely tame, nor will it ever be fully mine.

It begins to rain. The windows are shiny with tears. Periodically, I have to scrape the remains of suicidal birds from the floor.

I follow a path into the bedroom, intending to rest. Life in the forest takes a lot out of you. It is not the same bed my father slept in; I was wise enough to replace it. But it is in the same spot. I start to lie down when I notice blood has permeated the bedding. I search the sheets and blankets but find no signs of a corpse, and no signs of a wound.

The phone cries out.

I go to pick it up, but it has hidden itself, not wanting to be touched.

EACH DAY I woke up more tired than the day before. I couldn't keep my eyes open. Lying down for a nap only gave my father's dreams another opportunity for access. Every time I closed my eyes, I was pulled into another dream, losing any possibility for calm.

After many of these dreams, I woke up to an overwhelming stench of booze and urine. It was a smell I knew well from my childhood living with my dad. This stink eventually faded, leaving behind a devastating sadness.

I THINK I HAVE AWAKENED, and perhaps I have. My bed is in the backyard beneath an overcast sky, surrounded by withering trees. I know they are dying, but I have no idea why. Some turn into smoke even as I am watching them.

The bed begins to sink into the ground. I try to get off, but the sheets are wrapped around my legs holding me down. I can barely move.

The bed continues to sink with increasing speed. Walls of mud rise around me, and as the bed descends into the pit it begins to shrink in size. Finally, I am able to kick the covers loose and stand at the center of the ever-diminishing bed. I try to leap for the opening above me, but it is now too far away.

The bed continues to dwindle until it is less than two feet on a side. The walls are closing in. I spin around seeking a solution and come face to face with the skinny little boy again, this early version of my father. This close I can see just how thin he is, so sickly, pale, and trembling from the cold. He is shirtless, and his torso is layered in bruises. Despite our proximity, I try not to touch him.

"Am I going to die now?" he whispers. "I think I am going to die."

I interlace my fingers in front of me, palms up. "Step into my hands. Hurry! I'll boost you up!"

He steps into my hands, and I am shocked by how light he is. He weighs no more than a dream. I jerk my arms upward and he is flying. A few seconds later, his head appears in the tiny opening above. "But how will you get out?"

I sit down on the tiny patch of bed, close my eyes, and try to wake up.

I can feel the rumbling beneath me, a steadily building pressure which makes my ears pop. Within moments I am rocketed upwards in an explosion of mud and water. When I open my eyes again, I'm lying in the muddy field, this diminutive version of my father hovering over me.

"Thanks," he says. "Are you okay?"

I don't want to speak. I struggle to my feet and look around. I am surrounded by shadows, shimmering as they breathe. Above us the sky rolls by so quickly the clouds begin to smear, creating white streaks across my eyeballs. A storm is rapidly descending, full of ragged, squawking birds.

"We should get inside the house," he says.

"Just so you know," I say. "Even with understanding, I can never forgive you."

He stares at me blankly. Of course. He has no idea what I'm talking about. He turns and starts toward the house, and I follow. We cross over numerous holes with their little boy heads protruding. Like eggs, I think, and perhaps just as fragile. I accidentally kick one or two.

"I'm so sorry," I say, but none of them answer.

In our father's house, there are many doors. We're both confused. But finally, we find the front door, the one which leads outside. I race ahead of him. When he doesn't follow, I turn around.

"I can't. I just—" he says, fading into the light. "This is where I live."

AFTER MANY MONTHS, I felt settled in. It seemed as if I had lived in this house forever. And after weeks of seemingly dreamless sleep, I had my father's final dream.

The big man is giving me a bath, but he always forgets I can't breathe underwater. Perhaps other children can—I don't know—but I sure can't. Maybe the big man has made an honest mistake.

The big man holds me under and holds me under until the giant black bubbles arrive. The black bubbles take up more and more space until I can't see anything else. I close my eyes. They aren't doing me any good, anyway.

When I open them again, I am at the bottom of the sea. What a wonderful place!

There are caves full of eyes! Trap doors in the seabed hide creatures which peer at me with curiosity. There are fish which are all skeletons, with enormous eyes and teeth! They have the oddest appendages imaginable. If I am going to die—and surely this is what is happening—I might become one of these strange fish myself, if I am lucky.

Sometimes I am chased by bigger fish. There are creatures within shells, and I want to join them. I hide inside a large one. The big fish swim back and forth looking for me.

When the world looks a bit safer, I swim out from the shell, and I swim as far as my diminutive fins will permit. Below me lies the vast ocean floor, and the bodies of the pale little boys who came before me.

To be yourself you must remember who you are. It's not as easy as you think it's going to be.

# NIGHTTIME RITUAL
## CYNTHIA PELAYO

One can drift. One can sleep. One can dream, really and truly dream, and I dreamed of you.

No, you're dreaming of me. Maybe we're dreaming of one another. It's all a great spindle, spinning thread, and we'll be weaved in and out, layered onto this great golden tapestry of design. Life and death, and what is death but sleep? Because when I close my eyes I cease to exist on this plane.

In that darkness, I am launched into a boundless realm that holds such a tender name—*dream*. In that wilderness, I wander, and in that wild, the night is king. The twilight commands all. In that blackness, I am free to roam, free to create. Well, I was...until I met you. You changed my life's course, and my motivations. My movements and measures were completely flipped. You changed the chemical makeup of my brain.

I'm in bed now, and I'm drifting off finally, thinking of you, hoping you'll think of me, and find me.

I regret none of this.

The only light I know is you.

SLEEP AND DEATH ARE TWINS. I want to believe you and I are interconnected like that somehow, and that it's in sleep I shall find you again. Or, something more.

Everyone dreams. We may not all remember our dreams, but when we arrive at that dream door, we step into that watery world. In that plane, faces can take on any form, blurred, those from our living lives, or faces that are completely unknown to us. It's those people, the ones whom we've never seen before, save for our dreams, that are the ones that made me question the existence of an out there, of a something more.

These strangers in our dreams smile at us, they talk to us. Yet, where did they come from? I do not believe our minds merely crafted these people from a composite of thoughts. At least, I don't believe that anymore. My doctor, Justin Lewis, told me to be careful with the melatonin and the teas, and the sleeping pills. He begged me to take pause. How could I? Dr. Lewis refused to listen to me, to believe in that space out there. He did not want to believe in you, but it's because of you everything changed.

We want to believe the other realm is some reflection, a mirror, highlighting our fears and our anxieties, but that's not fully so.

Yes, many of us share similar dream scenarios. Many have found themselves back in high school, falling from a great height, or having a tooth pulled or plucked in this midnight world. Some of us have found ourselves lost in harsh, cold liminal spaces, that are empty and gray, lined by long corridors, and florescent lights. One can even dream of real places in their slumber that they've never visited—white sand beaches and glittering caves with stalactites strung across cavernous auditorium ceilings like holiday lights.

Then we awake. The dream fizzles, disintegrating into a cloud of feeling, formless and shapeless, until the memory is gone. Sometimes a hint of that emotional state from that dream remains. Rarely, if ever so, does that dream imprint itself on us so we remember it like a fully lived memory.

I met him in a dream—in the very dream I'm chasing right now.

IN THAT DREAM I was on a bus as it stopped. I gathered my bag, and I looked out the window. He had been waiting for me for a very long time, and I knew we did not have long at this transfer.

Seconds. Minutes. Dream time is snowfall landing on hot concrete.

I rushed down the steps and ran across to the next platform and stood in front of that bus. He stood there, smiling, expecting my arrival, waiting for me, for this night.

He was wearing a gray hoodie and dark pants, and the way he smiled at me, I just knew. I knew him. I had always known him. He threw his arms around my neck, and I remember his smell. He smelled like all the soothing scents I had ever inhaled in my lifetime.

What lingers was the smell of citrus, and on my tongue, I tasted olive oil. Even with my eyes closed in that dream, I had a memory. I saw vast tiered gardens. Lush pomegranate trees bursting with red bulbs, large leafy fig trees with fruit hanging from branches, and then there they were, olive trees, rows and rows of olive trees extended into brilliant fields.

He then stepped back, looked at me with this warm smile and said, "My name is Ezekiel. I love you. I have always loved you. I will always be with you."

He hugged me once again and what I felt in his embrace, I have never experienced before. I felt loved, cared for, and accepted. He knew me, really and truly, and I never wanted him to let me go, but then he did.

He took a step back, and said, "I will always be with you." He then boarded the bus and was gone, swallowed by a mass of distorted faces.

I woke that next morning, and in my bed, it was as if Ezekiel was there with me. I felt his energy pulsating, vibrating all around my room. I raised my bedsheet to my nose and there it was, the fresh smell of citrus.

I licked my lips and there I found it, the taste of olive oil.

My room was charged with his current. The electricity in the air was so hot, I believed I'd be electrocuted just for thinking of him, and I wanted that.

I want that now here in bed. I want him to pull me into this mattress and rip me out of this living world.

I've been begging for it since that night I met him.

The biblical connotations of that name are there. I read. I read and read, and found the name Ezekiel appears in monotheistic religions. I didn't care for organized religion, nor did it care for me. What I did find interesting is that the Ezekiel often referenced in Abrahamic religions lived in exile in Babylon. What set Ezekiel apart from other prophets were the number of visions, trances, and even symbolic actions which he was associated with, like eating a scroll on which prophecy was written.

Symbols. Visions. Trances.

It was no surprise then that it was him who appeared in my dreams, the prophet who entered dream-like states, and saw visions. And I was the woman who fell in love with him, and I could not move on without him.

THAT NEXT MORNING after the dream with Ezekiel, I alerted my job that I was ill, and there was no concern given I had worked there decades and rarely, if ever, took sick days. I brushed my teeth, bathed, combed my hair, changed into a clean new pair of pajamas, and returned to bed, deciding I would not leave that comfort for the rest of the day.

I stayed there and willed myself back to sleep, cycling in and out throughout the day, hoping to arrive at that bus stop again, to catch Ezekiel before he departed, to beg him to stay. That night, I did not dream of him.

The next morning, I woke, showered, dressed and went off to work, in a steady, foggy, disjointed haze. I ordered my usual coffee, but after a single sip my stomach turned, as if rejecting the caffeine. It tasted foul, but still I forced it down. I soon found myself throwing it all up in the bathroom. I rinsed my mouth, splashed water on my face, and looked at myself in the mirror. My eyes were dull. My skin was dry. Sleep, I needed sleep, and him.

I paced my office.

I paced the work floor.

People typed away nonsense onto screens, and all of it felt so empty and useless and pointless, numbers and letters launched into the abyss. I wondered then if we had it all wrong, were our waking lives nightmares? Were our dreams then the only path to real salvation and peace?

I left work early, citing illness, and it was true. I was sick of being awake.

When I arrived home, I researched which teas would help me fall asleep fastest.

Chamomile. Lavender. Valerian. Passionflower.

To sleep. To dream. To fall away.

I went out to the market and purchased them all and more. My basket was filled with whatever little box of tea presented a name like 'Sleepy time,' or 'Calm,' or 'Dream Dust,' or 'Bedtime.'

I took a warm bath. Then brewed two bags of chamomile tea. I sipped the hot liquid sitting in bed until I finished the cup. I then read and reread Anne Sexton's poem "The Gold Key."

Then I drifted off to a sad and dreamless sleep.

I woke to my alarm clock signaling it was time to restart the program of getting ready for the day, work, and all the insignificant things that take up time but hold little meaning. I left work early once again. There was no reason to tell my boss I had taken sick, because the entire work floor saw me vomit up the morning's black coffee in the center of the office.

The pounding of fingers against keyboards and gross conference call chatter buzzed in my head like angry wasps until I unlocked my front door at home.

When I entered my house, I knew then I would never leave.

That night, I tried lavender tea, and while I enjoyed the scent, the effect was too mild. Later on, I brewed valerian and the taste was too medicinal. I messaged Dr. Lewis explaining simply that I was having trouble sleeping and asked what he would recommend.

That next morning, I found a message from him suggesting melatonin, which I ordered and it arrived that same day. Before

# NIGHTTIME RITUAL

I ingested the recommended ten milliliters, I emailed my boss with my resignation.

There was enough in savings to sustain me until I found Ezekiel. My new occupation, my new purpose was only in locating him. I chose to sleep and that's what I did.

I treated it as a profession. More, a mission. A purpose. A spiritual calling. I trained my body to sleep twelve, fourteen, sixteen-hour days, more. Yet, the teas soon proved ineffective, and the melatonin useless.

I explained to Dr. Lewis my struggle, that I needed a restful sleep so I could work effectively. He warned me of the mixtures, the teas and melatonin, but I begged and pleaded. I needed to work, I said. He suggested I visit his office, but I pressed that I was too busy, my profession was demanding, and asked if he could please make an exception, and he did. The prescription for the sleeping pills was forwarded to the pharmacy, and once completed, the order was shipped to my home with instructions. One pill per night, but what was a single night? That definition no longer existed to me, because night could and should consume everything.

Time became murky, muddy. I discarded all clocks and watches. I ordered blackout curtains. It would be forever night outside and inside. Night and day, a rhythm did not matter, because all I needed and wanted was sleep. I didn't need much food. I didn't want so much energy, and so I trusted only things that were sweet and simple and promoted the drowsiness I required—almonds and cherries, oats and milk. Whatever could help lull me and sustain me to sleep.

I woke, showered, and washed and dried my bedsheets and lit soy candles with the scent of sandalwood, ylang-ylang, cedarwood, anything that stimulated the body's response to rest. I kept the lights in the house off or dim. This was a

181

monastery devoted to the land of nod and that was the entire purpose of this home.

In time, I forgot about the outside world. Useless things were discarded. Almost everything in my house was offered for free to a consignment shop, and they sent over a truck and their people to pack and carry it all away. I didn't interact with them. I stayed in the bedroom because I was not real; nor were they. The most precious item in the house now was my bed, with beautiful white sheets and comforters I washed and changed out regularly. Candles were kept lit on my nightstand and on the floor of my room, where tiny flames danced and cast long shadows, ushering me off to my slumber.

My room was bare, as was the house.

This was no longer a house for living, but of dreaming.

I make very little noise and so sound is kept to a minimum. This entire house quickly became more than a monastery, but an altar in this ritual to transport me back to dreamland.

I had broken free, in a way, from the outside world, but I was still not close to that inside world. I would sleep, yes, but I had still not dreamed. I had prepared my home and trained my body. My mind and more were given away to this great hibernation I sought. I lived and breathed in this world now for just four hours daily, sleeping twenty hours each day. No longer did I conform to the rules of those awake.

In those hours I did not sleep, I read about dreams. I read how in Greek mythology dreams were personified by Oneiros, how in Homer's *Iliad* Zeus delivered wicked dreams to an enemy, how in the *Odyssey* there was mention of a land of dreams, past the vast ocean.

World mythology spoke of how monsters brought us nightmares, the Sandman from Scandinavia who would steal the eyes away from little children who refused to sleep, the Baku from Japan, the Mara from Germany who sits on the chests of the sleeping, constricting their breath and ushering bad dreams, and the Djinn from parts of the Middle East who do the same, the Melino from Greece, the Caer Ibormeith from Ireland and more, so much more. There were creatures who hovered over us as we fell away into the dreamscape, but there were those great beings who commanded the locks and gates of night.

When my body did not feel tired, I would call to the god of dreams, Morpheus, and I would chant his name again and again. If that did not work, I then would call on his brother, Hypnos, the god of sleep. If sleep still did not come, I would call on Phobetor, father of nightmares, hoping he could turn the key and open that door.

When I awoke each time, again and again without dreaming, I resigned to the fact that I would have to add him to my call, the one I knew who could ferry me off.

The next time I proceeded with my ritual of a bath and clean sheets, candles, tea, melatonin and then a sleeping pill and chanting, "Morpheous," "Hypnos," "Phobetor," I added to my call "Thanatos, father of death, take me to Ezekiel."

Because if dream, nor sleep, nor nightmares could bring me Ezekiel—then perhaps death would.

When I woke from that first try of adding Thanatos to my call, I sat up, shocked, because while there was no dream, there was that charge, that rippling electricity and that smell. Ezekiel's smell. I raised my bedsheet to my nose and caught the scent of lemons. I licked my lips and tasted olive oil. I looked over to my nightstand and I knew, I knew I was close. So close and I needed to fully commit to this, commit to finding him.

I longed for him while I was awake and prayed for him as I drifted away. He was more real to me in a dream than anyone was to me in this wicked waking world. He and I, we're like a point in the ever-expanding universe that you cannot reach, you will never reach, no matter how much you tug and pull. You can't disconnect me from him, just like you cannot disconnect him from me. We are bound together in this great cosmic cycle we call a single human lifetime. He and I know that. Both of us know we are here and that we will meet again. It's not karma, or a curse in which we will repeat again and again until we've learned some lesson. There are no lessons to learn, there is just living, and feeling, and hurting, and life, and nighttime and sleep. And I know now that great course ends with dreams. So I pray to starlight and magic and command the Sandman to bathe me in sparkling fine dream dust, to transport me to where I truly belong, to him.

And how did we get here? Me manifesting him or him manifesting me? It doesn't really matter as we'll eventually settle as two bright points back against the backdrop of the galaxy once we mark our oblivion. For now, I refuse to allow him to evaporate like mist against the rising sun, and so I've resigned to this, to him, to that bus stop where we met in that other realm.

The dream world is real. It's not blips of the real world, or a composite of stress. The dream world is as real as the waking world. More so.

Even ancient philosopher Plato knew dreams were one of the ways gods communicated their messages to mankind. Dreams can hold meaning, but they can hold so much more. The past, present, future, are whispered to us, and shown to us in clips and flashes of images by demons, ghosts, and gods. The dream world is beautiful, but it's dangerous. Because they know when we slip into that reality, we glow like fireflies to the beings that occupy that space. We sparkle and burn bright to those entities that are not human nor ever will be. Some of us will travel there and return, unchanged, but me, I choose to sever the cord and slip away into that domain.

Our dreams are prophecies, and meeting Ezekiel prophesized my end.

I wake, and the world feels an incomplete haze. The living world is a mirage, one I beg will vanish.

I REPEAT THE RITUAL. Bath. Candles. Teas. Melatonin. And this time, with a fully refilled prescription bottle of sleeping pills. My commitment to this will see me through. Turning the cap carefully on the bottle, I close my eyes and then take pause. Carefully I tip the bottle into my hand and there a single pill settles. I place it on my tongue and take a sip of water. Then I call "Morpheus, Hypnos, Phobetor, Thanatos." I take another pill, sip water, and repeat their names—"Morpheus, Hypnos, Phobetor, Thanatos"—again and again, begging, pleading the god of sleep, dreams, nightmares, and death to take me to Ezekiel, to please please please take me back to that bus stop and take me back to that moment in which I felt so real.

A pill. Water. Chant. Repeat.

Sleep.

Dreams.

Nightmares.

Death.

Again and again and again.

I fall heavier now against my pillows. I smell the scents of sandalwood and cedar, bergamot and rose, jasmine and chamomile and all the soothing scents I have ever come to know.

A pill and water, the gods of sleep, dreams, nightmares, and death.

Again and again.

I smell fresh lemon now.

I hear the rustling of leaves from great pomegranate trees swaying in the breeze. The taste of olive oil spreads across my tongue. Again and again I repeat, until I sense a hand on my shoulder and feel a cheek pressed against mine.

I open my eyes, and finally, finally I am here, and so is he.

# ONEIROPHOBIA

## TODD KEISLING

The fluorescent lights here in the basement of St. Joseph's are noisy by design. You wouldn't think it of lights, the kind of noise they put off, but the ones down here have a hum that digs into your ears like a gnat. You don't think you hear them, but you do, and now that I've told you about them, all you're going to hear for the next hour is that lifeless drone.

*Mmmmmm.*

That's the sound of this room. It's the sound buzzing away in the background of the world, an involuntary reaction to existence that goes on and on in its tiring way, leeching time from you, stealing life. For many, the noise is the sound of bureaucracy, consumerism, corporate toil; but down here, one floor away from all those Hail Marys, it's the sound of consciousness. The dull buzz of being awake.

Like I said: by design. The folks who come down here to our little meetings twice a week do so with the expectation of avoiding sleep. It's why you won't find any cots, quilts, or pillows left over from when this place was used as a shelter.

187

It's why all we have are these rusty metal chairs that squeak when you unfold them and a couple of card tables near the entrance for carafes of coffee and other goodies.

Anyway, hello. Come on in. Help yourself to some refreshments. The coffee is good and strong. No decaf here. There may even be a few pastries left if you're lucky. I hope you're not diabetic or have a heart condition. Nothing but sugar and caffeine on that table, believe me. Oh, and the theater masks. I'll get to them in a minute.

I'm getting ahead of myself. Where are my manners? Let me welcome you. I'll take your coat. When you're ready, please take a seat in the center of the circle.

Huh? Everyone else? Don't mind them. I promise they aren't being rude. Facing away from the circle is how we do things down here. As long as you're in the center—like you are now—no one will look at you, and no one will interrupt. It's a precaution, just like the masks. Did you take one from the table? You'll need one—but don't put it on yet. Not until we're done.

It's one of the rules, see? You come in, take your coffee and treats if it pleases you, take a mask, and take a seat. If you're new, or it's your turn to share, you sit in the center. Everyone else faces away from you in masked silence. You don't put on your mask until it's no longer your turn to speak.

And since it's your first time here, well, you get to speak. But not yet. I'm not done explaining things yet.

So, the odds are good you know why you're here and what we do down here. It's no secret. You probably saw the flyer on the community board upstairs, or maybe you saw it downtown at the YMCA. Maybe your doctor or therapist sent you here, just to try things out, see if it helps.

We do help, in our own way. We're all here for the same reason, after all.

I can see you're anxious, uncomfortable—that's the idea, remember—so how about I start, show you what we do?

We're all here because we see the Face in our dreams.

Yes. A face. *The* Face.

This face, it could belong to anyone you know, or it could be someone you've never met. Most of the time, it's a face with which you're all too familiar. The mug you see staring back at you in the mirror every day. Yes, sometimes this Face looks just like you or me, but wrong somehow.

You know that game you used to play as a kid? The one where you stand in a dark bathroom, stare at your reflection, and say "Blood Mary" three times. Ever do that when you were a kid? The point was, you'd freak yourself out because your face would appear to shift or change in the mirror. Just slightly off, a grin too wide, or cheeks that sag a little more than they should.

That's the kind of wrongness I'm talking about. We've all seen the Face staring back at us in our dreams. A smile too wide. Eyes too far apart. Features just out of focus. But always there, sometimes in the background, sometimes right in front of us.

So, the masks—yeah, you get it. Hiding our faces keeps us from manifesting others in our dreams. One less face, one less person to dream about, limits the possible archetypes in which our mystery person might appear. I could go into Jungian dream concepts, but that would probably put us both to sleep, and that's the last thing we want, isn't it?

Right. We're at risk of dreaming about every person we've ever known or met or seen. Worse, we're at risk of dreaming people who don't even exist, conjuring them out of the ether of the collective unconscious. And no matter who we meet in our dreams, no matter how they appear or manifest, we must remember they are always suspect. *We must remember it is always us or them.*

Which leads me to the purpose of our little group. Contrary to what you may be thinking, we aren't here to avoid sleep—that is impossible and altogether unhealthy—but to better understand the nature of our dreams.

See, most people regard the Face as another dream presence or concoction of the subconscious mind, but that couldn't be further from the truth. The Face is an interloper in the natural course of our sleep cycle, and it exists solely to kill us in our dreams.

No, not like that horror movie. This is worse.

The Face isn't an external factor. It comes from within. It is, to some degree, a part of all of us—but its purpose is far more sinister. The Face, however it chooses to appear, is the part of us that has yet to be.

Yes, exactly right: It *is* us. The us of tomorrow. And the Face's sole purpose is to become us. To take our place. Every night we die and awaken as someone new. Every sleep is a "little slice of death," as often misattributed to Poe.

The Face is who we become, if we allow it to have its way. Every night we are murdered and every day we become a copy of our former selves, but changed. Diluted. Sometimes drastically and sometimes barely at all, but the fact remains: we aren't who we were before we went to sleep.

We're someone else.

Someone wearing the Face. And every Face you see is someone else trying to murder you in your sleep. The last time you dreamed and saw the Face, odds are good that who you are now isn't the same person you were before you fell asleep. Just like me and everyone else here.

We've come to identify the "Face" as the one who will steal our lives and take our places in the waking world. Our dreams have become a game of cat and mouse. Jungian espionage, if you will.

And you're here because you've seen the Face. Maybe you've avoided it, but it's more likely you haven't. None of us have. Not all the time. And the sad irony is that even when the Face is victorious, another Face will be waiting to take its place. As if life isn't difficult enough, our dreams are a battleground, and we must do everything we can to remain who we are for as long as possible.

And to do that, I come here twice a week and lead the group. We talk about our dreams, the many forms the Face will take or has taken, and how we can prepare for its coming. Maybe you don't see it every night, in every dream. Hell, maybe you don't remember, which is an even scarier prospect.

My first time? Yeah, I remember it. I don't think anyone forgets the first time they noticed the Face. Me, I was still a young man in college. In my dream, I was back home in my childhood room, curled up in bed. Right away there was a faint sense of familiarity and foreboding, like I'd been told a terrible secret that I can't remember, a horrible something on the tip of my tongue if I could only recall the words to speak it. And there, right there in front of me, was the real reason for my terror.

The Face sat across from my bed, and it looked just like me. Like I was staring into a mirror of hairline fractures just small enough to distort the image slightly. No expression. No words. Just staring and staring, into me and through me, an almost perfect clone or doppelganger. Good twin or evil twin, I wasn't sure. I'm still not.

I tried to scream, but the Face was faster and fell upon me in an instant. It shoved its hand—*my* hand—into my mouth, and I suffocated on the pressure and pain of its arm reaching deeper down my throat. The last thing I remember is the terror of dying. Panic and adrenaline flooding my body as fire burned my lungs, the sensation of neurons sparking into nothingness, and the blistering cold of a vast sea of darkness crashing over me.

When I awoke the next morning, I felt different, looked different. My body was a foreign entity and felt like driving someone else's car or wearing their shoes, one size too big. The light was harsher, the sun brighter, and everything hurt just a little more. Some would say I'd become aware of entropy, that I'd just grown a day older and somehow felt the change, and maybe they're right. Maybe that's what the Face is, in a Jungian sense—an archetype representing the death and rebirth of ourselves.

Apologies. I'm rambling. Any questions so far? Why do we resist the Face?

Great question. An argument is to be made that the Face is simply a part of the natural order of things. Maybe we're supposed to die every night. Maybe the point of life is death and rebirth. That very well could be true, you know.

But...think about the last time you saw the Face in your dreams. You were repulsed by it, weren't you? Its not-quite-right features, its thin and knowing smile, the blank stare it gave you from across a room or street or crowd—*everything* about it looked familiar and wrong.

Maybe you woke up in a cold sweat, reeling from a simple dream that was far more terrifying than anything you could call a nightmare. At least with a nightmare you know it isn't real, but when you see the Face, its existence feels *possible*. That dread you feel when you awaken is the knowledge that this uncanny thing wants to step inside your skin and wear you —*become* you.

That chilling fear you feel is the pure, heart-stopping knowledge that if the Face takes over, who you are will *cease to be.* Who you are will be a facsimile of who you were, ad nauseum. Death of the self in perpetuity.

Death of *your*self, over and over again, every night into every day. You are here because of your innate sense of self-preservation. Just like the rest of us. You would rather fight to exist than to be overcome.

How, then, do we fight when we are in our most vulnerable state?

Many of us have trained ourselves in the ways of lucid dreaming to control our actions and better prepare ourselves should the Face make an appearance. That's one such skill we develop here in the group. It could prove useful to you if you haven't learned it already.

How? Mnemonic induction, rehearsal of a phrase as you fall sleep, can train your brain to recognize when you are dreaming. Think of it like training yourself for meditation. You're teaching yourself a trigger to reach a mental state on command.

A word or phrase is common, but some of us utilize a sound.

A click of the tongue, snap of the fingers, or a gentle hum.

*Mmmmmm.*

This takes practice and doesn't always work. Sometimes we go into our dreams believing we're in control when it is the Face who has the upper hand. You know the falling dream? The one you have where you're always falling is one of the Face's most effective traps. It's sudden, you never know how or why you're falling, and the rush of primal fear as the ground fast approaches is all-encompassing. That's a dream you can't control. The same goes for the dream where you're late to a final exam for a class you can't remember attending, or when you have to give a presentation on a topic you know nothing about. Classic Face scenarios. We've all fallen prey to them.

But a lucid dream where you're in control? You have the upper hand by default. The setting, the rules, the scenario— you determine everything. All you have to do is wait for the Face to appear and spring a trap of your own making.

An example?

Well, it could be anything, but enclosed spaces work best. Kind of like a wasp trap, where the victim can enter but can't leave. A classroom, for instance, or maybe a burning house or crashing airplane. It's always fun to turn the Face's scenarios around and use them against it. The point is to create a space that doesn't look suspect. You'd never want to use a police station or a jail, for example. Too obvious, and too easily used against you if things get out of hand.

No, you want something inviting and familiar. Even if the space isn't warm, the premise should be—like a therapist's office, or maybe a church. And once the Face arrives, make it feel at home. Welcome it with open arms. Be friendly. Don't let it know that you know what it is and why it's there. By the time the Face realizes what's happening, it's likely too late. There's no escape from this place you've created. Remember, it's trapped in here with you, not the other way around.

Unlike the Face, you'll want to give it a reason for being there. It's your dream, but the less it feels like one, the better your odds of success. Context and premise go a long way here. Rather than imitate the Face's scenarios that dump dreamers into the thick of things with little time to react, you want to flesh things out, make everything seem plausible. Ground your dream in reality and give yourself a reason for being there. If your trap is a doctor's office, for example, then maybe you're the doctor or nurse, and the Face is the patient. Of course, you'll have better success if you approach the Face from a position of authority.

Oh, there is one thing I left out. Your mnemonic trigger can give you away if you aren't careful. The people who fail at this often rely on actual words for their mantra. It's the repetition, I think. The Face isn't just an impulse; it has sentience, to a degree, and with that comes a sense of self-preservation. You must still have your wits about you and be ready to improvise if the need arises.

Personally, this is why I rely on a sound for my trigger. Something that easily conforms to the scene. White noise, like from an oscillating fan or a refrigerator. A mechanical drone that's always there, and because it's always there, you barely notice it. Even when it's pointed out, you might hear it for a moment before it slips back under your radar.

It's why I hum.

Sounds just like electricity in the lights, doesn't it? Fits perfectly here in a church basement.

Do you need to top off your coffee? I think there's a pastry or two left on the table. Please, help yourself.

Oh, do be careful—

Were you born with two left feet? Ah, now see what you've done? I knew I should've done a better job of tying those bodies to their chairs. And the mask is off, isn't it?

Yes, you're right. Those people are dead. And they all look the same. Just like you. Do keep the mask, though. It's how I hide your face when another Face inevitably strolls in here, looking for me.

Why? Haven't I explained myself? You know, there was a moment when I thought you'd figured me out. Just after you arrived, while you were standing in the doorway looking around the room, I'd swear you caught on. Was it the bodies? The masks? Fine, be that way. Doesn't matter if you tell me or not.

I have to say, though, there was a point when I thought I had convinced you of the evil inherent in your being. When I was explaining everything like you were one of me, another terrified soul looking for answers and a way to defeat their dreams.

Oh, don't try to run. Where are you going to go? The door isn't there anymore. It hasn't been for quite some time—

Easy there. Steady. Coffee's got a hell of a kick, doesn't it? Made it myself. Worked great for these other iterations of you. Go on, take a load off. No pillows or blankets, I'm afraid, but that mask in your hand does a great job of blocking out the light.

Want some more coffee? It'll speed things along, get you to where you're going a lot faster.

No? Sure? All right.

I'll see you when you come around again, Face. You can put on the mask now. Close your eyes. Focus on the sound and dream a little slice of death.

*Mmmmmm.*

*Mmmmmm.*

*Mmmmmm.*

# PRAYERS TO CHTHONIC GODS

## LYNDSAY E. GILBERT

S omnus grows his own harem. Deep, down, deeper still, here under this decrepit castle—fragile and dull as ancient spider's web—we, the butterfly girls, are wrapped in our cocoon.

There are twelve of us. But do not mistake us for dancing princesses. We do not wear our pretty shoes to tatters on a fairy ballroom floor each night. No gossamer gowns, no fine silk shawls for us. Our naked, sinewy bodies meld with the sebaceous walls of our chrysalis. We are soaked in acid. It burns away our past and turns us **Other**, ready for a new world —a god's bed.

Here we must keep dreaming. It matters not what dreams may come, so long as they come. Without dreams, we will die. I dream only of how I came to be here, of why he chose me. Over and over, it runs inside my mind, a circle of events that cannot change. Nothing is linear anymore; there cannot be an end to this tale until Somnus releases me.

～

I'M RUNNING FROM DEPRESSION—a series of episodes, each lasting months and months. Doses of psychosis that worsen over time. I lose touch with reality; it wriggles free from my tightly clasped fist and then floats above me in the air, just out of reach as I leap and twist and contort. I'm trying my very best to get a hold again.

I agree to electroconvulsive therapy, and it changes my life. All the stigma in the world will not stop me from trying it. I have nothing to lose. I trade memory for life, and I rise again. No longer do I need to chase after reality. It lies safe in the palm of my hand, or perhaps like a wedding band, a perfect circle attaching me to my new husband—hope.

It works. They don't know why or how, but it does. Just like the many pills I have tried over the years; some remedies work for some and not for others. I am ecstatic, and I start to put my life back together. I leave the house, I dance, I write, I read. It is glorious to eat without guilt, to look at my body without wanting to dice it up and garner fifty stitches a pop. And better yet, they say I can obtain maintenance ECT should I need it. A top off. I hope I never need to use it, but the knowing is a safety net that wraps me up like a mother's arms.

But this mother is cruel.

Sometimes she withholds her love.

"WE DON'T OFFER maintenance ECT. I don't know who told you that. No, there's no point. You need to be very much worse." My psychiatrist doesn't look at me; she looks at her computer screen as she metes out my sentence.

*You need to be very much worse.*

I have been fighting the nine voices in my head again for months. I am diligent. I take all my pills. I try not to engage when they tell me to hurt myself, when they bombard me with insults. When they dance with my OCD and make me believe my loved ones will die unless I perform pointless, exhausting rituals.

Tears trail down my cheeks. I dash them away.

*You need to be very much worse.*

She is just the puppet of the system. Her hands are tied behind her back by vampire politicians. The health service is being brought to its knees. The voices laugh. They say, *It's because they want you to kill yourself. You're a drain on society. You are useless. Your education was wasted. You couldn't stay in your job. You can't contribute. You are pathetic.*

Very much worse means surviving a suicide attempt again, being on your knees. Needing months of hospital again. Surely that will cost the system more.

The voices are right.

I'm supposed to get the next attempt on my life right.

ALONE IN MY HOUSE, the voices crowd me. And the visions start. A woman with the face of a ruined watercolour painting, dressed in a long, heavy black gown, walks up and down my stairs like a sentinel. She stops at the top and gazes into my bedroom. If she touches me, I will die. I don't know why or how or when; I just know that I will. She doesn't feel malevolent. She just feels inevitable. I am scared to sleep. I am scared in case she slips into the empty side of my bed. So, I stop taking my night medication. I lie awake, barely leaving my room to eat or drink.

The voices get stronger. And the woman takes a single step closer to my bedroom each time she comes up the stairs. This is all in my head. That doesn't make it any less real.

I pass out. I cannot avoid sleep any longer.

In dreams, the woman tiptoes across my threadbare carpet and slides her long, thin body under my covers. She gathers me in her stick-like arms and pulls me close to her. The quilt lifts on the other side of the bed, behind me. Another body presses up against me—a man's—hard and lean. I am like a child sleeping between its mother and father. But I didn't come here to escape my nightmares.

My nightmares came here for me.

Somnus leaves a copy of my body in my bed. A soulless changeling that needs no medication to function. A miracle cure before my family's very eyes. He shows me how happy they are, a vision reflected in the waters of the river Lethe. If I drink from it, I will forget. And I want to forget.

I cup the cool liquid in my hand, but Somnus jerks me away. "No, no. Your memories are what will make you potent. They will keep you strong enough to survive the change."

He holds my face between his cold, sickly grey fingers and appraises me with pit-dark eyes. His long black hair frames the angles of his razor-sharp face, skin taught over bones that threaten to slice through. He is exactly how I imagined the brother of Death should look. What a disappointment. Those memories of mine he thinks so important—they are full of disappointment. My father's cruelty, the casual and not so casual abuse of man after man. I should have expected the gods to look and act as I imagined they would.

I have been fashioned to make this god a satisfying concubine. I have been fattened on agony, a prize pig. Every trauma inflicted on me has been a prayer to chthonic gods.

I CHANGE FASTER than the other girls. I already know a little about metamorphosis, about changing states and losing myself only to find myself again, somewhat different than before. Somnus visits every day to check our progress, but he cannot peer within our walls. He waits only to see if we will emerge.

Now, I am only half asleep. I dream and yet I am awake. The girl to the very left of me is still. Her purpled eyelids do not flutter, and her body remains fully human. I try to tap into her mind, and my consciousness creeps through the veins of the wall to enter her inner world. I see a pill slipped into a drink— the world gone blurred at the edges. The world gone dark. She does not dream in this state. I cry out to wake her, to bring her back to the living. And she opens her eyes.

I see him then as though he lies on top of me. I feel the roiling sea of nausea. She wants to close her eyes again. She wants to pretend to still be asleep—too terrified of what this coward will do if he realises his potion is failing. His sleeping beauty is awake.

My newly-grown sharp teeth begin to ache. I run my tongue along them, cutting it so blood sweet as nectar floods my mouth. I want to bite, to devour, to feast, but the image of the boy fades away as the girl forces her eyes shut again. She wants to die here. She will not lie beneath Somnus in any form.

"We will fight him," I tell her.

"We are not strong enough alone," she whispers. I look through my own eyes to see she has turned her head toward me. "Take my heart. Devour it. Let my vengeance live in you."

I shake my head but, as she speaks, the sucking pressure of the wall releases me and I step out and stand on my new legs for the first time. I am taller. My arms are long and slender, and each finger ends with a deadly blade-sharp nail.

"Do not be afraid," the dying girl croaks. She is growing weaker.

I step toward her, but something tugs me back. I spin, ready for violence. It is only the wings at my back sliding from the cocoon. They shudder, sending a thrill of gooseflesh over my naked body. They rise, then the slime and acid sloughs away and splatters the fleshy floor underfoot.

I go to the girl, half by step and half by stuttering flight. She refuses to open her eyes but reaches out and takes my hand, caressing the blade at every fingertip. She presses my forefinger to her heart, between her breasts. I sink it into her flesh. Then I am twisting my entire hand inside, and it feels so natural. As though I have been clawing out hearts for all eternity. I break bone and sinew, clasp the warm, beating muscle, and haul it from her body.

She no longer breathes. But she still lives in the walls of our cocoon. *Eat*, she commands.

I obey and sink my pointed teeth into her heart.

THE COCOON IS DRYING UP. I stand in the centre and look up. My escape is through a mouth at the top. Somnus will consider even one girl a success. It is hard to create a creature like me. He regularly wastes thousands of girls on this process. I lick my lips, still tasting my sister's heart blood.

Ten other girls whisper, "Take us with you."

I know the pain of every one of them. The memories of her life, blighted by constant nightmares, flashbacks, suffering. Suffering to add to my own. I look around at the girls. Some of them are half-changed, some have gone wrong. A half-formed wing has climbed from one's eye socket and is covered in a hundred tiny insect eyes, but all of them are still as the host loses the power to dream, hour by hour.

Can I bear to look inside each of their minds? Can I stomach their pulsing, too-full hearts?

Yes, I am strong. My suffering has shown it. They call us weak, but all we have ever done is survive. Survive, only to keep on reliving the pain.

I go from girl to girl, see the mark of Somnus already on them, laying claim in every way he can. Sleep is dangerous, night is treacherous. I swallow down drug-fuelled horror, the weight of unwanted men in the dark, insomnia, sleep paralysis, hideous nightmares and flashbacks that promise not to end, that promise to be the only arms that will keep on holding on.

I lie down now, heavy with the flesh of my sisters. Full to the brim of nightmares.

Full too of dreams.

I FLY UPWARD and burst from the top of the cocoon. It collapses under me, smouldering in a cold, blue fire before sifting to ashes. I am both butterfly and phoenix. I can feel my own horrendous beauty—the power in my long, thin limbs. My deadly grace as I land before Somnus. Every time I blink, I look through a new pair of eyes: hazel, emerald, brown, azure.

I cycle through my sisters over and over again. Their bodies are in the pile of ash behind me, but their thoughts are in my ears. I hold them easily, as years of hearing voices has taught me to do. *Spit on him. Cut him. Fly away. Fly far away.*

Somnus rubs a thumb under my right eye. "This is different. So many colours."

*We are your end. Yes. We are different.*

I smile, a wide and empty gesture. He runs a hand through my tangled dark hair and his gaze reads every inch of my body. I want to flinch, to hide away, but I remain upright and only giggle, coquettish. The girls throw me advice, the collective works of performing femininity. *Look through your lashes. Bite your lower lip. Hold eye contact. Break it first. Look down. Sigh gently.* It is a heavy set of shackles. It is a deadly weapon. It is a sturdy shield. It is whatever we make of it. Or whatever men decide it is.

Somnus smiles, his sharp teeth a mirror of my own—I, the coquette; he, the wolf. My teeth are just for show, surely the only bite they make is one of love. He turns and leads me from the stone chamber, empty now of my second womb.

I follow, obedient.

I AM at the bottom of the pecking order. Somnus has no wives and among thousands of concubines, I am the newest. Still, I have his interest. This makes me the lowest, the most hated—and the most powerful. For now. Until he's had me.

Many lounge in great cavernous halls, underworld gardens with withered, ghost-stemmed flowers and trees pendulous with overripe and rotten fruit. There are great pools of water, but they are not formed from the river Lethe. Their waters do not offer the boon of forgetting.

Instead, the water belongs to the Styx. It flows slowly here, full of souls forbidden from rebirth. In the pools of Somnus' harem, they stagnate. The winged creatures, the women like me, submerge themselves in the water and the hands of the dead attempt to hold them under, grab their hair and clutch their wings.

They scream and splash in fake fear, laughter echoing off the walls when they inevitably break free and climb from the water. It is a game. The voices of the dead wail and moan in response.

A human servant girl takes me to a private chamber, and I am relieved to see the bath is simply water. I do as she asks and clean the last of the cocoon's fluid off my skin and wings and out of my hair. She sprays me with heady perfume and dresses me in a loose swathe of white satin, fastened at my shoulder with a butterfly pin.

"Why are you here?" I ask her. "Did he not try to change you?"

She backs away from me as if I have turned to flame. Fear and confusion dance over her features, shattering the dull nothingness that was there before.

"You aren't supposed to ask questions," she says, and glances behind her at the door. "I must inform the master."

My sisters' voices rush my mind. *Silence her. Kill her. Now. He cannot know.*

I grab her wrist, and in my new hands, it is tiny and frail. "He already knows." I lean down so my face is level with hers. "Look." I blink so she can see my changing eyes. "He made me slightly differently. I'm...an experiment."

She relaxes after a tense minute and looks once more at the door. I release her, and she takes out a comb and begins to arrange my hair. I say no more, and the voices in my head settle, sated.

When she leads me to his bed chamber and ushers me inside, I wait for them to come back to life, as bloodthirsty and ready to kill as they were before. The bed dominates the large room, carved from the same grey stone as the walls, engraved with the faces of demons, incubi, and night terrors. And at the very base, a naked maiden whose blood is flowing from each wrist, curling and twisting to make the form of Thanatos on one side and Somnus on the other.

There is utter silence in my head. The stillness of a creature caught in the sight of a predator.

SOMNUS PLAYS NO GAMES NOW. He backs me toward the monstrous bed. I am the girl with her wrists slit. I am the blood, the sacrifice. I am the beginning of sleep and death as much as I am the beginning of life, of birth. I am woman.

His hands clamp around my waist and hoist me onto the mattress. Now those hands slide up my thighs, pushing my dress upward. He presses his lips to mine, hard. His tongue invades my mouth, still sweet with the hearts of my sisters. They remain silent. I listen hard but hear only the sick, dull thud of every heartbeat.

I turn my head to the side, away from him. His tongue hits my cheek, and he draws back. "What's this now?" There is laughter in his words.

He grips my face and turns it back to his. My resistance delights him. I put my hands against his chest. "No," I say.

"No?" Again, comes the laughter.

My sisters awake from their paralysis as that word repeats. *No. Never. Stop. Please.*

There is no please now. There is simply *No.*

He grabs each wrist and pulls my hands to either side of me. And then he puts his weight on me. On us. We know this weight, this powerlessness. He need not even hold our hands. We may pull at his hair, pound on his back—it will make no difference.

But I did not eat eleven broken hearts for nothing. I am different. I am a creature he grew. He made me to be supple, pliable, giving, soft. Instead, I am hungry, unyielding, grasping, hard.

I rip my hands into his back and sink them deep. He pulls away, and my hand only sinks deeper. His eyes are wide. The terror in them thrills every nerve in my body.

"You can't kill me. I am sleep. Without sleep there is chaos." Words spill from him. *You can't. You can't.* "The world will end in madness."

"Then let it end," I say. And my sisters say the same thing at the same time, and we are truly one. I am not afraid of madness, or chaos. I was fed into this hell because the world refused to help me.

It is his turn to lie very still.

I grip his heart, surprised that it is cold and does not beat. I rip it out, spraying frozen blood and shards of bone. He collapses on top of me, still, dead, powerless. I roll him off with one hand and climb from the bed.

My legs are shaking, but I walk to the door and push it open, stumbling out into the harem. They turn and stare at me. The smiles on their faces shift, no longer soulless and vapid. Instead, there is hunger in their eyes. They stand together, and a pregnant silence falls.

I hold the heart up, and they gasp as one.

I know what I must do. I bring it to my mouth and devour it in front of them. It tastes nothing like the hearts of my sisters. It is icy and brittle and crumbles between my teeth, melting into a paste that burns as I swallow it down.

*What have you done?* His voice is now in my mind. My sisters laugh, closing in around him. He is ours now.

I see the future, the present, the past. Every nightmare. Every dream. Every touch of madness where the night infects the day. I feel the call of the souls in the Styx and I hear the waters of the Lethe gushing nearby. I have the power to release those that wish it, to let them forget and live again.

*You can't do this.*

In the underground palace, Sleep's harem bows to me.

Oh, but I think I can.

# OUR DARKEST THOUGHTS ARE INKED IN CARBON

## CATHERINE MCCARTHY

Charred fingers pluck feebly at the oxygen cannula in Cheryl's nose but fail to muster the strength to remove the foreign body. Her hand gives up the ghost and returns to her side, IV needle intact. Beneath pale lids, salt-caked with tears, her eyes flutter in an attempt to open, but exhaustion prevents them from doing so. A spluttering sigh, and the drug induced sleep ensues.

THE RHYTHMIC WHOOSH of a mechanical ventilator plays accompaniment to the beep of the heart monitor, neither of which are attached to Cheryl. Not today. Yesterday, and the five preceding days, yes, but not today. Because last night she started to breathe on her own. The news made both her parents cry tears of joy. Her husband, too, though it might not make her feel the same way. Not when she learns the truth. Too drugged. Too sleepy. She will rest a while longer in counterfeit reverie, plumped on pillows and narcotised on novo-caine, for reality, when it comes, will be a bitter pill to swallow.

"Keys." One word, croaked by smoke damaged vocal chords and an inflamed trachea. Eyes flutter, and this time remain open. Pupils like pinholes, sclera threaded with bloody tribu-taries and full of fear. Then, "My boys?"

What is it she wants to hear? The truth, or a pack of lies? The first could kill her, theoretically. The second might act as a temporary reprieve from the first. Nothing more. So which is kinder?

She attempts to sit up, but a stabbing pain shoots through a pelvis held together by titanium rods and screws, and she cries out. Broken glass lacerated the femoral artery on the right side of her groin as she jumped, and she'd almost bled out. She should be careful. The last thing she wants is to reopen that wound. The paramedic saved her life by applying pressure, but was it the right thing to do? Would it have been kinder to let her go?

A nurse approaches, all doe-eyes and white teeth. "You're awake," she says. "I'll get the doctor."

"My boys?"

But the nurse is already walking away, too gutless to face the music alone.

The doctor takes Cheryl's bandaged hand in his and looks her in the eye. "Hello, Cheryl. I'm Doctor Kathri. I'm taking care of you."

"My boys?" The hand is snatched away, the heel pushed into the mattress as she makes a second attempt to sit up. Left arm in plaster, unable to assist. A cry of agony escapes cracked lips, face contorts and eyes squeeze tight, so the doctor steals a moment to gather his words, while Cheryl gathers her breath.

"Easy now, Cheryl. We've done our best to put you back together, but you mustn't exert yourself."

"Keys," she murmurs, and the charred fingers on her right hand flex and straighten as though trying to grab hold of something. "In the kitchen…behind the door."

Doctor Kathri glances at the nurse who stands beside him, her head bowed like a funeral mourner. He pulls up a chair, and gentle as a lamb, takes hold of Cheryl's hand again.

And she looks into his eyes…and knows.

"All of them?" A whimper. A whimper that grows louder and louder. She wants to scream, but the nurse is stroking her damp forehead and hushing her like a mother does a young child. She should know; she's done it often enough.

"What do you remember, Cheryl?"

"Fire. Window keys. In the kitchen, behind the door." The last words spoken are a punch to the guts. "My boys!"

NIGHT HAS FALLEN. The blinds are drawn, and a lamp shines a halo of light on the nurse who sits at a desk in the far corner. Light at the end of the tunnel, of which there is none. Cheryl has not opened her eyes once since the doctor left—perpetual darkness of her own choosing. Even when her husband, Rob, visited, she refused to open them, so she did not see the bandages swaddling blisters on the palms of his hands, the jagged gash on his forehead. Nor did she witness the shame in his eyes. But she heard the rasp of his voice, sore from smoke and emotional strain.

She flinched as he held her hand. Turned her face to the

pillow as his tears dripped onto her bare neck unhindered. Couldn't bear to speak to him. Because she can't forgive him.

Eventually the Diazepam kicks in and she drifts to sleep, the restless kind, all jerky movements and indistinct whimpers.

FALLING...

Falling through the air, arms and legs flailing, and the cooling wind on smouldering skin, then *crack*! She hits the pavement and her sacroiliac joint splits in two, left ulna fractures and pierces the tender flesh beneath her lower arm.

Blackness.

A distant siren. A woman dressed in green looms over her. The woman's mouth moves but issues no sound. Then, nothing.

CHERYL JOLTS AWAKE WITH A GASP, stares wide-eyed into the darkness, heartbeat to match a hare's when the gun goes off. Only then does she notice the figure sitting on the edge of the bed. No fear, just curiosity, because the worst has already happened.

The smell of smoke fills her nostrils, and something more acrid, like burned flesh. The figure is naked—charred skin, black and flaking, hair singed to a crisp, and eyes that smoulder not with lust but dying embers. Beneath the skin, his veins pulsate red and amber as fiery blood courses through his circulatory system. He says nothing, just sits there...watching.

"Who are you?"

A smirk. A hungry flame darts from his tongue, licks the air as he speaks. "Come now, Cheryl. I think you already know."

She drinks him in, wondering if her time has come and hoping it has. Beneath the burning embers something vaguely familiar lurks. Something she can't quite put a finger on, but she's too numb to search for it.

A twitch at the corner of his mouth. "Have you got it yet?"

A shrug, a dismissive sigh. "What do you want?" Her face contorts in agony, breath comes fast and shallow, because speech requires effort.

He grins and his irises glow bright. The heat from his body is so intense it embraces her in its arms. "I want the same as you, Cheryl."

"Then you want to die." No hesitation.

He tuts, each click of the tongue emitting a wisp of smoke. "And why might that be?"

Narrow eyes fix on him; hatred oozes from every pore. "My guess is you already know."

A slow nod of the head; his blistered skin crackles as he moves. He takes her hand in his, his skin so parched she imagines it might disintegrate to the touch, but she doesn't pull away. "And you'd do anything to change it, right?"

A lump forms in her throat, and for the first time since it happened, she thinks she might cry tears of sorrow instead of pain. "Anything. Anything at all." A dry sob shudders through her torso, stops at a chin that quivers.

"Because of the guilt?"

"Guilt. Pain. Emptiness. Christ, all of it." Eyes dart to the nurse who remains at her desk in the far corner, oblivious. Does she not hear? The nurse senses her looking, so she stands and approaches.

"You all right, Cheryl? Any pain?"

Pain? Christ, does she not see the charred being sitting on

the edge of the bed? Can she not smell the smoke, the reek of charcoaled flesh?

He's still there, holding Cheryl's hand with an amused look on his face, but she's not afraid. Not of him, at least. "No, I'm okay." When Cheryl closes her eyes, the nurse sighs and turns her attention to the comatose old guy in the bed opposite.

"You were saying?" His blackened forefinger traces the pale skin along Cheryl's collarbone, intimate, both right and wrong. "Before we were so rudely interrupted."

"Help me die. Please!"

A pause, and then in the self-assured manner of a psychiatrist he says, "You know, Cheryl. I'm not so sure it's what you want. Not really. Otherwise it would have happened."

The urge to punch him in the face is strong, but all she can do is snatch her hand away from his embrace, though the pain is a tear from a lion's claw. "You're wrong! How can I live without my boys? I killed them. *We* killed them when we locked the bedroom windows and hung the keys in the kitchen. I mean, how could we be so fucking stupid?" She expects the nurse to come running, but she doesn't.

Perhaps she should tear out the IV line. That might do the trick. All it would take is one quick tug, so why does she leave it intact? A moan of frustration and with her right hand, she tears a handful of singed hair away instead. Such pain when she moves! Sixteen stitches at the shoulder where broken glass tore soft flesh. Third-degree burns to the forearm and palm, cosseted in gauze and bandage. But at least the bone's intact, unlike the left arm.

And all the while he watches, an amused smile playing on parched, flaking lips. He pinches his bottom lip between thumb and forefinger, deep in thought, and a fragment of blackened skin loosens and spirals onto the white sheet. "What would they want, Cheryl? The boys, I mean?"

"To be with me. Their mother. Christ, my youngest was only three."

"I know, I know. So young..." His sigh is a gust of Saharan wind. "And Jonathan, what would he want?"

Jonathan was the eldest, but still only seven. Jonathan's sweet face clouds her vision, close enough for her to reach out and touch, and she fails to suppress the moan of longing that rises to her throat. "Look, if you can't help me, then fuck off!"

He waits for the tantrum to pass. "But when you locked the windows you believed you were protecting them from falling, right?"

She nods her head and whimpers.

"Everyone makes mistakes, Cheryl."

"Yeah, but not like this. Buy the wrong flavour potato chips, perhaps. Marry the wrong guy, possibly. But murder their own children? I think not." Her words are a vial of poison.

He raises an eyebrow. "So let's get this straight. You would sacrifice your life for theirs, right? And what about Robert's? Would you sacrifice his life, too?"

"Of course. It's what he would want."

He inhales smoke deep in his lungs then says, "So you'd sacrifice your life, and that of your husband, so that the boys might live without a mother or father."

"Mmm." Put like that it doesn't sound so appealing. She can't bear the thought of them living without her. "My parents would raise them." Her stomach lurches at the thought, and she grabs for the kidney-shaped sick bowl. A spatter of bile and a string of mucus is all she can produce because she hasn't eaten in days.

The nurse hurries over, but Cheryl holds up a hand. "I'm all right."

"Sure?" She backs off, frowning with concern.

He strokes Cheryl's brow, wipes away a stray tear, and the

smell of barbecued ribs makes her retch again. "I'll leave you for now," he says. "Give you chance to think about things."

HER STATS HAVE STABILIZED, so the following morning they move her out of I.C.U. and into a small, private room. How can being wheeled in a bed along a corridor be so exhausting? Eyes closed all the way, because she cannot bear to see people. Real people, like visitors and other patients, because they're alive and her boys are—

She can't say the word. Can't even think it.

New faces, different nurses, and a plump and cheerful orderly who reminds her of her grandmother come and go throughout the day. The orderly can't have been told about the accident, because if she had she wouldn't make a joke about burned toast now, would she?

Bedpan (because she won't be allowed to put any weight on her legs for at least six weeks), wash down, then change of dressings, the new nurse—the pretty one with hair in a chignon who looks like Snow White—asks if she's ready to look in the mirror. Couldn't care less. Her appearance is the least of her worries. Puckered skin, burns, and scars don't matter. She shrugs dismissively, and the nurse blushes.

When Rob walks through the door wearing a fake smile and carrying a bunch of bright yellow daffodils, she turns her face to the wall. "We have to talk, babe." His voice is choked, the words lodge in his throat like a lump of gristle. "*I* need to talk."

A few moments silence, then, "Good for you." Words spat, vengeful. Her face buried deep in the pillow, she refuses to look at him.

He shuffles around the bed like an old man, burden heavy

on his shoulders. He stoops to kiss her forehead, and she shrinks back. The love is still there though, because at the same time part of her wants to hug him and never let go. A sob rises in her throat, and the next thing she knows, it escapes along with a torrent of tears that stream down her face and soak her nightdress. He kisses the salty wetness, and his tears mix with hers to form a sticky mass.

"W-we k-killed them, Rob."

He wraps his arms around her and the pain in her shoulder —the shoulder torn by the glass—is excruciating. But at the same time, enjoyable, because she deserves it—murderer. As he lets go, she sees his bandaged hands and looks at his face for the first time. Minor abrasions, singed eyebrows, but he got away light. There's love in his eyes, though—pain, and love, and desperation.

He pulls up a chair, holds the tips of her fingers, and for the first time she listens to his side of the story. He'd fallen asleep on the sofa, woken to the smell of smoke. He breaks down again when he speaks of how hard he tried to get to her and the boys, but the staircase was ablaze. He holds his bandaged hands up to her face to prove how hard he tried, but all she can think about is the big bad wolf in the fairy tale, the part where it dons white gloves and pretends to be the baby goats' mother by holding its paws up at the window.

*Mummy's home, let me in.* That was from Nathan's favourite story, the middle child, the neediest of her three boys. Poor thing. Sat right there between Jonathan and Callum, just two years between them all. Didn't stand a chance really, did he?

She doesn't say a word, just lies still and listens, and lets him get it all out. She'll judge for herself whether or not he tried hard enough to save them.

Deathly silence fills the room when he finishes. Can't fill the gap, because what the hell is she supposed to say to that?

She considers mentioning the smouldering spectre who visited last night but decides against it. He'll think her demented.

AFTER HE LEAVES, the nurse comes in and asks if she wants to talk. It's the last thing she wants. She needs time alone now, time to think about all the things Rob told her.

Two things bother her most: when he couldn't get up the stairs, he ran outside to try to get help. The door slammed behind him, deadlocked. Fucking stupid! Ah well, he has to live with the consequences, as does she.

What did she do, though, to try to reach the boys? The palm of her right hand oozes sickly-yellow pus that seeps through the bandage. An injury incurred when she tried to open her bedroom door to reach the boys. The handle was molten. Burned straight through her palm. And what was the use? As soon as she opened the door, the backdraft hit her full in the face. Knocked her off her feet and forced her back inside.

No window key, so she yanked a drawer free from the bedside cabinet and threw it at the glass. It rebounded onto the floor, so she picked it up and used it as a weapon. Bang! Bang! Bang! time and time again, and all the while she screamed the boys' names. "Callum!Jonathan! Nathan! Please, God. Please!"

But their screams outdid hers. "Help, Mammy! Help!"

Thick smoke, and the heat. Unbearable! The skin on her arms sizzled. Lungs fit to burst.

Eventually, the glass gave and there was Rob, in the street, tearing his hair out by the handful and screaming for her to jump.

"Not without the boys!" she'd said.

The other thing that bothers her is the lie. She might have forgotten the lie if he hadn't reminded her, but now it's too late. "Someone's coming for them," he had said. "Jump, Cheryl. For Christ's sake, jump!"

A moment's hesitation as she listened for the boys' screams, but the only sound she heard was the roar of the flames and the occasional bang as some household object succumbed to the heat. She convinced herself, then—the boys were not screaming because they'd been rescued, so she climbed onto the windowsill, grabbed the broken glass with burned palms, and jumped.

THE MORE ALERT SHE BECOMES, the more the pain kicks in. Off the morphine drip and on oral meds now, each stab of pain, each throb of agony, she embraces whole-heartedly, because no one deserves to feel pain more than her. It's a taste of penitence for her crime.

She stares at the blank walls. It's more peaceful here than on I.C.U.—fewer nurses back and fore, and no other patients. Time alone, to think.

Night falls and the lights are out, just a dim celestial glow from the recessed ceiling panel above her head. She reaches towards the glow with her right hand, face to the heavens. "Take me to my boys, please!"

She feels his body heat before she sees him. Tonight, the molten lava within his veins and arteries glows a little dimmer.

"How are you feeling?" he asks.

Small talk, no point answering.

He tries again. "So, did you think about what we discussed?"

"Thought of nothing else."

He pats her hand like an elderly relative, leaving behind traces of carbon on her skin.

"And?"

"Yes, I'd sacrifice my life; Rob's, too, if my boys could live." She reads doubt on his face. The hiss of a twitched lip, the crackle of a raised eyebrow. "And before you say anything, I'm under no illusion that life would be tough for them without us both, but at least they'd have a life."

He pauses for a moment. "And what about their injuries? Would it be fair to make them suffer the pain and torment of living with such horrific burns?"

The thought bends her double. She clutches her belly and moans. Her answer, when it comes, is a viper. "I-I thought you meant—"

He raises a hand to stop her, and the fire in his eyes rages. "I know what you're about to say... You're happy to sacrifice your life, and that of your husband, as long as the boys are healed, right?"

A nod of the head, barely noticeable. "I can't bear to think of them in pain." Silent tears slide down her face, unhindered.

He sidles closer, bringing the scent of woodsmoke with him. As he touches her wet cheek with the tip of his finger, the skin sizzles, like bacon in the pan. "Do you think that's possible, though? That *anyone* has the power to make such a thing happen?"

A sob, a shake of the head, because deep down she knows it's impossible. She'd live in a cardboard box on the street for the rest of her life in exchange for the boys. Live for them, die for them, sacrifice the lives of everyone she knows by means of barter, but deep down she knows it cannot happen. All the *if onlys* in the world can't bring them back.

"I understand your pain, Cheryl. Hear every single thought that enters your head, even the most perverse, those demons you cannot yet give voice."

"Such as?" An impulsive retort she doesn't want answered.

"Well, since you ask... Thoughts such as the funeral arrangements and how you will find the strength to part with their belongings. If there are any belongings left, that is."

Each word he speaks makes her flinch, because it's all true.

He watches her closely, a look of empathy on his face. "And what about the darkest thought of all? That which nestles deep within your womb. Shall I give it voice?"

"What good would it do?" She smooths the sheets, terrified, because it's the sickest thought of all. The one she retches at every time it creeps in.

He sighs, and his out-breath reminds her of when they took the boys on a camping holiday: the smell of the fire-pit, toasting marshmallows and telling ghost stories beneath the stars while Callum, the youngest, slept in her arms, the heat from his body keeping her warm. She'd give anything to kiss his damp forehead right now, the transparent skin on his eyelids.

"Not a lot, I admit, but I assure you that you're not alone in thinking such things. Any parent in your position would do the same."

She seethes beneath the surface, ready to pounce. "Go on then, say it. If you're so fucking clever, say it."

A long pause, and his fiery eyes flash red to amber before settling for gold. The blackest of pupils. Deep, dark tunnels that reach right inside her soul, the darkest of all places.

He clears his throat before speaking, spraying the air with sparking fireflies. "All right..." A pause. "What if you could only save one son? Which son would you choose?"

The words congregate in the air, forming a child-sized plume of smoke. Her fingers clutch the bedsheet tight, bone-white knuckles and bitten nails. Her throat constricts, like someone's squeezing tight, stealing her last breath. *Take it,*

221

*you're welcome.* Can't bear to look at him, because she knows he sees the truth in her eyes.

"Trust me, Cheryl. It's natural to think such things. Plea-bargaining. All part of the grieving process."

"I-I could n-never choose between them, n-no matter what." A streak of snot trickles from her nose, settles on sore lips before she realizes it's there and wipes it away with a bandaged hand. Eyes meet, and she sees pity reflected in his, and for the first time she allows herself to feel a little of the same.

"Of course you couldn't." He tries to smile, but the shriv-elled skin around his mouth is too tight, so instead he wraps his arms around her, holds her close as she breathes in the toxic fumes of carbon and sulphur. Head to sternum, she listens to the crackle of flames that hiss and spit in his lungs. The sound reminds her of nursing Jonathan, her eldest. Diag-nosed with asthma at the age of two and always poorly with his chest.

He strokes her hair, his fingers light as dust. "They'll always be with you; mark my words. They'll find a way to show you." His words are cold comfort, served in warm arms.

The floodgates open and she thinks she'll never stop crying, because she's remembered their little faces, their distinct scents, the innocence in their eyes. She remains wrapped in his arms for some time, rocked like the child she is, because when tragedy occurs, each and every one of us reverts to childhood, the primal need for comfort.

Eventually, she falls asleep, until dawn breaks.

SHE SENSES it rather than sees it because the blinds are drawn. Instinct.

He's gone. Perhaps she imagined it. The whole thing is just her subconscious playing tricks.

The nurse enters, opens the blinds with an enthusiastic whoosh, and greets her in an overly cheerful manner. "Let's give you a nice wash, hey? We need to take the stitches out of that shoulder today."

The nurse whips off Cheryl's nightdress with expert hands and begins the cleansing process, soothing, healing. She pats her dry, then places a change tray on the bedside table: sterile gloves, tweezer, scissors. "It might tug a little, okay?" She removes the dressing and frowns. "Hmm, strange shape to this scar," she says. "Bit of an odd colour, too."

"Is it infected?"

"I don't think so." She begins the process of removing the sutures, one at a time, *umming* and *ahhing* as she deliberates over the wound.

Cheryl wishes she could see, but the scar's on the back of her shoulder.

"Well now, look at that. I think there's a little message here from your boys, you know."

A gasp as the nurse holds the mirror in position. Three curved lines, diminishing in size, a semi-circular gash at the top of each, like three little heads. The wound is still red and angry, but it's filled with soot, too. A permanent memorial etched on her skin, like a tattoo.

She remembers what he said...

*They'll always be with you; mark my words. They'll find a way to show you.*

He waits until the witching hour to pay his final visit. It's the smell of stale smoke that wakes her, not the heat, because the fire inside him is extinguished. The molten lava that ran through his veins has crystallized; his flesh has turned to ash. His carbon outline waits at the end of the bed, watching.

She sits up, and switches on the night light. Breathes in his fragile state to prove her strength.

He points a shadowy finger. "Didn't I tell you? The boys will sit on your shoulder 'til you breathe your last." His voice is a faint whisper, and as he speaks fragments of ash fall from his lips and come to rest on the white sheet.

"And what then?" She wants him to promise they'll be reunited, mother to sons, but he has never lied, no matter how painful the truth.

He sighs, and the effort of doing so causes his lungs to disintegrate so that his chest implodes. Particles of ash float in the air. One lands on her cheek, and she sticks out her tongue and tastes its acrid tang. And in that moment, she knows he has given all he can.

A deep inhale, and with no trace of bitterness or resentment, she puckers her lips and blows. Dandelion seeds on the wind, until he is nothing more than dust.

# LEONORA DRIVE

## GWENDOLYN KISTE

T t's half past noon when a veil of nightmares descends on downtown.

"Right on schedule," you whisper, and with your hands in your pockets, you wander out of the auto shop where you work and onto the sidewalk, watching the gray inkblots dart about the air. All around you, the other townspeople are screaming, their mouths contorted, their eyes gone wild and dark. You almost laugh. They act like they've never seen a thing like this before.

They're running in all directions, fleeing a nightmare on the corner and another by a mailbox, but one thing every-body's got in common: they keep turning back and staring at the smudged bay window in the duplex across the street. Sadie's window.

"Somebody wake that girl up," a voice calls out, maybe the pharmacist next door or the barber on the other side of the block. They already know Sadie's to blame. That's because every sentient dream in this town belongs to her.

She doesn't even have to be asleep for this to happen. A simple daydream can do it.

Up and down the street, the nightmares swirl and shimmer on every surface, their misty bodies twining around lampposts, their murmuring cries like a most hideous lullaby. You can't help but smile. From where you're standing, it's oddly beautiful.

Of course, you can't find a single person in town to agree with you. They're too busy swearing and sobbing. A scream cracks the sky, maybe from a man, maybe from a monster, but it must be enough to break the spell, because all at once, her front door swings open, and Sadie emerges, her eyes bleary, her cheeks blossoming red.

It's been twenty years since the two of you were in high school together, but in moments like this, it's as though she hasn't aged a day. The same long red curls, the same distant expression on her face.

"I'm sorry," she says, not looking at you, not looking at anyone. Nearby, the nightmares let out one final screech before dissolving into the afternoon like sea foam.

"It's all right," you say, but nobody hears you. They've all gone back to their middling day, the shops on Main Street swallowing them whole.

Sadie returns to her day too, vanishing inside her lonely house and back into her lonely life. You want to go after her, to tell her this isn't her fault, but another voice rises up to stop you.

"Get back to work, Renee," your boss says to you, his hulking figure leaning against the doorway of his namesake establishment. Jerry's Auto Repair. You're an apprentice here, the same job you've had since you were seventeen, since before this town became a living nightmare.

You nod, ready to do what you're told. Except something

else has caught your attention. It's twitching on the cement, no bigger than a fist, its vacant eyes trained on you. A brittle remnant of a nightmare, curled up and writhing, as if in pain.

You watch it for a long moment, feeling so very sorry for it, so very sorry for all of you.

"Go to sleep now," you whisper, and bring your boot down hard on the sidewalk. The creature lets out a little yelp before disintegrating into dust.

Then with Sadie's dreams dead at your feet, you turn and go back to work.

It's closing time when the next batch of nightmares arrives. You're the only one left in the repair shop, and it seems like these creatures are made just for you, nuzzling at your throat, sticking in your hair, thick as gum.

With a sigh, you swat them off like common houseflies, but they hardly notice. Instead, the swarm follows you as you count the drawer and turn off all the lights.

Outside, you lock up and head toward the sidewalk. Even though you work all day as a mechanic, your hair stinking of Valvoline and chrome, you have to walk everywhere you go. That's because your own car doesn't start—you don't have the right parts to fix it, and in a town of nightmares, it's not easy to find what you need.

As you start across the street, the thin curtains flutter in Sadie's upstairs window. For a moment, you're sure she's right here, gazing out at you, her eyes pleading with you, pleading with anyone who will listen. But then you blink once, and like a phantom, she's gone. So are her nightmares, dissolving into the evening like fog. You reach out for them, but they slip right through your fingers.

Sadie lives in a plain white duplex, the first in a row of them, all identical, all built in the last thirty years. This is the so-called new part of town, back when everyone had hope, when you honestly believed you had a future instead of just a past.

Up ahead on the sidewalk, there's one dream left floating in the air. It's flickering like a firefly, like a beacon to light your way. You know you shouldn't bother with it. You should head home. But you can't help yourself. It leads you along, twisting through back alleys and backyards, and even before you make the last turn, you know where it's taking you. To the place this whole mess started twenty years ago.

The last house on Leonora Drive.

It sits as empty as heartache, nestled on a dead-end street in this dead-end town. If you ask the old timers, this house was born haunted. Nobody ever lived here, not so far as you can tell. It was supposed to be someone's dream house, and to be fair, that's exactly what it's become, just not in the way anyone expected.

Because it was always vacant, it was transformed into a dumping ground of sorts, a junkyard for everyone's failures. Stacks of tires piled sky-high in the backyard. Boxes of old family photo albums in the attic, gone yellow with time. From what you hear, there are probably bones buried in the garden, forgotten secrets tucked away in the horsehair plaster.

But that was the problem. This place learned all about your dreams. It learned about your nightmares too. And the house on Leonora Drive has an impeccable memory. Your town gave it all the things you loathed until finally it demanded something that you loved.

For a while, it just seemed like good fun. When you were in high school, kids used to sneak in here on a dare, guffawing and guzzling cheap pints of Mad Dog 20/20 like it was ambrosia of the gods.

Not you though. The other kids never dared you to do anything, because they never seemed to know you existed. You were a nobody, all hunched shoulders and smudged eyeliner, your mom's Marlboros tucked in your back pocket. A sneer on your face and a thorn in your heart, you pretended you were the reincarnation of James Dean, but you were much less than that, and you knew it. Just the wrong kind of girl from the wrong kind of family.

On Friday nights, a group of kids your age always went to the house, the quarterback and the running back and all the other backs it takes to make up a football team you never watched on the field. You only watched them when they came here. That's because they brought Sadie with them.

As they went upstairs into the main bedroom, you lingered in the hallway, unseen and unwelcome, eavesdropping on their party, make-believing you were part of it too. The way they would dance and drink and dream. The house seemed to come to life with them inside, especially when Sadie was here, the walls vibrating around her, pulsing just so they could be closer to her. The prom queen to be, the most popular girl in town.

"It likes you, Sadie," the quarterback guffawed, and you could practically hear the ugly grin on his golden boy face. "Maybe it wants you to stick around and be its little housewife."

"Knock it off," Sadie said, and when they wouldn't stop teasing and taunting, she stormed into the hallway, quick as a jackrabbit. So quick that you didn't have time to duck inside one of the empty rooms. Instead, there the two of you were, you at one end of the hall and her at the other.

You braced for it, for her to cry out, to tell the others about you, an intruder, a pest. But she did something else. She smiled at you. In spite of yourself, you smiled too. Her friends called for her, but she didn't look back. Without a word, she took your hand, and the two of you disappeared down the stairs and out of the house.

"I hate it in there," she said, as you walked her home, her hand still clutching yours, her body so close you could almost hear her heartbeat.

"Then don't go back," you told her, but you already guessed that she wouldn't listen. Her friends came here, which meant she would too. Everyone was drawn to Leonora Drive.

And now here you are, alone in this house, alone with the past. The dream has vanished, abandoning you with the most abandoned place you've ever known.

Your hands shaking, you reach into your jeans pocket. Back in high school, you used to smoke, a pack a day, maybe more, but there aren't enough cigarettes left in town now, so you begrudgingly gave up the habit years ago. One habit you never surrendered though—carrying a red Zippo lighter in the frayed front pocket of your hand-me-down Levi's.

You take it out, and with a calloused thumb, you flick the flint wheel, igniting a spark in the shadows. You try once again, even though you've tried a hundred times before. Even though you already know how this will turn out.

The flame touches the floorboards, but nothing happens. That's because the last house on Leonora Drive won't burn. It won't splinter. It won't budge.

This property will outlast all of you. That's its promise and its curse.

You shrink back into the hallway. "Leave her alone," you whisper. "Leave us all alone."

But the house won't listen. None of this will end, not until it gets what it wants.

Not until Sadie stops dreaming.

It's Thursday afternoon, and you're lingering at the city limits, waiting for this week's deliveries.

A few others are waiting with you. The regulars, you call them. The pharmacist, the grocer, the gas station attendant. They're always eager to load up supplies, to do their best to sustain you all for a little longer.

But that isn't easy. The truckers always stop in an old dusty lot just before they reach town. None of them are brave enough to venture further. The outside world knows all about what happens here, the same way people always hear about urban legends. Through a friend of a friend, the details as murky as midnight. And they know they want to stay clear of you as much as they can.

Today's deliveries all come on the same truck, the bespectacled driver a guy named Chris McLaren who used to know your father back when you had one. As soon as the engine cuts out and he flicks open the door, a nightmare darts down out of nowhere and splats on his windshield like bird shit.

"What the hell—" he starts to say, but then his face goes still as stone, as if he suddenly remembers where he is.

The sun in your eyes, you do your best to ignore the nightmare. Besides, you've got other things on your mind.

"Could you bring a catalytic converter and maybe some spark plugs next time?" you ask, and Chris gives you a shrug.

"I'll see what I can do, Renee," he says, but you already know what he really thinks about you.

"Everyone tells us not to bother," he confided to you once when he was delivering a shipment of Firestone tires. "The people in the neighboring counties want us to let you all die out. Like you're some kind of invasive species."

You let out a sharp laugh. "I don't know what we are," you said.

You pay for today's supplies in cash and then you start walking. On your trip back to town, there's someone hiking on the other side of the road, those red curls glistening in the afternoon. Sadie. You watch her, your heartbeat quickening, everything in you as lovesick as a schoolgirl. She's different than yesterday when you saw her on the street. This time, she doesn't look away from you. Instead, she smiles. You smile back. You wish you could stop and talk to her, but the others are right behind you, the pharmacist and the grocer, driving their beat-up jalopies, and you know they can't spot you together. It isn't safe.

So you just keep walking, your pride in your shoes, past all the sleepy houses in this sleepy town, a white-walled hellscape of conformity you can't seem to escape. No one escapes these days. Plenty of people in town have tried of course, and with vile visions chasing them around every corner, who can blame them? But no matter which road you take, you can never leave for long. Sadie's nightmares follow you wherever you go.

You deliver the supplies to the auto shop, a box of motor oil and a few new wrenches. Then you clock out early and head home. You rent a room downtown above the old funeral parlor, the heady scents of sorrow and embalming fluid wafting through the air like a department store perfume.

You curl in bed, pretending there's a way to escape. Pretending you could be someone or somewhere else. Pretending you could take Sadie with you.

What does it mean to grow up? What does it mean to grow old? You don't really know the answer. You thought by now you would. You thought you'd know a lot of things. It's strange how time can keep passing but also pass you by.

Evening leaks down from the sky, but you don't drift from this spot. Instead, something drifts closer to you. A new batch of nightmares, their claws sharper than ancient bodkins. They're stronger than usual tonight, seeping inside through gaps in the ceiling and between planks in the wooden floor, their heavy figures everywhere at once.

One by one, they descend on you, and suddenly, the stench of embalming fluid is replaced with something else, sweet and whimsical like the scent of wildflowers in bloom. Sadie's scent.

"I miss you," you whisper, but the nightmares don't care. Neither does the house on Leonora Drive. It knows what's happening to you, and even from across town, it savors every moment, the weight of the past suffocating you.

You part your lips to scream, but no sound comes out.

THE NEXT MORNING, you're under the chassis of a '78 Gremlin when Sadie's dreams shift.

"Look," your boss says, and you crawl out from the dark and glance up at the sky, your chest tightening.

A living dream is playing out for anyone to watch, flickering like a movie against the clouds. This has happened before, and you always hate it. The way Sadie's secrets are on display for the world to witness.

Your neighbors emerge from the grocery store and the post office and every other business on Main Street, all of them huddling together, gawking at the spectacle. At these private images flashing before you. Today, it's Sadie's body, stripped naked, her figure wandering through shadows.

*Renee*, her voice echoes in the dream. *Please help me.*

Everyone turns toward you, as if you're to blame. You look away, both from them and from the vision of Sadie.

"Wake up," you whisper, and she must hear you because the dream slowly ebbs away. The others roll their eyes, their glares and gossip as eternal as the sun.

"That girl was always trouble," they say, but that's a lie. For years, everybody adored Sadie. The perfect smile, the perfect grades, the perfect girl. She was the one they all wanted. Now she's the one they all want to hate. She's become this town's sacrificial lamb, a maiden for the slaughter.

"Maybe it's this town that's trouble," you say, your hands tightening into fists, and the others grimace at you, but you're suddenly not looking at them. You're looking at the pale duplex across the street. Sadie's watching you from the front porch, and in an instant, you know what she's thinking.

*You don't have to do that, Renee. You don't need to protect me.*

But you both know that isn't true. You did have to protect her once. That's what caused this mess.

Her head down, she disappears back inside, and regret blooms inside you.

You wish you could help. You've always wished that. Back in high school, after that night you walked Sadie home, it became your secret ritual. Every weekend, she would go to the house on Leonora Drive with the others, but she'd always make an excuse to leave early. You'd wait for her in the dark, hidden in a bedroom or a backroom, and she'd find you, the two of you lost in ways nobody else could see.

"We should run away together," you'd whisper, as you took detours through every narrow alley in town.

"It's not that simple, Renee," she'd say, but you knew she was wrong. You could run. It might not fix everything, but it would have fixed what happened next.

It was prom night, all streamers and hormones, and as

everyone expected, Sadie was crowned prom queen. She beamed from the stage, with her pink dress and pink cheeks, and you watched from the back of the auditorium. You went alone, arrayed in a rented tux and scuffed dress shoes, and afterward, you followed the boys and Sadie to the house, tracking the glint from her bejeweled crown, watching as they passed around a flask, making sure Sadie drank more than her fair share.

Upstairs, you waited for her in the darkened hallway, but she didn't come to you. Instead, all you could hear were the boys' voices, rising up in the bedroom, their laughter like a cat puking.

Your jaw set, you peered inside after her. Something had gone wrong. Her eyes were closed, her body limp on the floor. And there they were, her dreams projected on the wall like a liquid lightshow. You could see everything happening inside her. You could feel it too, deep down in the marrow of your bones.

The house was coaxing her dreams out of her. It was coaxing the life out of her too. It wanted the same thing as everyone else in this town: to have Sadie to itself. Sadie as always got no say in the matter. With her breath hitching in her chest, she was slipping away, and you knew you had to wake her. You had to bring her back, or else she'd never come back at all.

Your hands clenched, you emerged from the hall and pushed the useless boys out of your way. They cursed at you, but that didn't matter. All you could see was Sadie. Kneeling at her side, you took her hand, and at once, she opened her eyes.

"Renee," she whispered, and you grinned back at her.

"Way to ruin our fun," the quarterback seethed. Except what he didn't know—what none of you knew—was that the house's fun had only just started. It wouldn't be satisfied until it got its way. If the house couldn't have her, then she couldn't have herself either. She belongs to it now, every secret in her heart laid bare, the house coveting her like a jealous boyfriend.

This is the ultimate revenge porn. She wouldn't fade into the floorboards, so now she's on display for everyone to see.

Across the street, her front door slams shut, and something settles in your guts like buckshot. Because for the first time, it feels like you can't reach her.

As if Sadie is disappearing in plain sight.

On Sunday morning, when all the churchgoers are praying to their plastic Jesuses, there's a knock at your door. Sadie's waiting on the other side.

"Can I come in?" she asks, her voice no more than a wisp.

With the morning light peeking in through the threadbare curtains, you curl up in bed together.

"I have an idea," she says, her head resting on your chest. "For how we can stop this."

You wait, already knowing she's going to tell you, already knowing you won't like it.

"If we recreate that last night in the house," she says, "just you and me, I think we can fix it."

"You mean, we can end it." You won't look at her, grief tightening in your throat. "We can end *you*."

"It's what I want, Renee. It's what everyone wants."

She never asks what you want. Nobody ever does.

You wrap your arms around her. "Why now?"

"Why not?" she asks, trembling. "At our age, we both know it's too late to start over."

You want to tell her that's not true. You could still run away. Except maybe for her, it is too late. She's never tried to leave. This is her penance for being what the town wanted. For being the girl everybody loved and loved to hate.

"I wasn't supposed to survive high school," she whispers.

"What if that's not true?" you ask, but she's already closed her eyes, her dreams draping around you like velvet. You should wake her, but in her sleep, she clings to you, and even as the shadows coil around your bodies, thick and heavy, you won't let her go.

IT'S THURSDAY AGAIN, and you're pacing at the city limits.

Right on schedule, Chris pulls up with the other truckers. He brings out a box of supplies for the auto repair shop and takes his payment in cash. You're ready to walk away, but once he's sure nobody's looking, he passes you a small plastic bag. "Those parts you asked for," he says.

A flash of hope brims in your chest. "How much do I owe you?"

"On the house," he says with a small smile. "Good luck, Renee."

You head back to the shop and start working on your car. You don't listen when your boss threatens to fire you. You don't listen to anything except the clanging of your wrenches against metal.

It's after dark when you tighten the last bolt and climb behind the wheel. The engine murmurs for a moment like it's telling you a secret. Then all at once, it roars to life, the heartbeat of the throttle thrumming deep inside you.

At last, your car is fixed. For all the good it'll do you now.

Behind you, Sadie materializes in the doorway, clutching her dusty crown from prom.

"Are you ready?" she asks.

Without a word, you walk together along the sinuous streets of this forgotten town, headed toward the place you wish you'd never gone. The end of Leonora Drive.

This is the inverse of all the journeys you made with Sadie before, escorting her home after she'd left the house. Now you're taking her back to stay.

Upstairs, the empty bedroom is waiting for her.

"Are you sure?" you whisper, as Sadie reclines on the floor.

She reaches up and entwines her fingers with yours. "This is for the best," she says, her hand falling away, as she closes her eyes.

All around you, the house trembles with glee, because it's about to get what it wants. The dreams start unfurling from her, a thousand of them at once, gray figures seeping out from every direction, their hazy fingers clasped around her throat.

Sadie struggles to breathe, her body convulsing, her prom crown slipping to the floor, but you already know the rules. You aren't allowed to stop it this time. But you don't want to watch either.

You could run. That's what you've always wanted to do. And it would be so easy now—just turn toward the hallway and disappear into it.

Then you see it, projected on the wall. The dream that's drifting inside of her. It's the two of you together in this house, you at one end of the hall and her at the other. The moment when you really looked at each other for the first time. The way she smiled at you. The way you smiled back.

Sadie's fading away, evaporating into oblivion, yet this is the memory she's still clasping to her heart.

You stand frozen, hating this house and everyone who built it. Why should a girl have to suffer so that others can live? Who makes these rules anyway?

Your hands unsteady, you take out your red Zippo lighter,

and you conjure a flame, holding it to the wall, willing it to burn. As always, nothing happens. You wish it could be different, but you already know the truth: the house won't fall. It'll stand forever, longer than you.

But something surges through you, as you realize you've been wrong. For all these years, you've wanted to escape, to be free of the past. Except that's not possible. You'll never be rid of this house or this town, not really.

But they'll never be rid of you either.

"It's not too late," you whisper, and through her dreams, Sadie must hear you, because you don't have to take her hand. She opens her eyes on her own. It's her choice this time and no one else's. Together, you see each other, understanding at last what you should have done all those years ago.

Let the nightmares come. Let them follow you wherever you go. Let everyone see what this town has done. Nobody protected you and Sadie. Now you'll force the world to witness what that feels like.

With dawn brimming through the smudged windows, you march together down the stairs. The house shudders around you, splintered doors slamming shut, wallpaper peeling back like a thick skin to encircle you. But you just keep walking, out onto the street and back to the auto repair shop.

With the keys in hand, you climb into your car, and Sadie buckles herself into the seat next to yours.

"Where do we go now?" you ask, and Sadie grins at you.

"Anywhere but here."

The world out there might not want you, but you want each other, and that's all that counts.

You head onto the road, the engine humming, the sun rising in the pale sky, and with her gaze set on the horizon, Sadie wraps her hand around yours, the two of you trailing laughter and nightmares in your wake.

# SPECTER

PHILIP FRACASSI

The last present.

It's wrapped in black paper embossed in silver cycles of the moon, crisscrossed with a glittery string tied in a loose bow. Holding the box in her small hands, Jenna looks up at her nana, who sits stoically among a few straggling parents clutching plastic cups of cheap wine. A smattering of young girls grow restless and bored watching Jenna open gifts. Jenna's mother stands to the side, arms folded, a tight smile on her face, as if nervous.

"That one's from me," Nana says, sucking on a cigarette and ignoring the side-glance grimaces of some parents, each of them surely debating whether to discuss the effects of second-hand smoke with the old woman.

Jenna, sitting cross-legged on the living room carpet, gives her nana a smile. "Thank you, Nana," she says.

The old woman nods, frowning. "It's not another dress; I can tell you that."

Jenna's eyes flick instinctively to her mother in time to see her face harden, her eyes shift momentarily downward. Jenna has opened three new dresses, all of which she adored. She was eleven years old now. Next year, she'd leave her middle school for junior high, which was practically high school.

Clothes were essential.

In addition to the dresses, she's been given absolutely *perfect* gold-colored ballerina flats and a gorgeous pair of cherry-red Mary Jane's with a matching red leather belt. She doesn't like that Nana makes her mother feel bad about giving her new clothes, especially since it's what—frankly, *all*—she'd asked for.

Her friends have mainly given her jewelry—a pair of earrings, a charm bracelet, a set of pretty hairclips decorated with fake pearls. Her best friend, Esther, always eager to surprise, gave her a mahogany jewelry case that, when opened, played music and revealed a twirling ballerina. Esther's mother, gushing with pride at having delivered the knockout punch of 'best gift,' announces the tune to be "March of Wooden Soldiers" by a Russian composer whose name she couldn't remember.

"Tchaikovsky," Nana says through a haze of smoke, "killed himself with poison, but wrote beautiful music."

"Mom, please," Jenna's mother says nervously, avoiding eye contact with any of the other parents.

Some of the girls giggle into their palms.

Nana simply shrugs, like she always does when chided.

Despite her nana's age (Jenna didn't know it exactly but had a shaky memory of an 80th birthday being mentioned when she was a few years younger), she was an intimidating woman. Small, thin, and bony, but with a spine straight as a yardstick and hard gray eyes to match shiny silver hair (which was always perfectly coiffed in a backswept style that made Jenna think of Disney villains, although she'd never admit such a thing).

Jenna studies the package a moment longer, then gently frees the hand-tied bow at its center. She runs the tips of her fingers lightly over the embossed moons, knowing full well her nana's love of the stars, which she once told Jenna: "revealed all the secrets of the universe, if you only knew to read them." In addition to studying the stars (which she'd repeatedly informed Jenna was called *astrology,* a word Jenna could never quite remember), Nana also enjoyed telling fortunes using a deck of special cards. Jenna's favorite of these was one called *The Empress*—the woman in the image seeming so powerful with her revealing clothes, her horns of hair, her golden scepter. But Jenna also thought her beautiful. The kind of woman she'd like to be when she was older—sexy, sure. But *strong.*

Flipping the box over (*too thin for shoes, too heavy for a belt*) she pulls the paper apart at the neatly taped seam to reveal a black cardboard box. She turns it back over, right-side-up. Another half-moon—this one stamped gold into the box's lid —stares back at her. Intrigued, Jenna pulls off the top... and, at first, her heart sinks.

*A book?*

Momentarily thinking she might have said the word aloud, she quickly glances up at her nana, who studies her with cold, indifferent eyes, her black turtleneck and halo of cigarette smoke giving her pale head an almost detached look. Jenna has a flash memory of the bulbous floating head that was the Great and Powerful Oz. *All she needs is flames shooting from her ears.* Jenna feels a wash of shame and drops her eyes once more to examine the gift.

"What is it?" Esther asks, with all the giddy coyness of someone knowing the event has finished, the last challenger falling short of competing with this year's winner: she who brought the musical jewelry box with the twirling ballerina.

"A book," Jenna replies, doing her best to shovel a modicum of enthusiasm into her response.

"What kind of book, hon?"

Jenna looks up at her mother, whose seemingly innocuous question sounds rife with tension. Worry.

"It's a dream journal," Nana announces before Jenna even has it out of the box. "You put it next to your bed when you're sleeping. When you wake up, you write down your dreams before you forget them. There's a guide in there, as well, at the back, that tells you what they mean."

"Cool," Jenna says excitedly, meaning it this time. She lifts aside a fold of black tissue paper and studies the cover.

The book is large, almost like a dictionary. The cover is black leather, and there's no title. No words at all. There are designs, however, carved into the leather. Intricate, beautiful designs: a pair of large hands holding sand that spills between cupped fingers; a snake eating its own tail; a large, closed eye in the center; stars, moons, planets...

Jenna lifts the cover to reveal a neat inscription written in the center of the first, blank, page.

*For Jenna,*
*When you dream, dream of me.*
*Nana*

"It's beautiful," Jenna says, part of her wanting to leaf through the book then and there, feel the thick pages within, read the different meanings of dream symbols...

But her friends are already standing, antsy and ready for the cake and ice cream portion of the event. The final meal before the party is officially over and they can go home to daydream about their own childhood birthday parties, the wonderful gifts they'll hope to receive.

Jenna carefully sets the book back into the sturdy black box, her eyes unable to leave the cover.

"Jenna?" her mother says. "Come on, let's blow out the candles."

"Okay," she replies, and begins to fold the thin tissue paper back over the book's cover, when she pauses.

The embossed eye in the center—the one she would have sworn was closed only a moment ago—is now open wide. As if watching her.

As if seeing her for the very first time.

Realizing she must have seen it wrong the first time, Jenna dismisses the chill that climbs up her spine at the sight of the open eye. She dutifully covers it with the paper, replaces the cardboard lid, then heads for the kitchen to have cake and ice cream with her friends.

She doesn't notice Nana watching her as she passes by the table, a rare smile curling the old woman's lips.

LATER THAT NIGHT, Jenna is settled in bed, turning the interior pages of her new journal, when her nana comes to say goodbye.

"I'm not good at gifts for little girls," she says, sitting primly as a perched crow on the edge of the bed. "My Thomas always hated getting clothes on his birthday."

Jenna smiles, having grown used to the old woman referring to him in those words: *My Thomas.*

Never *your father* or *my son.* Almost always—and especially when speaking to Jenna's mother—it was simply: *My Thomas.*

"You like the book?" she asks.

Jenna nods. "I've been reading the descriptions. Did you

know, in dreams, a horse symbolizes strength? And losing your teeth means you're anxious."

"That's right," Nana says, sniffing. "But it's more than that, Jenna. You must put things in context."

Jenna studies her for a moment, brow furrowed. "What do you mean?"

"For instance," Nana says, with a small sigh, "a horse in a blizzard can mean perseverance, which could represent finding the strength to meet your goals in life. But a horse that's kicking you in the face, smashing all those little bones," she says, running a cold finger down the bridge of Jenna's nose, "well, that might mean something completely different."

Jenna scowls at the idea of her broken face, annoyed at Nana for saying such a horrible thing, but curiosity forces her to continue. "Like what?"

The old woman shrugs. "Like you don't have the strength to go on," she says, gray eyes intent on her granddaughter.

Jenna closes the book, runs her fingers over the grooved designs that decorate the leather cover.

"I almost forgot," Nana says. "One more gift before I go."

She reaches into her clutch and brings out an ornate pen, the casing dark wood, the trim silver and bright. "It's a nice one, the kind you refill the ink when it runs out instead of throwing it away. It's a good pen for your journal."

Jenna takes the offering, loving the heavy feel of it. She pops off the top, studies the glistening ink coating the tip. "Cool. I'm going to write my name in it now. There's a page for it."

The corners of Nana's lips twitch, and Jenna doesn't know if she's genuinely pleased, or just trying to hold in a mean-spirited smirk. "You do that. Now give Nana a hug. It's past time we all go to sleep."

JENNA WAKES THE NEXT MORNING, eager for school, excited to show off one of her new dresses. It isn't until she's out of bed that her eye catches the dream journal on the nightstand. "Oh, shoot," she says, realizing that in her haste she hadn't given herself time to recall any dreams she may have had. Taking a moment (and forcing herself to forget about school and which dress she might wear), Jenna sits on the edge of her bed, curls her fingers into fists, squeezes her eyes shut tight, and tries to remember.

Seconds later, her eyelids shoot open and she snatches the journal, and the wonderful new pen, from her nightstand. She quickly flips past the opening pages (including the one where she'd written her name, the precise handwriting encircled by the image of celestial, dancing figures she thinks of as angels) until she reaches the first blank journal page. At the top, it says DATE, followed by a thin line. She writes the date then, just below, she writes what she remembers of her dream.

*I'm standing on a seashore watching giant waves coming in from a huge, gray ocean. I hear a noise and turn around to see a tall, rocky cliff. At the bottom of the cliff is the opening of a large cave. I walk closer to the cave, then stop when I see what's making the noise.*

*A bear.*

*He's huge and black as night. He's also very fat, as if he'd just eaten a family of campers. I watch him walk slowly into the cave, and I know he's going there to sleep.*

Jenna takes a moment to think of the right word.

*To hibernate. Like for the winter.*

*I keep watching until he disappears inside the cave. I'm about to follow when I hear a scream from behind me. I spin around fast, frightened, but see nothing except the crashing waves of the ocean.*

*I think now that I must have heard a bird. Like a seagull.*

*At this point I notice that my feet are itchy. I look down and see they're covered in tiny spiders. Thousands of them! The wet, dirty sand is moving because there's so many of them. It was like I'd stepped on their eggs and they'd hatched beneath me. I see a hand coming out of the sand, fingers clawing through the mass of spiders.*

*I start to scream.*

*And then I wake up.*

*It sounds weird but, thinking back, I wonder if the scream I heard was me. Dreams are weird like that, aren't they?*

Jenna stops writing, solemnly puts the cap back onto the pen. She makes a mental note to look up "bear" and "spiders" after school. She doesn't like the dream, and she's curious what it all means.

She closes the journal, sets it on the sheets of her unmade bed, and all but runs for the bathroom and a hot shower.

While she's getting cleaned up, she decides to wear the yellow dress.

HER MOTHER WATCHES from the porch as Jenna walks to the corner. This was the first school year Jenna had been allowed to walk alone to the bus. A rung on the ladder of independence climbed with being a year older, combined with the facts it was only a block from her front door and there were always a few other kids from the neighborhood waiting there, including Esther, who gawked like a fool when she saw Jenna in her new dress.

"Looking good, baby!" Esther says, loudly enough that a couple of the other tired-looking kids momentarily glance up from their phones.

Jenna laughs, then shivers. She hadn't wanted to wear a

coat over her dress, and the day would warm up soon enough, but at seven o'clock in the morning it's still chilly, even for early fall.

"Thanks," she says. "And thanks again for the jewelry box. I love it."

Esther nods and loops her arm through Jenna's as the bus pulls up, followed quickly by the sharp stink of exhaust and the high-pitched rumble of the chatting children already aboard. "I knew you'd love it. Better than a stupid book, anyway," she says as the girls climb aboard, navigate the narrow walkway before reaching their usual bench.

The vinyl seat is icy on the back of Jenna's legs, forcing her to suppress another shiver.

Jenna thinks Esther's remark is more a test than a statement, as if making sure the dream journal hadn't somehow trumped her own gift now that the dust of the party had settled. "I actually wrote in it this morning," she says, amused at Esther's grimace. "I dreamed about a bear, and spiders. Isn't that weird?"

"I don't like spiders, and I really don't like bears," Esther says, looking out the window as their familiar neighborhood drifts away like a mirage. "They eat people."

When Jenna arrives home that afternoon, she's in a foul mood.

For starters, a rotten boy named Steven Duane Allison Junior, who was rumored to be the neighborhood serial killer of stray cats and squirrels, knocked over his fucking chocolate milk during lunch and some of it leaked over the table and spilled onto her dress. She'd spent ten minutes in the bathroom crying and trying to clean it out with water and paper towels, which *then* made her late for fifth period, and snotty Mr. Jensen gave her a tardy slip even though she'd told him what happened, and it was *obvious* she'd been crying about it.

To make the day a total disaster, Esther's mom picked her up at school to go shopping. They invited Jenna to come with them, but she was so embarrassed about her dumb dress (complete with the stupid brown stain from Steven Duane Allison Junior's goddamn chocolate milk) that she'd said 'no,' and then nearly cried again on the bus ride home. *Alone.*

"Mom!" she yells as she walks through the front door, glancing into the kitchen, then the living room, but not seeing her mother. Because *of course* she's not there, waiting for her (or waiting on the porch, like she usually was).

Instead, Jenna finds her mother in her bedroom, sitting on her bed.

Reading her dream journal.

"Mom?"

Her mother audibly *squeaks* in surprise, almost dropping the oversized book to the floor as one hand clutches the fabric in front of her heart. "Jesus, honey, you scared me."

Jenna's eyes narrow. "What are you doing?"

Looking embarrassed, her mother closes the book and sets it gently on the nightstand. "I was curious about your book. I wanted... Well, I wanted to read about some of the meanings, you know? For dreams."

"Why? Also, look at my dress."

Her mom glances at the small stain (*because it is,* Jenna realizes in the aftermath of her day from hell, *small*) and gives a tired nod. "That'll come out in the wash, honey."

Feeling suddenly foolish, Jenna goes to her dresser and pulls out a pair of jeans and a T-shirt. She pulls off the yellow dress and hands it to her mother, who glances once more at the stain, then clutches the dress to her breasts, as if it needed comforting. "And to be honest, I had a very strange dream myself last night. It was...upsetting. So, I don't know, I wanted to see if there was something about it..."

Jenna pulls on her jeans, tugs the shirt down over her head (mildly annoyed at how much more comfortable she feels out of the dress), then sits on the bed with her mother, crossing her legs beneath her. "What was the dream?"

She wants to ask: *Was there a bear? Were there spiders?*

But her mom only sighs, absently runs her fingers down the arm of her blouse. "It was about your father. He was talking to me...but I couldn't understand what he was saying. It was like he was behind glass, or something... but he kept talking, and gesturing in a crazy way, like he was upset, or in pain."

"Whoa," Jenna says quietly. Her mother didn't mention her father often, and Jenna herself has no memory of him, since he died when she was just a baby. But she knows her mom had loved him very much, and that he had been Nana's only child.

Jenna thinks part of the reason her mom doesn't talk about her father is because Nana had helped them after he died. Gave them money for the house, to live. It was as if they'd made an agreement, her mother and her nana: money for silence. A pact she thinks quietly, slowly, broke her mother's heart. Like a hand pressed against cracked glass, each splintering *snap* a beat closer to shattering it completely.

The other reason, Jenna knew, was because Nana blamed her mother for his death. As if it had been her mother's fault her dad had...done what he did. Jenna only knows the details because Esther once overheard their mothers talking late one night, an empty bottle of wine between them. Jenny remembers the flushed cheeks of Esther's excitement when she relayed the information.

That her father had hung himself in the bedroom of their old home.

"Anyway, when I woke up," her mother continues. "I could have sworn he was trying to tell me something important."

She looks over at Jenna then, almost expectant, a half-smile appears on her face. "Stupid, huh?"

"Let me see the book," Jenna says, and her mom hands it over.

"What are you doing?"

Jenna opens the book on her lap, begins flipping pages until she gets to the back portion that contains the dictionary of meanings. "Looking up ghost. Why, what did you look up?"

Her mother looks confused for a moment, then sighs. "Husband."

"Here!" Jenna says, finding the entry. "Ghosts can often symbolize fear," she recites. "Or a strong paranoia about death."

Jenna glances up at her mom, who stares at the far wall, her expression blank.

She shrugs, continues. "It can also symbolize loss. As of a loved one through divorce, or death."

"That's enough, hon..."

"Maybe you were dreaming about Dad because you're afraid of something."

Jenna's mother stands up, brushes down the front of her wool skirt, then kisses her daughter's head before turning away. "I'm always afraid," she says.

FIVE DAYS after Jenna's eleventh birthday, Nana is found dead in her kitchen.

Firemen, responding to a neighbor reporting the smell of gas, find her on her knees, wearing a formal black dress, head bowed into the open door of an antique oven, the pilot light purposely extinguished.

She'd done herself the courtesy of laying a blanket beneath her head.

At the funeral, Jenna overhears a cousin saying, "The fussy old bird probably didn't want rack lines on her cheek." The person he's talking to laughs.

The day after her grandmother's funeral, Jenna wakes up crying. Her bedroom window is a hazy gray, the sun having not yet fully risen. She takes deep breaths in the dusky light of her room, recalling a most vivid dream.

She clicks on her bedside lamp and plucks up the journal along with the ornately engraved pen.

*Just had the most horrible dream EVER.*

*I was at Nana's funeral, and at some point I walked out of the room and into the lobby. There was a man there with his back to me. He was staring at the large photo of Nana that the funeral people had put out front on an easel. I said, "Hello?" but he didn't turn around or anything. He just stood there, wearing a dirty brown suit. He was breathing heavily, his shoulders lifting up and down. I could hear his breathing getting louder, like he was getting angry. Then he turned around and his face was blacked-out like a shadow. Like his head was empty.*

*I ran back into the room where Nana's coffin was but there was nobody there. All the pretty flowers around the coffin had turned black. I started to cry and yell for Mother. I didn't want to leave the room because the man was out there. Then I heard my name.*

*"Jenna."*

*I spun around to where the chairs were and Nana was sitting there, smiling at me. She held out her arms and I ran to her and hugged her. She was stroking my hair and calming me down. Then I realized she* couldn't *be there because she was dead.*

*I said, "Nana, why aren't you in the coffin?"*

*She smiled even wider, and it was creepy because Nana hardly ever smiled, and she said, "That's not me in the coffin, honey. That's your mother."*

*Then she took my hand and stood up, walking towards the coffin, which was open like it had been for Nana. She was dragging me toward it.*

*"You should join her," she said.*

*I started to pull back and scream. I didn't want to be anywhere near that coffin so I yelled, "Stop! Stop!"*

*But then I heard the man behind me, breathing like a horse, and he smelled bad, like rotten but also like dirt. And Nana pulled me right up next to the coffin and my mom was in there, but she wasn't dead. She was alive! She was alive and she turned to look at me, and her eyes were wide and scared and she wanted to open her mouth but the stitches inside kept her from talking. The stitches inside her mouth stretched. Unable to open her mouth, she moaned horribly. Tears ran from her eyes.*

*And then I woke up, and now I'm crying and I hate this stupid journal.*

JENNA SLAMS the journal closed and tosses it onto the nightstand. She's been recording dreams every morning since her birthday, and mostly it's been fun remembering the crazy, fantastic things that happen in her mind while she sleeps. The ominous bear hadn't returned (*or the spiders,* her inner voice reminds her, *the ones that were crawling all over your feet*) and, until this morning, hadn't recorded a single nightmare.

She climbs out of bed to use the restroom, then debates whether to put a sweatshirt over her pajamas and go watch television, preferably curled beneath a blanket (it was chilly in the house), or just go back to sleep, since it was Sunday and not quite 6 a.m.

Yawning, she decides on sleep versus television, and crawls back into bed.

When she wakes for the second time that morning, her window glows with warm yellow sunlight. She tilts the face of her charging phone toward her and is shocked to see it's past 10 a.m., both pleased and surprised her mother hasn't come in to wake her for breakfast. She stretches and folds back the covers, feeling more alert and relaxed than when she'd woken earlier, and is excited for a free day of doing whatever she wants.

She didn't dream in the short window of her second sleep and has a hard time remembering the details of her initial nightmare, the one so awful she'd woken in tears. Curious, she opens the dream journal to reread her entry.

As the details come back, she feels her mood dampen, mad at herself for rehashing the stupid dream in the first place.

But it's not until she reaches the end of the entry that a chill of pure terror fills her chest like ice water, freezing her lungs and causing her heart to beat faster, faster…

Below the neatly printed words of her nightmare are two lines of flowing cursive.

*That wasn't a dream, my sweet.*

*Your mother is dead.*

Wide-eyed, Jenna reads the second line again.

*Your mother is dead.*

The handwriting is easy to recognize. She'd seen it on birthday and holiday cards; once on a postcard sent to her from Italy.

It was Nana's.

Jenna throws the book aside and leaps from the bed. She pulls open her bedroom door and runs into the house screaming, "Mom! Mommy!"

When she sees her mother sitting at the kitchen table,

reading the newspaper and having coffee—the mug caught midway between the table and her mouth, her face a mask of surprise at her daughter's distress—Jenna runs to her and throws her arms around her, crying her heart out.

"My God, Jenna, what's wrong?"

Jenna shakes her head, rubbing tears into the shoulder of her mother's soft robe. "Had a nightmare," she says, and decides it's best to leave it at that.

DURING THE REST of that Sunday, Jenna avoids going to her room.

She calls Esther from the living room couch and they talk about nothing and everything. She watches a movie while her mother makes dinner, then reads a book at the dining room table once the dishes are stacked away, the kitchen cleaned. As nine o'clock rolls around, she knows she can't stay out of there forever, and—with a heavy heart—goes into her room to get ready for bed.

Everything seems the same. The bed is still unmade, and there's nothing hiding beneath it (she checked). The lone window is closed and locked. The lights aren't flickering, and there's nothing in the closet other than clothes (also checked).

The journal is on the nightstand, closed and harmless.

She takes her bath, puts on her pajamas, kisses her mother goodnight, and climbs into bed, offering a silent prayer to the darkness that she won't dream.

Before she has the chance to fall fully asleep, or to dream, something—*someone*—walks into her room.

The floors of their house are old, bare hardwood, and she plainly hears the creaking of every step as they move around at the foot of her bed.

Jenna's face is turned away from the door, toward the far wall, but she doesn't open her eyes. She doesn't want to know. Doesn't want to see.

The footsteps are beside the bed now.

Moving from her feet to her head.

Jenna hears soft breathing, followed by the faint rustle of pages, the light scratching of pen on paper. The almost inaudible *thump* as the book is placed back on the nightstand, the *click* of the pen cap being secured.

There's a pause which—to Jenna's terrified mind—lasts an eternity. She waits, shivering with fear, to feel a cool hand on her head, or shoulder; for the sheets to be pulled slowly off her body, down past her hips, her feet. Exposing her to whatever stands beside the bed.

But then the footsteps are retreating across the floor, back toward the door, which gives a creak of protest as it's opened, then softly shut.

Jenna doesn't know how long she lies there, shaking, breathing fast, her mind numb with fear. She doesn't know because at some point—somehow—she falls asleep, and doesn't wake again until morning, the tweeting birds of her phone's alarm telling her it's time to wake up for school.

Bright daylight fills her room through the window, as if the sun itself was hunched low in the backyard, one eye brought down just far enough to peek in at Jenna's sleeping form. In the sobering daylight, she decides the nighttime visitor was a dream.

Because it *had* to be a dream.

A dream Jenna has no wish to write about. Or remember.

Instead, she has breakfast with her mom, then puts on white stockings, a pink dress, and her new cherry-red Mary Jane shoes. She puts her hair in a ponytail and clips it with a pink bow that matches her dress *exactly*.

It's only when she's at her bedroom door that she turns back, sees the dream journal on her nightstand, recalls the sound of rustling paper, the click of the pen cap, the scratching of someone writing inside of it.

She lets out a breath and, without allowing herself time to overthink it, walks briskly to the nightstand, lifts the book, and opens it—somewhat roughly—to the point of her last dream, marked with the black ribbon bookmark.

And sees...nothing. Just her last entry. Something about swimming in a big pool with a bunch of other kids. How it started sunny but then got dark and began to rain. How cold it was and how she was afraid of lightning striking the water, but she couldn't get out, couldn't swim to the sides or to a ladder, so she kept swimming and swimming and praying she wouldn't be electrocuted by a white blast of high voltage.

On a whim, she turns the page, expecting to see the blank page that follows.

But it's there she sees the writing.

*I know you're not asleep.*

It's in that same spidery hand she recognizes immediately, and as she reads the message, something in Jenna's mind snaps like a broken power line. She can almost hear the *fizz* of the loose end buzzing behind her ears.

She reads the line once, twice, then (*gently*) closes the book and sets it down on her bedspread. She knows she must hurry to make the bus, so she runs out of the room and heads for the hallway where she hangs her backpack, yells 'goodbye' to her mother as she bursts out the front door.

Walking to the corner, and seeing her best friend wave cheerfully as she does so, Jenna forces herself to smile.

She also decides that later, when she gets home, she's going to throw that fucking journal in the trash, and never think about her dreams again.

DURING SEVENTH-PERIOD STUDY HALL, it's Esther who changes her mind.

Jenna hadn't planned on telling her best friend about the strange journal, but Esther commented on how tired she looked, and Jenna confessed to having nightmares. When Esther asked if Jenna had been writing the nightmares down in her new journal (and subsequently hinted at wanting to read such entries), Jenna broke down in tears, revealing all that had happened since her nana's funeral.

"I think that's the coolest thing I've ever heard," Esther says, eyes bulging, cheeks flushed red. "Are you sure it's not, I don't know, your mom playing a trick on you?"

Jenna, wiping away tears, shakes her head. "She'd never. Never ever."

Esther nods, as if in agreement. "Well, I think it's kind of spooky, for sure. But it's also pretty neat, don't you think? I mean, come on Jen, your grandma is sending you messages from the beyond. Do you know how awesome that is?"

Admittedly, Jenna hadn't thought of it as cool, neat, or in any way positive in the slightest. She'd thought it terrifying.

But now, in the light of day, surrounded by students and the extreme normalcy of school, she thinks maybe, in a way... it *is* a little bit awesome.

"What do you think I should do?" she asks. "Honestly, I was planning on chucking the stupid thing."

"What? No! Jen, you can't do that. You'd be throwing away an incredible gift. I mean, you loved your grandma, right?"

Jenna realizes she doesn't honestly know the answer to that question, but she sniffs, wipes drying tears from her cheeks, and nods.

"And she died in that horrible way, you know?" Esther

says, her enthusiasm growing, contagious. "Offing herself like that? Don't you want to know why she did it? Think about it. You could *ask* her, and she'd *tell* you. That's insane!"

Jenna laughs at her friend's enthusiasm, suddenly feeling better than she had in days. She especially likes the idea of the journal not being something bad, per se, or scary. But something incredible. Like a miracle. "You think I should?"

Esther nods madly. "Or whatever. Ask her what the afterlife is like. Is there a Heaven? A Hell? Jenna, this is the chance of a lifetime."

"I'm surprised you even believe me," Jenna says.

"Well, and I hate to tell you this, but you're a terrible liar," Esther says, giggling. "There's no way you're lying about this. You should have seen your face when you finally told me what was going on. Jesus, dude. You were white as a ghost."

When Jenna gets home that afternoon, her mother is sobbing on the couch. Jenna wants to talk to her, to comfort her, but when she tries her mother pulls away, red-faced and ugly. "I'm sorry, honey. I just need to be alone."

She goes into her bedroom and shuts the door. Jenna, confused and concerned, grabs a banana off the counter and goes into her own room, quietly shutting the door behind her, not wanting to hear the hitched, muffled sobs of her mother coming from just down the hall.

She sits at her small oak desk, an antique her nana bought for her when she turned ten, then opens her laptop to watch videos while she eats, part of her mind always thinking about the journal sitting quietly on the opposite side of the room. Just behind her.

When she's done with her snack, she closes the browser and walks around her bed to the nightstand. She plucks up the journal, opens it to the page where Nana had written her last, cryptic message: *I know you're not asleep.*

Beneath it, she writes: *What happened to my dad? Why did he kill himself?*

She closes the journal, sets it on the nightstand, and leaves her room to pull her homework from her backpack, deciding she'll do it at the dining room table. Between sitting in her room with the journal—which feels to Jenna how it might feel to have a loaded gun sitting next to your bed—and listening to her sobbing mother, she chooses the latter.

After pulling her binder from the backpack, she turns on the television and sits at the table to work. She quickly discovers that if she turns the volume up loud enough, she no longer hears her mother crying.

THE NEXT MORNING, Jenna wakes to the soft sound of a tinkling melody.

She sits up, stares past the foot of her bed to her vanity, the smeared reflection of her torso in the oval mirror perched on its top.

In front of the mirror, her jewelry box is open. The ballerina twirls slowly as "March of Wooden Soldiers" plinks gently from deep inside the box. For a moment, she can only stare at the raised lid, the spinning ballerina.

Her mind, her *body,* fills with conflict: excitement mixed with fear.

She turns and quickly, almost absently, checks the screen of her phone. It's not yet 6 a.m., but that's fine. That's okay.

Jenna grabs the leather journal, opens the cover and flips to the page neatly marked by the black ribbon.

She sees her note: *What happened to my dad? Why did he kill himself?*

And, below that, in the unmistakable, spiraling handwriting of her dead nana: *Ask your mother. Tell her he's waiting for you both in Hell.*

For the remainder of that morning, Jenna's mother doesn't come out of her room. Doesn't make her daughter breakfast, or kiss her cheek, or stand on the porch as she walks for the bus. After eating cereal and getting herself dressed, Jenna knocks on her mother's bedroom door.

"Mom? Mom, are you okay?"

There is a *shifting* sound from the bedroom. As if her mother was sliding furniture from one place to another.

"I'm fine, baby," her mother replies. "Go to school."

Jenna thinks about opening the door to see if her mother really is okay or just pretending to be. But something stops her from turning the doorknob. A premonition. A fear. She worries about what she'll see. Will her mother be in bed, under the covers? Or will she be standing atop the bed, the sheets thrown to the corners of the room?

Jenna has the strange thought that she might find her mother huddled in a shadowy corner, naked and dirty. Maybe even bloody. Jenna imagines her mother leering toward the voice at the door, wild-eyed, teeth bared, perhaps hoping her daughter *would* come in...come into the bedroom so she could show her little girl what she'd become, what she'd turned into.

"Okay," Jenna says, and pulls her hand from the cool door-knob as if burned. She runs for the front door, desperate to be away.

When she reaches the corner where the bus stops, Esther notices the distress on her friend's face and pulls her into a hug. A few minutes later, as they climb onto the bus, Jenna tells her friend about the message, about her mother's increasingly strange behavior.

Just as they're pulling into the school parking lot, Esther grips Jenna's hand tight in her own. "Don't worry," she says. "I have an idea."

THE NEXT DAY, Esther comes over to Jen's house to hang out. As they enter the front door, they see Jen's mom at the kitchen table, hair messy, work clothes wrinkled. She gives them a blank-eyed stare as they walk past.

"Hello, Mrs. Crane," Esther says politely. "Anything new at the shop?"

Jenna's mother works the opening six-hour shift at a gift boutique in their small downtown, primarily selling knick-knacks and candles, handmade soaps, stationary, and artisan items that came primarily from local residents. She'd been there for as long as Jenna could remember.

"Hello, Esther," she says, ignoring the question. "I'm sorry, hon. I didn't know you were coming by. Are you girls hungry?"

"No, thanks," the girls say in unison, as if fully expecting the question.

Jenna's mother nods and her eyes grow distant once more. "Okay. I'll order pizza later if you want to stay for dinner. I'd cook, but I haven't been sleeping well. I'm very tired lately."

"It's fine, Mom," Jenna says, and tugs Esther away.

In her bedroom, Jenna closes the door and looks at her friend meaningfully. "She says she's been having nightmares. She cries a lot, and sometimes I hear her talking. Like she's having a conversation with someone in her room. Oh, and the other night I heard her scream in her sleep. It was scary."

"Weird," Esther says, walking to the jewelry box she'd

given Jen on her birthday. She winds the small brass crank on the side a few times, then lifts the lid. The ballerina dances and the music tinkles softly. "You said this was playing when you woke up the other night?"

Jenna nods. "And don't forget the footsteps. And the messages, of course."

"Speaking of which, did you write down your dream this morning?"

Jenna laughs. "You mean did I bait the hook? Yes, ma'am. It was a very pleasant dream in which my bed slowly submerged into a roomful of black water. According to the book, it means my conscious mind is sinking into my subconscious mind."

Esther dumps her backpack on Jenna's bed and digs inside. "That's some deep shit," she says, then pulls free a small black device about the size of a remote control. "This is what I was telling you about. It's a camera." Esther points to the lens. "It has night vision and a motion sensor. My parents use it when we go on trips because they don't trust the pet sitter. There's software you need to download, and you have to connect it to your network, but I can help with that."

Jenna holds out her hand and Esther hands the small device to her.

"Careful," Esther says, "that thing's worth a couple hundred bucks. If my dad finds out I borrowed it he'll kill me."

"It's so small," Jenna says, impressed.

"Right? So look, once you hook it up, it'll record any movement and save the video to your laptop. You can also access it from your phone, if you want, but I'm not sure how to do that."

"That's okay," Jenna says, handing it back. "Laptop is fine."

Esther closes the music box, snuffing the soft plinking sounds of Tchaikovsky. She looks around the room, then nods her head toward a bookcase next to the window that faces the

264

bedroom door, and Jenna's bed. "That should work. It's a wide lens, so it should see that whole side of the room."

Jenna nods. "This is crazy, huh?"

Esther smiles. "Yeah, but it's also kind of cool, right? I mean, if someone is coming into your room at night, writing stuff in your dream journal, this will catch them red-handed."

"Unless it's a ghost," Jenna says.

Esther's smile grows even wider. "Even cooler," she says. "If it's a ghost, it might catch that, too."

ESTHER STAYS FOR PIZZA, then calls her mom to pick her up.

Jenna informs her mother she has homework, then locks herself in her room to test the camera.

She turns off the lights, steps carefully to the center of her bedroom—making sure to be in full view of the camera's lens—and begins doing jumping jacks. After ten, breathing heavily from the exertion, she turns the lights back on and goes to the laptop. A folder on the screen reads MICROV22_CAPTURE, and she double-clicks it. There are two video files inside. One she knows is her and Esther dancing and waving before breaking out into a fit of giggles, their initial test run saved forever. She double-clicks the second file and a window pops up. It shows her standing in the middle of her bedroom, the night vision washing the room in shades of gray, her eyes full white.

"Creepy," she says, and plays the file.

She laughs at the bizarre image of watching her digital twin do jumping jacks in the dark, decides to save the file to show Esther the next time she comes over.

Satisfied everything is in working order, she gets ready for bed.

Jenna sleeps soundly that night, and she doesn't dream.

She isn't woken until her alarm goes off at 7 a.m. She feels rested, even cheerful. She glances toward the bookcase, sees the nose of the camera sticking out from beneath a stack of books, the laptop closed on her small desk by the window. Excited despite herself, she throws her legs out of bed, ignoring the chill morning air on her skin, and grabs the dream journal off the nightstand.

Flipping to her last entry, she looks for further messages. A response.

But there's nothing.

She turns the page. Then another.

Nothing.

Disappointed, she sets the book down and hurries to the laptop. She opens it, types in a password, and her desktop image—a close-up photograph of a bouquet of roses—appears. The folder containing the camera's captured videos is already open.

There are two new files.

Feeling a surge of jagged nerves, Jenna opens the first file, which is time-stamped as the earlier of the two videos. Her breath catches at the image of her room, the exact same framing from when she was doing her jumping jacks, except now she's nothing but a lump under the covers of her bed.

Her bedroom door, securely closed when she went to bed, is partway open.

She takes a deep breath, needing to pee but willing to hold it (for now). Biting her lip, she glances behind her to make sure the door is (currently) closed, and then plays the video.

On the screen, the door continues opening, the beginning motion of which must have cued the camera to begin recording. The hallway beyond is mostly dark, but there's a ghostly figure standing in the doorway, a shadow in contrast, pale shades of gray instead of black, its head turned toward Jenna's bed.

It's a woman. She's dressed in a pajama top and shorts, her hair wild, her eyes glowing that same, unnerving pure white.

Jenna's mother.

She enters the room slowly, walking in small, shuffling steps, until she's standing at the foot of the bed.

Jenna holds her breath, staring, wide-eyed, at the bizarre (and unsettling) image of her mother looking down at her. Watching her sleep.

Slowly, her mom bends over, puts her hands on the bed, palms resting a few inches from the misshapen lump of Jenna's feet. Moving carefully, as if not wanting to wake her sleeping daughter, she *crawls* onto the bed, pale skin shimmering white in the camera's night vision, her hair a tangle of shadows. She continues upward until her head is even with Jenna's, then she settles down next to the blanket-covered body...and goes still.

"She sleeps with me?" Jenna whispers aloud, not quite knowing how to feel about the strange revelation. Could it have been her mother this whole time? Creeping into her room to write bizarre journal entries, mimicking Nana's handwriting?

The video stops, and Jenna quickly slides the cursor over and clicks open the second file. She has a good idea what she'll see.

The second video plays, an odd reversal of the first. Her mother rolling gingerly off the bed, then standing to face the direction of the camera.

Jenna's eyes flick to the time stamp on the video: 4:35 a.m.

Her mother had only lain with her for an hour, and Jenna feels suddenly ashamed of herself—ashamed of thinking her mother would do something so cruel as to write those things in her journal, ashamed of seeing her mother's vulnerability, her obvious, desperate need to be comforted. Distraught, she'd come to lay beside her daughter for a bit, find some temporary solace against whatever was inflicting her mind as of late.

Jenna closes the laptop. She needs to get ready for school, and when she sees Esther, she's already decided to lie.

She'll tell her the camera didn't record a thing.

That nothing had happened in the night.

"WELL, you'll just have to try again," Esther announces when Jenna tells her about the initial failure of their project.

"I don't know if I want to," Jenna says. The two of them sit in the cafeteria, each picking at school-supplied cheesy pasta and limp green beans. "It's kind of freaking me out."

Esther shrugs. "More than the ghost of your dead grand-mother writing notes in your journal? Saying your dad is in hell and shit? That's what would freak me out."

"My mom feels guilty about his suicide, I think," Jenna says, finding herself thinking more about her father than she ever has. "In a way, I think Nana blamed her...blamed both of us, for what he did. They had a fight once, a couple of years ago, and I heard Nana say as much; said he'd still be alive if he'd never married my mom."

"Dude, that's horrible."

Jenna nods, pushes away her tray.

"Well, if that's true," Esther says, chewing thoughtfully on a green bean. "And assuming it's your grandmother writing those messages, I'm beginning to think you shouldn't mess around with it anymore. The journal, I mean."

"Why? You said it was cool."

"That's when I thought old granny was communicating with you because she missed you or something. But, based on the messages? I don't think she misses you," Esther says, swallowing the bean with a grimace. "I think she's pissed."

THE FOLLOWING MORNING, Jenna is eager to write down her dream.

She dreamed about the bear again. But this time he wasn't in a cave, but trapped inside a massive cage. He was roaring in frustration, pawing at the thick metal bars. The cage itself sat deep within a swampy, muddy patch of land, a great sea storming in the distance, just out of her sight. Jenna stood outside the cage, watching the frenzied animal pace, annoyed she couldn't figure out a way to free him. There was no door. No lock. Just thick, black metal bars.

Jenna walked to the cage, reached her hand between the bars.

The bear came to her, sniffed her fingers, pushed his giant head against her palm. Jenna scratched obediently. "Daddy?"

Wanting him free and relying once more on the bizarre nature of dream logic, Jenna realized she *could* help him escape. That she could, just maybe, *dig* him out.

Knowing she had to try, she began clawing furiously into the mud, pulling up giant clumps of wet dirt and weedy grass with impossibly powerful swipes of her hands. She dug deeper, and deeper, until she came to pieces of white rock lodged far below the surface. Knowing she had to go further, she kept on, pulling the white rocks free before tossing them behind her, a growing pile as she tunneled further into the earth, finally digging so deep that she could no longer see the sun overhead. At this point, she didn't know if she was getting closer to the bear, or further away.

Exhausted, she turned around and studied the large pile of

white rocks, and realized they weren't rocks at all, but bones. Her dream logic informed her quietly, calmly, that they were *human* bones.

Hastily, without rationalization, she began assembling the bones, like a puzzle, laying them flat on the floor of this tunnel —this cave—she'd created.

Legs. Feet. Ribs. Skull. Arms.

The skull, she noticed, was toothless.

Deep down in her heart, staring at the man-sized skeleton, she knew it was her father. Long dead and buried. Flesh rotted away.

There was a roar from above. Jenna ran back, looked up toward the opening—a pale sky staring back like a sightless eye, and then a face appeared at the jagged hole.

Nana.

She's dressed in black and crawling on all fours, like a spider. There's a roll of distant thunder and a heart-stopping scream from the clouds above, as if the sky itself is tormented by the jagged lightning. The screams continue as the storm above swells, and Jenna watches in horror as Nana scurries around the edges of the tunnel entrance, pushing down rocks and great piles of earth. The dirt began spilling down on Jenna from above, sealing her inside the tunnel, entombing her in the cold dark. Burying her with her father.

As the dirt squeezed in around her, and it became more and more difficult to secure a breath, the pressure on her chest and lungs increasing steadily, Jenna found that she wasn't upset, or scared.

In a way, she was happy.

When she woke, gulping in deep breaths of fresh air, Jenna felt sickened by her dream. She had a terrible headache and her stomach gurgled and burned, as if she were close to throwing up. She wondered if she was coming down with the flu, or a bad cold. Her entire body was achy, her nose stuffy, her eyes burning with exhaustion.

Still, through her exhaustion and discomfort, she slowly reaches out for the journal and pen from her nightstand, uses the ribbon to find the next blank page.

However, once she opens it, she finds someone has already written in the blank space where she'd hoped to record her dream.

*I'm coming for both of you.*

*Nana is waiting.*

And then, further down the page, scrawled with haste: *WE'RE ALL WAITING.*

Jenna drops the book to the floor in disgust, as if she'd lifted it to find it crawling with ants, or spiders. Then— remembering her precautions—she turns her head toward the camera set in the bookcase, to the laptop on her desk.

At the computer, Jenna double-clicks the new video file, the one recorded during the night. As with the last video, she's greeted by the frozen image of her bedroom submerged in ghastly shades of gray. A blur of frozen movement at the side of her bed, a finger smear distortion of reality.

She plays the file.

In the video, Jenna sees herself.

She's standing beside her own bed, wearing an oversized T-shirt a shade paler than the exposed flesh of her face, arms, and legs. She picks up the journal, opens it, and begins to write. A few moments pass, and she sets the journal back onto the nightstand. Turning fully around, she walks quickly across the room, past the foot of the bed, toward the dresser. Once there, she pauses a moment, as if thinking. Then she opens the musical jewelry box, watches the ballerina spin.

Then, in the blink of an eye, her head turns.

She looks directly at the camera.

Horrified, Jenna watches herself move toward the camera slowly, step by step. She gets close enough that the entire frame is filled with her head—white eyes glowing around dilated pupils, shimmering pools of silver. Her pale gray skin is sickly, corpse-like, her tussled hair a nest of ink-black snakes. She stares into the lens, as if staring not at the camera but at *herself*, and for a moment Jenna is held breathless as she stares back into her own haunted eyes.

Then, the Jenna in the video cocks her head slightly, her white eyes opening wide.

And she smiles.

Jenna cups a hand to her mouth to stifle a scream, and is about to slam the laptop closed when the Jenna in the video steps away from the camera, her movements now spasmodic, as if the video file has been corrupted, split seconds of time gone missing, causing the image of her body to move around the room in jerky, blurred movements.

Taking a breath, fighting back tears, it is only now that Jenna notices the shape in the bed, lying still as the girl in the video staggers across the bedroom floor. It's the shape of someone sleeping.

The face, poking free from the humped blankets, rests atop a blazing white pillow.

*Her* face.

Before she can begin to rationalize how there are *two* of her, the version of her moving around the room suddenly stops at the foot of the bed. Then, in those same, twitchy motions, it (because Jenna can only think of the girl as an *it*, not a *she*, and certainly not a *me*) crouches low, knees bent like spider legs, her body impossibly close to the floor.

Then it crawls beneath the bed.

The last thing Jenna sees in the video is the image of her own feet disappearing, as if swallowed up.

When she leaves her room for breakfast, Jenna's only mildly surprised at not finding her mother already awake and at the table, smiling at her while holding a cup of steaming coffee, asking her if she'd prefer oatmeal or cereal.

She glances at the closed door of her mother's bedroom at the end of the hall, wonders what nightmare vision she'd find if she went inside to look.

A pile of bones? A giant spider? Something else?

Something that would drive her mad?

With a sigh, Jenna sits at the table, forces herself to eat a banana, a cup of yogurt.

As she eats, she sets the small doll she found beneath her bed on top of the table.

The doll had been wedged between the wooden slats of her bedframe and the box spring beneath her mattress. She hadn't found it earlier because she hadn't bothered to look *up* when checking under her bed for ghosts, monsters, whatever.

The doll is made from rough canvas, and it smelled, Jenna thought, of urine. The eyes are tarnished gold studs, earrings Jenna thought she had lost a few months back. The mouth is red cross-stitching, the glued hair wispy and real. The same color as her own.

Jenna had torn the head open at a loose seam, curious what the hard, lumpy things were beneath the cloth. It turned out to be baby teeth. Six of them. She couldn't be positive, of course, but she was almost certain they were hers. She'd had many visits from the tooth fairy when she was younger—a dollar here and there, left under her pillow in the night, no questions asked.

After she finishes breakfast, she takes a large pot from the cupboard and sets it on the kitchen counter. She places the doll inside (keeping the baby teeth in her palm, thinking she'll put them in her jewelry box for safekeeping), then finds the lighter fluid in the pantry; a large plastic, yellow bottle they sometimes use to get the charcoals going for the small grill on the back patio.

In a junk drawer, she finds a pack of matches.

Humming to herself, Jenna douses the doll with lighter fluid, then lights a match and drops it into the pot. She makes sure to turn the stove's overhead fan on to suck away a majority of the smoke, but as the doll begins to burn she opens a kitchen window as well, not wanting to set off the fire alarm.

As she crosses back to the smoking pot, she glances toward the hallway, where she can just make out the open door of her bedroom.

Her Nana stands there, watching her. Hunched and scowling.

Jenna sits down at the kitchen table once more, letting the doll burn, doing her best to ignore the old woman screaming at her from the bedroom.

Later, she'll go check on Mother. She is fairly certain who her mother has been dreaming of, and who she's been talking to. Jenna knows she will find another doll, similar to her own, hidden beneath her mother's bed, and that the head of her mother's doll is not filled with baby teeth, but adult ones, pulled from her father's dead mouth, and left to rot in their house like a cancer, a contagion.

A curse.

# NEVER WAKE

KENNETH W. CAIN & TIM MEYER

T's been a long, strange trip. Or so says the Grateful Dead, who often captured the simplicities of life in such vivid detail. Well, at least that's what I say...

This is Ken starting this out, by the way. Tim will add his thoughts here and there, and hopefully, after some blending of styles, this whole afterword turns into more of an "after work." Because I think the theme deserves a little back-and-forth commentary.

How ironic for me that Tim should ask me to co-edit an anthology with him that had this theme. See, I'm terrified of sleep. I dread waking up not being able to breathe; more so after watching my own dad pass, losing his breath. I suffer from insomnia, too, and often, I've even seen things that may or may not have been there. Yes, folks, there's something within that fold of darkness in the corner of your room, hidden by a thin veil of reality. What lurks there, who knows? But whatever it is, most of it isn't good. I know that for a fact, having witnessed some pretty haunting stuff throughout my life.

So, let's get on with it then, shall we?

Dreams can seem so much like real life. We recall distant memories, believing we experienced this or that... But did we really? Or were our dreams merely so vivid that the familiarity we experience, that feeling of déjà vu, seems like it really did happen—perhaps in a past life even? Or are we instantly transported to another time, another place, somewhere far far away...if only for a moment? Are dreams gateways?

That, in and of itself, is something people have written about for ages—the dream world. It's fascinating, isn't it? It's understood that 80% of Earth's oceans remain unexplored. If that's true, how much of the un-waking hours remain unexplored? If there is something more to this world than what is right in front of us, perhaps some of the secrets lay there, in the unknown of our minds. Do we have power enough in that state to create new worlds, explore strange, new places, or are we merely powerless to some omniscient being, dangling our lives upon a delicate thread that could snap at any moment?

One thing is for sure, we put this challenge to the writers, and they came through with flying colors. After hundreds and hundreds of submissions, we managed to narrow it down to what you've found here in this single tome. And as Ken often says at the end of these calls, we could have put together three or four solid anthologies for your enjoyment. Alas, our budget allowed for only one, and even then, we stretched ourselves thin.

And the path forward wasn't always an easy one. As many of you know, we were supposed to have a Laird Barron story in *Never Wake,* but Laird took ill and had to be hospitalized for a long time. He ended up not being able to contribute, but hey—life happens sometimes. We are elated that Laird is recovering quickly, as his health is way more important than any anthology. We knew immediately that we would have to dedicate the anthology to him, since he was so supportive of the concept in its early stages, and instrumental in getting this thing off the ground.

Anyway, we don't want to keep you awake. It's time for that dream world, for your adventure. May these stories serve as fuel, carrying you far and wide into a mysterious realm. May you flourish there and overcome the hidden evils within. As Ken often signs...

Pleasant nightmares,

Kenneth W. Cain and Tim Meyer
March 10, 2023

# THANK YOU

SPECIAL THANK YOU

Huge thanks to our Kickstarter backers. *Never Wake* would not
exist without you!

Theresa Derwin
Steven Duane Allison Junior
Scott Casey
Justin Lewis
David Swisher
Catherine Hargrave
Bonk
Chad Grider
Chris McLaren
Derek Chaput
James Boyer
William Fisher IV
Kelly Snyder
Mari Merino
C. F. Page
Joseph Pesavento
Steve Pattee
Jesse Rohrer
Alexander C. Bailey
Shrader Thomas

Lord TBR
Robert Brown
Parker
Stephen Chappell
Maryanne Chappell
David Niall Wilson
Drew Cook
Austin Hoffey
Michael Feir
Lisa Westenbarger
Kristina Meschi
Paula Limbaugh
David Lars Chamberlain
Susan Jessen
Cathy Green
Kayla Holliday
Nicholas Stephenson
Simon Dick
Stanley Bowles
Bailey Meeker
Drew Cox
William Jones
Steven Byrd
Trip Space-Parasite
Becca Futrell
Jason Levesque
J. Arndt
David Myers
Sarah Duck-Mayr
Ravyn Bryce
Alex Pearson
Armand Rosamilia
Kenneth Skaldebø

Michael Cieslak

Steve Loiaconi

D.S. Ullery

Vulpine

Tripp Ritter

Ben Thomas

djerra

Karin A. Jeffery

Bridget D. Brave

Cat Treadwell

Michael Miller

Paul Buchholz

Karmen Wells

Cameron Jones

Yusa

Kenny Endlich

Josh Buyarski

Paul Rylott

Rebecca Stefoff

Mark Musante

Colton Terry

M. T. Hall

Emily Lutringer

Alison J. McKenzie

L. G. Merrick

Laura Nettles

R.J.H.

Robert Helfst

Robian

Anthony J. Rapino

Cemetery Gates

James Aquilone

Joel McCandless

Jodee Stanley

Benet Devereux

Alan Lastufka

Darrell Z. Grizzle

Jonathan Gensler

Steve Ingleston

Michael W. Phillips Jr.

Alexa K Moon

Greg Greene

bennett hudson

John Rowe

Bruce Baugh

Stina Marie Patton

Richard Leis

Michael Axe

Jay Charles

Emiliyan Gikovski

Kari J Wolfe

Brennan LaFaro

Brynhild Corona

John Fahey

R. D. DeMoss

Pete Gerard

John MacCarrick

Rae Knowles

Roni Stinger

Elana Gomel

Tanya Pell

Vincent N. Darlage, PhD

William Kurt Malkames, Esq.

K. M. Sanders

D. Gworek

Case Chow

H Casper
Ash Phelps
Chris Wolff
Max Stottrop
S.D. Vassallo
KT Wagner
Lee-ann Oleski
AJ Franks
Anas Abusalih
Thomas Barragan
Alice Austin
Amberly Lynott
Shannan Ross
Michael J. Riser
Brit Hill
Nicole Coster
Shaun Jacob Cobble
Patrick Barb
Matt Ramsey
Eric Hendrickson
Nicholas Serrato
Robert Fleck
'Joseph Jerome Connell
Rex Burrows
L.P. Hernandez
Beth Lee
Justin Moritz
Jenny Underwood
Audrey Z. Boytim
Zach Low
Christopher Bowers
Emmy Teague
Zyon Johnson

Kristin Peterson
Ernesto Pavan
Richard Fairbanks
Grant B.
Micheal Jeramy Lee Perez
Moe McBane
KJ Stark
R. B. Wood
Sean Ford
James W. Thomas, PhD
Dave Urban
Nathan "Moonbeast" Skank
Christina Castle
Michael Harris Cohen
Karen Bayly
Artifact Books, Encinitas, CA
RS Redman
Frank Edler
Katrina Carruth
Amanda Headlee
Janelle Janson
John WM Thompson
Michael G Little
Zin E. Rocklyn
Aaron Sabin
Chris Phillips
Donald Brawley
KJ Stark

# About the Authors

**Michael Bailey** is a recipient and eight-time nominee of the Bram Stoker Award, a four-time Shirley Jackson Award nominee, and a multiple recipient of the Benjamin Franklin Award, along with over thirty independent publishing accolades. He has written, edited, and published many books. Along with serving as a Senior Editor and a mentor for emerging writers, his nonfiction book *Righting Writing* is used as curriculum. He is also the screenwriter for *Madness and Writers: The Untold Truth*, a creative documentary series about writers, and lives in Costa Rica.

**TJ Cimfel** is an award-winning screenwriter, author, and creative director based in Chicago. His films include Blumhouse Television's *There's Something Wrong with the Children* (2023), *Intruders* (2015), and Bloody Disgusting's *V/H/S Viral* (2014). He has appeared on Hollywood's Blood List and Young and Hungry List. You can find him online @TeaJaySee on Twitter, @tj_cimfel on Insta, and yes, even at linkedin.com/in/tjcimfel.

**Anaea Lay** lives in Chicago where she engages in a numinous love affair with the city. She haunts zoning committee meetings in search of high drama, makes annual pilgrimages to every branch of the public library, and hasn't been outside the city limits since March of 2020. Her lovebird familiar, Allium, stole her feathers from a T-rex. You can find more of Anaea's work in places such as *Apex*, *Nightmare*, and *Beneath Ceaseless Skies*. For a full bibliography, check out her website, anaealay.com. To talk to her online, find @anaealay on Twitter, or look her up on the Dream Foundry discord server.

**Philip Fracassi** is the Bram Stoker-nominated author of the story collections *Behold the Void* (named "Collection of the Year" from *This Is Horror*) and *Beneath a Pale Sky* (named "Collection of the Year" by *Rue Morgue Magazine*). His upcoming novels include *A Child Alone with Strangers*, *Gothic*, and *Boys in the Valley*. Philip's work has been translated into multiple languages, and his stories have been published in numerous magazines and anthologies, including *Best Horror of the Year*, *Nightmare Magazine*, and *Black Static*. *The New York Times* calls his work "terrifically scary."

**Lyndsay E. Gilbert** hails from Northern Ireland where she lives beside an ancient castle looking out to see. She has stories published in a number of zines and anthologies and works away constantly on novel writing. Lyndsay loves fantasy, horror, Dungeons and Dragons, cats, dogs, playing the fiddle and the ancient art of bellydance.

**Sadie Hartmann** aka Mother Horror is the co-owner of the horror fiction subscription company, Night Worms and the Bram Stoker Awards® nominated editor of her own horror fiction imprint, Dark Hart. Her non-fiction book about horror books titled, *101 Horror Books to Read Before You're Murdered* for Page Street Books is coming, August 2023. She lives in the PNW with her husband of 20+ years where they stare at Mt Rainier, eat street tacos, and hang out with their 3 kids. They have a Frenchie named Owen.

**Laurel Hightower** grew up in Lexington, Kentucky, and after forays to California and Tennessee, has returned home to horse country. She's a fan of true life ghost stories, horror movies, and good bourbon. She is the author of *Whispers In The Dark, Crossroads, Below*, and the short story collection *Every Woman Knows This,* and has more than a dozen short story credits to her name. *Crossroads* was the recipient of an Independent Audiobook Award in 2020 in the category of Best Horror, as well as the This is Horror Best Novella Award for 2020. She has also co-edited three anthologies: *We Are Wolves*, a charity anthology released in 2020 by Burial Day Press, *The Dead Inside*, an anthology of identity horror released in 2022 by Dark Dispatch, and *Shattered & Splintered*, a charity anthology released in 2022 to benefit the Glen Haven Area Volunteer Fire Department, who saved the historic Stanley Hotel from wildfires in 2020.

**Pedro Iniguez** (He/Him) is a Mexican-American speculative fiction writer and painter from Los Angeles, California. His fiction and poetry has appeared in *Nightmare Magazine, Helios Quarterly, Worlds of Possibility, Shortwave Magazine, Star\*Line, Space & Time Magazine*, and *Tiny Nightmares*, among others. He can be found online at Pedroiniguezauthor.com

**Todd Keisling** is a writer and designer of the horrific and strange. His books include *Scanlines, The Final Reconciliation, The Monochrome Trilogy,* and *Devil's Creek,* a 2020 Bram Stoker Award finalist for Superior Achievement in a Novel. A pair of his earlier works were recipients of the University of Kentucky's Oswald Research & Creativity Prize for Creative Writing (2002 and 2005), and his second novel, *The Liminal Man,* was an Indie Book Award finalist in Horror & Suspense (2013). He lives in Pennsylvania with his family.

**Gwendolyn Kiste** is the three-time Bram Stoker Award-winning author of *The Rust Maidens, Reluctant Immortals, Boneset & Feathers, And Her Smile Will Untether the Universe, Pretty Marys All in a Row*, and *The Invention of Ghosts*. Her short fiction and nonfiction have appeared in *Nightmare Magazine, Best American Science Fiction and Fantasy, Vastarien*, Tor's *Nightfire, Black Static, The Dark, Daily Science Fiction, Interzone*, and *LampLight*, among others. Originally from Ohio, she now resides on an abandoned horse farm outside of Pittsburgh with her husband, two cats, and not nearly enough ghosts. Find her online at gwendolynkiste.com

**Joe Koch** writes literary horror and surrealist trash. A Shirley Jackson Award finalist, Joe is the author of *The Wingspan of Severed Hands, The Couvade*, and *Convulsive*. Their short fiction appears in publications such as *Vastarien, Southwest Review, Pseudopod*, and *Children of the New Flesh*. He's been a flash fiction judge for Cemetery Gates Media as well as co-editing the art horror anthology *Stories of the Eye* from Weirdpunk Books. Find Joe (he/they) online at horrorsong.blog and on Twitter @horrorsong.

**Eric LaRocca** (*he/they*) is the Bram Stoker Award-nominated author of several works of horror and dark fiction including the viral sensation *Things Have Gotten Worse Since We Last Spoke*. A lover of luxury fashion and an admirer of European musical theatre, Eric can often be found roaming the streets of his home city, Boston, MA, for inspiration. For more information, please follow @hystericteeth on Twitter/Instagram or visit ericlarocca.com.

**Angela Liu** is a Chinese-American writer from NYC. She researched mixed reality storytelling at Keio University's Graduate School of Media Design in Japan and now works in IT consulting. Her stories and poetry are published/forthcoming in *Strange Horizons, The Dark, Fusion Fragment, Clarkesworld, Dark Matter Magazine,* among others. Read more of her work at: https://liu-angela.com. Or find her on Twitter and Instagram @liu_angela

From her 19th century Welsh farmhouse, **Catherine McCarthy** weaves dark tales on an ancient loom. She is the author of the collection *Mists and Megaliths* and the novella *Immortelle*. Her short fiction has been published by Black Spot Book, Alienhead Press, Dark Matter Ink and others. Her love of dark fiction has been an ever-present ghost, and she enjoys haunting others with her words. 2023 will see the publication of a Gothic novel, *A Moonlit Path of Madness* (Nosetouch Press), a novella, *Mosaic* (Dark Hart Books), and a YA novel, *The Wolf and the Favour* (Brigids Gate Press). Time away from the loom is spent hiking the Welsh coast path or huddled in an ancient graveyard reading Poe. Find her at https://www.catherine-mccarthy-author.com or at https://twitter.com/serialsemantic

**Lee Murray** is multi-award-winning writer, editor, and poet from Aotearoa-New Zealand, a four-time Bram Stoker Award® winner, Shirley Jackson Award winner, and a USA Today Bestselling author. Read more at https://www.leemurray.info/

**Jara Nassar** is a writer and performer based in Berlin, Germany. Her works explore the boundaries between reality and fiction and what amazing or horrifying things can occur when these boundaries become brittle. She has previously been published in *Wizards in Space, Glitter*, and the upcoming anthology *Tangle & Fen*; and regularly performs as Drag King

Angelo Dynamo. You can follow her under @jaramachtsachen (there will be cat pictures).

**Cynthia "Cina" Pelayo** is a three-time Bram Stoker Awards® nominated poet and author. Her novel *Children of Chicago* won the International Latino Book Award for Best Mystery (2021). She lives in Chicago. Find her online at www.cinapelayo.com and on Twitter @cinapelayo.

**Kristin Peterson** (she/her), originally from the Cascade mountains of far-northern California, has had work published in *Vastarien* and *Thinking Horror*. Follow her on Instagram and Twitter: @krpeterson77

**Michelle Tang** writes speculative fiction from Canada, where she lives with her husband and children. Her short stories have been published by Cemetery Gates, Escape Pod, and Flame Tree Publishing, among others. When she's not writing, Michelle enjoys eating carbs, playing video games, and lurking on social media.

**Steve Rasnic Tem** is a past winner of the Bram Stoker, World Fantasy, and British Fantasy Awards. His novel *Ubo* (Solaris Books), a finalist for the Bram Stoker Award, is a dark science fictional tale about violence and its origins, featuring such historical viewpoint characters as Jack the Ripper, Stalin, and Heinrich Himmler. He has published over 500 short stories in his 40+ year career. Some of his best are collected in *Thanatrauma* and *Figures Unseen* from Valancourt Books, and in *The Night Doctor & Other Tales* from Macabre Ink.

# ABOUT THE EDITORS

**Kenneth W. Cain** is an author of horror and dark fiction, and a Splatterpunk Award nominated freelance editor. To date, he has had over one hundred short stories and thirteen novels/novellas, as well as a handful each of nonfiction pieces, books for children, and poems released by many great publishers such as Crystal Lake Publishing, JournalStone, and Cemetery Gates Media. He has also edited eight anthologies, with two more coming in 2023. He lives in Chester County PA with his family and two furbabies, Butterbean and Bodhi. His full publishing history is available on his website at kennethwcain.com

**Tim Meyer** dwells in a dark cave near the Jersey Shore. He's the author of more than fifteen novels, including Malignant Summer, The Switch House, Dead Daughters, Limbs, and many other titles. When he's not working on the next book, he's usually hanging out with his wife and son, shooting around on the basketball court, playing video games, or messing with a new screenplay. He bleeds coffee and IPAs. You can learn more about his books at timmeyerwrites.com.

# THE END?

**Not if you want to dive into more of Crystal Lake Publishing's Tales from the Darkest Depths!**

Check out our amazing website and online store or download our latest catalog here.

We always have great new projects and content on the website to dive into, as well as a newsletter, behind the scenes options, social media platforms, our own dark fiction shared-world series and our very own webstore. Our webstore even has categories specifically for KU books, non-fiction, anthologies, and of course more novels and novellas.

Readers...

Thank you for reading *Never Wake*. We hope you enjoyed this anthology.

If you have a moment, please review *Never Wake* at the store where you bought it.

Help other readers by telling them why you enjoyed this book. No need to write an in-depth discussion. Even a single sentence will be greatly appreciated. Reviews go a long way to helping a book sell, and is great for an author's career. It'll also help us to continue publishing quality books.

Thank you again for taking the time to journey with Crystal Lake Publishing.

You will find links to all our social media platforms on our Linktree page.

# Other titles by
# Crystal Lake Publishing:

## MISSION STATEMENT

Since its founding in August 2012, Crystal Lake Publishing has quickly become one of the world's leading publishers of Dark Fiction and Horror books in print, eBook, and audio formats.

While we strive to present only the highest quality fiction and entertainment, we also endeavour to support authors along their writing journey. We offer our time and experience in non-fiction projects, as well as author mentoring and services, at competitive prices.

With several Bram Stoker Award wins and many other wins and nominations (including the HWA's Specialty Press Award), Crystal Lake Publishing puts integrity, honor, and respect at the forefront of our publishing operations.

We strive for each book and outreach program we spearhead to not only entertain and touch or comment on issues that affect our readers, but also to strengthen and support the Dark Fiction field and its authors.

Not only do we find and publish authors we believe are destined for greatness, but we strive to work with men and woman who endeavour to be decent human beings who care more for others than themselves, while still being hard working, driven, and passionate artists and storytellers.

Crystal Lake Publishing is and will always be a beacon of what passion and dedication, combined with overwhelming teamwork and respect, can accomplish. We endeavour to know each and every one of our readers, while building personal relationships with our authors, reviewers, bloggers, podcasters, bookstores, and libraries.

We will be as trustworthy, forthright, and transparent as any business can be, while also keeping most of the headaches away from our authors, since it's our job to solve the problems so they can stay in a creative mind. Which of course also means paying our authors.

We do not just publish books, we present to you worlds within your world, doors within your mind, from talented authors who sacrifice so much for a moment of your time.

There are some amazing small presses out there, and through collaboration and open forums we will continue to support other presses in the goal of helping authors and showing the world what quality small presses are capable of accomplishing. No one wins when a small press goes down, so we will always be there to support hardworking, legitimate presses and their authors. We don't see Crystal Lake as the best press out there, but we will always strive to be the best, strive to be the most interactive and grateful, and even blessed press around. No matter what happens over time, we will also take our mission very seriously while appreciating where we are and enjoying the journey.

What do we offer our authors that they can't do for themselves through self-publishing?

We are big supporters of self-publishing (especially hybrid publishing), if done with care, patience, and planning. However, not every author has the time or inclination to do market research, advertise, and set up book launch strategies. Although a lot of authors are successful in doing it all, strong small presses will always be there for the authors who just want to do what they do best: write.

What we offer is experience, industry knowledge, contacts and trust built up over years. And due to our strong brand and trusting fanbase, every Crystal Lake Publishing book comes with weight of respect. In time our fans begin to trust our judgment and will try a new author purely based on our support of said author.

With each launch we strive to fine-tune our approach,

learn from our mistakes, and increase our reach. We continue to assure our authors that we're here for them and that we'll carry the weight of the launch and dealing with third parties while they focus on their strengths—be it writing, interviews, blogs, signings, etc.

We also offer several mentoring packages to authors that include knowledge and skills they can use in both traditional and self-publishing endeavours.

We look forward to launching many new careers.

This is what we believe in. What we stand for. This will be our legacy.

Welcome to Crystal Lake Publishing—Tales from the Darkest Depths.

**THANK YOU FOR PURCHASING THIS BOOK**